LANDER'S LEGACY

STONE SOVEREIGNS #1

C. S. WACHTER

Shadowfall Publishing

Lander's Legacy
Book 1 of Stone Sovereigns

Copyright © 2020 by C. S. Wachter
www.cswachter.com

Published by Shadowfall Publishing

Printed in the United States of America

Wachter, C. S.
    Lander's Legacy / C. S. Wachter
    Book 1 of: Stone Sovereigns
    ISBN: 978-0-9998861-9-9 (paperback)
    ISBN: 978-1-7340591-2-0 (ebook)

Cover Design by: Mountainview Books, LLC

Print formatting by: Mountainview Books, LLC

This book is a work of fiction. Names, characters, incidents, and dialogues are products of the author's imagination. Any resemblance to actual events or persons, living or dead, is entirely coincidental.

For Joe. Thank you for your patience and support. You are such a special blessing.

ACKNOWLEDGMENTS

Special thanks to Jan and Kelly.
The best critique partners a writer could want.

CHAPTER 1

The double doors whooshed open. A groan worked its way up from Lander's gut and poured between clenched teeth when he checked his watch. Flinging water from his shoulder length, shaggy brown hair, he dashed into the glass and steel entryway of City Line General Hospital. It had taken almost four hours to make the hour trip from Wharton to the hospital where he now stood—his heart thumping a wild rhythm as he blinked scratchy eyes. One missed bus, two wrong buses. So much wasted time.

Before him stretched an unfamiliar frontier painted in shades of white and silver; behind him, banks of floor to ceiling windows reflected massive overhead chandeliers on a backdrop of gray clouds and rain.

Lander had never been in a hospital before, never even seen a doctor. The prospect of finding his grandfather in this vast, impersonal space set his heart to racing faster. He stood, rigid and silent, as countless people rushed around him. He was a fixed rock in the center of a swift-moving river. Moving, always moving forward.

Pop-pop Ian told him people were like that. *Always in a hurry, those city people. You need to be careful around them, Lander.* But Lander was here now, surrounded … and alone.

He scanned the lobby for signs, seeking direction. At school, there were signs for everything. But here? No signs. Pulling in a deep breath and shaking out his hands at his sides, Lander took a step forward. When the surging crowd streaming around him passed without trampling him, he grabbed hold of his courage and approached a long, curved desk.

Like everything else in the pristine room, it looked cold and unwelcoming. Gray metal and glass. Several individuals stood behind the counter and answered questions for others standing on his side of the imposing obstacle.

No signs. He scanned again, then swallowed around the lump in his throat that he had struggled with ever since leaving Wharton.

I'll need to ask.

The directions were simple. His grandfather was on the third floor, room 319. The lady at the desk smiled; but no, she couldn't tell him anything about how his grandfather was doing.

Stepping off the elevator, he checked the sign with arrows pointing in both directions. Following the arrow for rooms 301-320, he turned to his left and, bouncing on his toes, controlled the urge to sprint up the wide corridor. He began to jog, his feet pattering on the shiny, gray, vinyl flooring. He prayed that whatever had caused Pop-pop Ian to set foot in this place wasn't serious.

Passing room 310, he saw them. Two official looking men in dark suits stood in the hallway near the door to room 319, like a pair of guards.

Don't trust anyone, Pop-pop had told him, *especially govern-ment-type strangers wearing black suits.*

Lander hadn't seen many suits growing up in Wharton,

just the old-fashioned ones the old men wore to Sunday church. Wharton was an old town, filled with old people. Even the high school had been built for the old people. Now, it sat mostly empty. Next year Wharton would be consolidated with the rest of the county. Lander would have to travel forty-five minutes each way to the big school in Harley.

He slowed to a walk, the men outside his grandfather's room set the hairs on the back of his neck on edge. He reached into his jacket pocket and pulled out Pop-pop's worn leather Bible. Holding it helped his jittery nerves settle.

Ducking into the open door of room 312, he concentrated. *They can't see me. They can't see me. Can't see me pass.*

Neither man noticed Lander as he approached room 319. Fingers twitching, he almost walked right past the door. But worry for his grandfather and guilt over taking so long to arrive propelled him past the two men and into the room, unseen. Deep in conversation, their focus on the hallway, they never noticed the door open just so wide and close without a sound.

Dark, heavy curtains covered the windows, blocking out any feeble light that might endeavor to corrupt the sanitary darkness. A series of beeps emanating from several machines between the bed and the far wall penetrated the tense silence. The muted voices of the men outside the door rumbled.

Sensitive to the dark silence, Lander crept forward to the side of the single bed. Pop-pop Ian lay under a white sheet and blanket. A clear mask covered most of his face. Lander had never seen him so still before. As he stood over the immobile form, the eyes blinked several times, then opened to pierce Lander with twin beams of brilliant silver.

Recognition blossomed in the orbs and Pop-pop tried to speak. He waved the hand that was free of tubes, prodding Lander to remove the alien-looking mask. Two straps held it in place and a long clear tube ran from the front of it to a piece of equipment. Reaching to the side of his grandfather's face, Lander undid the straps and the thing fell onto the pillow.

Pop-pop sucked in a harsh breath, rasping and choking. Lander panicked. Thinking he should put the mask back on, he reached for it. But with a weak shake of his head, Ian lifted his hand to stop Lander and wheezed. "No. leave it. I must talk."

"I'm so sorry. I got lost. I took too long. I'm sorry. By the time I got home and found the note ... Here," Lander stammered, "I can..."

"No," Ian rasped. "No time ... you can't heal me ... too late. You must go ... now. They know... Thought I'd have more time." Ian stopped, coughed again and sucked in a breath that rattled his chest. "Listen, Lander. Listen, now."

Ian's voice dropped to a breathy whisper and Lander leaned in closer. "Loose rock under oak ... find box. Everything's there. Must find ... box." He coughed again and the beeping grew louder, faster, insistent.

"Remember, Lander. You're special. Find the box. All the answers are in the box. Choose well ... not like ... Cyanne. Not like..."

Ian breathed out with a gurgle. All the machines began chirping and beeping and the door behind Lander flew open.

"Who are you?" The taller of the two men now standing in the doorway demanded. "How'd you get in here?"

Panic, like a jolt of electricity, zinged through Lander. His knees threatened to buckle. His limbs trembling, Lander focused once again. His form wavered.

The man cursed, took a step toward Lander.

Several nurses, and a doctor poured into the room and shoved past the two men, driving them to the side of the door in their haste. While the rest ran to Ian, one of the nurses turned back to the men and shouted, "Out. Now."

She herded them toward the door as one pointed to where Lander had been standing. "What about him?"

The nurse glanced over her shoulder. A look of disgust flattened her lips as she turned back to the man and waved toward the door. "Out. Now. Everyone else in this room is hospital personnel. Let us do our job."

The door slammed shut behind the suited men.

Lander stood like a posed statue in the dark corner next to the heavy curtains. He focused. His mind whirred as he struggled to remain invisible when a thin beam of sunlight snuck in through the gap at the edge of the curtain, striking his left cheek.

A soft mist had replaced the rain and the evening sun sent sparkling beams through the water laden air. Pain filled his chest as he watched the nurses and doctor work to bring his grandfather back.

But Lander knew he was gone. Watched as his spirit rose from the now empty husk of skin and bones. Pop-pop's spirit had smiled at him, and whispered, *I love you, Lander.* He pointed to the Bible, forgotten in Lander's hands. *It's yours now. Use it well.* As the spirit began to fade, he spoke one more time. The words were so quiet, Lander strained to hear them. *Find the box. It has the answers.*

Again, Lander was alone. He had never been truly alone before and the pain of it almost broke his concentration. If that happened, he would be seen.

Don't trust anyone. Pop-pop's words circled in his mind again. But now Pop-pop was gone, and Lander didn't want to stay hidden. He wanted to be normal; seen, accepted, allowed to give voice to his grief in front of others. He wiped his nose with the sleeve of his jacket and resisted the urge to sniffle. His emotions drowning him in a deep well of grief, he left room 319.

The men from his grandfather's room were waiting in the

chilly, mist-laden air outside the hospital, under the domed lights of the exit doors. Fear and sorrow fueled Lander's concentration and he walked out into the night, unnoticed among the many visitors leaving Center Line.

Somehow Lander made his way back home. It was the middle of the night. Penniless, he walked the final six miles. At least the rain had stopped. The evening turned cool and a full grinning-face moon lit the way.

Strange lights bobbed around in the old bungalow Lander called home. Several dark SUVs were parked on the drive and on the grass in the front yard.

Lander skirted the house and crept into the woods beyond, past the outer reaches of flickering flashlights. With all the activity around the house and in the yard, Lander kept his distance. With stealth born of experience in the woods, he made his way to the small storage container where he kept his sleeping bag and some supplies.

Grabbing what he needed, he jogged between the boles of hoary oaks and made his way toward a stand of hickory near the stream. He was home here in the deep woods. Here he could be alone with his thoughts and his grief. Tomorrow, after the strangers were gone, he would find Pop-pop's box. Then he would know what to do.

Lander had always known he was different. Pop-pop made certain he understood this fact. Because he was special, he was never allowed to play with the other kids when he was younger; or do sports or extra activities when he reached high school.

From grade school to now he stayed quiet and blended in at school. Always average, never standing out. A nobody who avoided bullies and friendship alike. Though he had acquaintances, there were no close friends at Wharton High School.

That was fine with Lander. Instead of an after-school job, his afternoons and evenings were spent learning woodcraft and other important life-lessons from Pop-pop. When he was younger, he resented the lack of friends and the need to do more *schoolin'* after school. As he got older, though, he came to just accept it as life with Pop-pop.

Lander knew all the woods and fields, hills and swamps within a twenty-mile radius of their bungalow. He knew how to hunt and trap, and, if necessary, could live off the land. But even more, Pop-pop Ian had taught him about the special things only he could do, like remain unseen when he focused.

He could also ignite a spark from his fingertips. It had taken him a long time to learn that very practical skill and, even now, he didn't always succeed. He considered building a fire tonight, but with the strangers around, he decided to stay shrouded in darkness.

In the shadows and faint moonlight, surrounded by the familiar chirping of crickets and the peeping of tree frogs, he settled with his back against a large old hickory tree and wept. The pain of loss seared through his soul and he allowed the grief to find release in his quiet tears.

Comforted by the deep dark that signals the coming dawn, and exhausted by the turmoil of the day, he shook out his sleeping bag and wormed into it without undoing the zipper. Within minutes, he was sound asleep.

CHAPTER 2

The next morning dawned cool and bright. Hickory leaves, a mix of greens and yellows, fluttered in the golden morning light, scattering pinpricks of shimmer among the shadows that dominated the underbrush. Lander, empty, drained and rung out, like a discarded, tattered old dishrag watched the show, numb to the beauty.

His stomach growled. Giving in to the physical need, he rummaged through his pack. At the bottom he found the broken remnants of venison jerky he and Pop-pop had dried last fall. Tears pooled and he blinked them back. Another part of his grandfather was lost to him as he swallowed the last bit of jerky, his stomach still growling its disappointment.

After washing up in the nearby stream, he gathered his things and crept to the edge of the woods surrounding the bungalow.

The cars were gone. The place appeared empty, desolate.

Breakfast? Lander left his day pack behind an overgrown, vine-infested clump of bottlebrush buckeye. He snuck up to the back door and peered in the small window. All was quiet. His hands trembling, he turned the handle, then inched the door open and scanned the kitchen before stepping in. Dark, silent.

When he got home yesterday afternoon, before he found the note, he had ignored the messy kitchen counter and still-warm, cast-iron frying pan, assuming Ian had run out to the garden intent on picking some forgotten ingredient. Then he found the note and his world narrowed to one thought—*get to the hospital.*

The phone receiver still rested on the floor where one of the intruders must have dropped it. Shaking his head, Lander replaced it.

Looking around at the trashed kitchen he struggled against the sting at the backs of his eyes and the burning lump in his throat. Not one of the strangers had hung up the phone; all apparently too bent on destroying things. Food, broken dishes, and forks, knives, and spoons littered the floor beneath the shattered wooden remains of what had been the silverware drawer.

With every step Lander took, stuff crunched underfoot. Breakfast was forgotten as he made his way through the four rooms of the tiny house: kitchen, living room, Pop-pop's bedroom, and the bathroom. Lander always slept in the living room on the pull-out couch that now looked as if it had been attacked by an angry cougar. The place wasn't much, but it was home. And now, it had been violated—torn apart. No room escaped the invader's touch; even the top of the toilet tank lay in pieces on the bathroom floor.

Lander stuffed shaking hands into his armpits, struggling to stem his trembling as a potent mix of anger and fear, pain and loss triggered an adrenaline rush. He couldn't stay. They would be back. Whatever they searched for had eluded them. They no doubt left angry and empty-handed. What they wanted must be in Pop-pop's box, hidden under the oak in the woods beyond the backyard.

The adrenaline bled off as Lander moved with swift purpose. He grabbed his school pack, dumped the contents, and strode back through the house, pieces of his life crunching underfoot. He slammed out the back door and marched to the shed. It too had been searched. The spade he sought lay out on the ground, wet from the morning dew, alongside the other tools Pop-pop always kept clean and stored in the lean-to. Picking up the shovel, Lander paused as, once again, grief tore through him.

"Not now," he whispered into the morning air. For a moment, he just stood, listening to the birds greeting each other and the slight breeze rustling the leaves of the trees. The small sounds of tiny creatures moving about surrounded him, just like they had every other morning.

But nothing was the same. It was different. He was different. And now, with that difference—and the danger that difference represented—weighing on him, Lander swallowed hard and paced to the buckeye to retrieve his daypack.

Returning to the yard, he turned toward the oak. He couldn't see it from where he stood, but it was there, towering above the adjacent woods, spreading wider than every other tree. Ancient. Different. Like Lander.

He dumped the contents from the day pack onto the ground. He stared at the small mound for a moment, his eyes landing on Pop-pop Ian's bible. Somehow with his grandfather gone it seemed foreign, unnecessary. He grimaced and stuffed the book, his spare clothing, a Swiss Army knife, and his few other belongings into his larger backpack. He tossed the empty bag back into the woods. Shouldering the pack, he moved down the path he had walked so often in the past.

The breeze stilled as Lander approached the oak. Memories of standing on Pop-pop's favorite balancing stone assailed him and he dropped to his knees.

"Stand on that flat-topped rock, the one there under the oak." Pop-pop's voice whispered through Lander. Ian's gnarled fingers pointing out the wobbly gray, lichen covered rock. "That's right boy."

Ten-year old Lander set his feet apart as the large stone teetered from side to side beneath him.

"Now keep it up boy, work on your balance. Don't waste time; practice what I taught you till I get back."

That day Lander had balanced for hours before Pop-pop returned from setting a track.

"Okay, Lander, you've got another hour till you lose sunlight. Follow the trail. I've left surprises. Find them all and we'll have peach cobbler for dessert tonight."

Did you practice? Lander could almost hear Pop-pop Ian's voice in the quiet morning. He always expected Lander to use his rock-balancing time well. *Focus.*

By the time Lander turned fourteen, he could balance on the tricky rock with ease and either practice his special gifts or quote whole chapters in Pop-pop's bible from memory.

His favorite game was to go still and quiet, then focus on turning invisible. He would keep track of how many creatures ventured close without even noticing him. Those were the times he felt most alive; the very heartbeat of the earth beneath him seemed to vibrate through him and he felt as if he belonged. As if he too was one of God's creatures.

Now, after prying the rock over with a fallen branch, exposing the underbelly of insects and dirt, he pulled out the stone that served as a fulcrum all those years, and dug in the soft soil and leaf litter.

The box wasn't buried deep, just an inch or so beneath the surface. A small metal thing with rusted hinges. Lander's jaw dropped at the smallness of it. He had expected something that held all the answers to be large, like a treasure chest. But the box was normal looking, just big enough to hold several books.

Sitting cross-legged on the ground next to the dislocated rock, he pulled the box to him and set it on his lap. The metal must have been painted green with gold trim at some time. Now, it was mostly brown with a slick layer of grit. Though it had a lock, it wasn't locked and grabbing the handle again, Lander pulled the top up.

The rusty hinges squealed in protest, scattering nearby birds in panicked flight. Inside sat a large, worn, black leather book, bundles of one-hundred-dollar bills, and two stones.

Lander shuffled the contents, thinking to find something more. But there was nothing else. He rifled through the bills, counting. Ten straps with one hundred bills in each.

Pop-pop had $100,000? Buried in the ground? A wave of anger surged through Lander. *Why? We never had enough money. We could have used this, and he kept it buried? Why?*

Setting aside the money, Lander picked up the stones. Like the box, they were crusty brown on the outside, but the moment Lander picked them up, energy from within pulsed, warming Lander's palms. They were potent stones. But what Pop-pop expected Lander to do with them, he didn't know.

Replacing the stones, he picked up the most interesting find in the box, the book. He ran his fingers over the old, tooled-leather cover attempting to sound out the unfamiliar word etched there. Leafing through the pages, disappointment birthed a lump in his throat. The first hundred pages or so were filled with small, elegant writing in the same language as that on the cover. Fanning past those pages, a folded slip of paper fell onto his lap. Unfolding the note, he recognized his grandfather's sprawling, irregular writing.

Lander,

If you're reading this, I'm gone. I hoped to explain things. I guess I shoulda done so sooner. This journal was your mom's. The stones belonged to your mom and dad. There's power in the stones and our story in the journal. I never taught you to read the old language. I guess I shoulda done that too. Someone else will have to now. I taught you what I thought you'd need to know.

Read what you can of the journal, it'll answer some of your questions. You'll have to ask Castor Elm the rest. Find him. He'll help you. He lives in Bethel. You'll have to travel to Camden, that's a hub for the bus line. You can catch a bus north to Sheridan, another hub. From there you'll need to go east to Greensburg where you can catch a local bus to Bethel. You're smart, you'll find it. The cash should come in handy. I hope I saved enough.

Love,
POP-POP

Also, remember DON'T TRUST ANYONE! (except Castor)

Keep the stones with you always. There's power in them, but only one of us can use them.

Lander read the note through several times hoping to learn something more. *Pop-pop, those are the worst directions. Bethel where? There must be millions of Bethels. And Castor Elm? What kind of a name is that?*

Powerful stones?

A journal I can't even read?

A person I never met?

Lander ground stiff fingers into his temples and his stomach churned.

And what do you mean by 'one of us'? You never told me. Who are we?

Stuffing the note into the journal again, he held it on his

lap, rested his forehead on the worn leather, and allowed his emotions to rage through him once again. The lump that blocked his throat earlier returned, now the size of a boulder. Pop-pop Ian had always been there for Lander.

"What do I do, Pop-pop?" he whispered into the still air.

Keep your wits about you Lander. You're strong. Even more than you think. You've got this. Pop-pop Ian's words from their boar hunt last spring whispered back.

After a few minutes, he sat up, opened the journal, and flipped pages until he found writing he understood. He didn't get a chance to read. The slamming of car doors startled him. Rising to his feet, he dropped the journal.

"Owl scat," he muttered. Lander snatched the stones and dumped them into his jacket pockets. One pocket had a hole and the stone dropped to the ground. Growling his frustration, he put it into the pocket with the other. Grabbing his backpack, he began cramming bundles of one-hundred-dollar bills in. He stopped and thought for a minute, then shifted two of the bundles into the pockets of his jeans. Last, he retrieved the journal and shoved it into the pack, closed it, and hoisted it to his shoulder.

Looking down, he growled at the upturned rock, disturbed earth, shovel, and box. The people who had torn up his home would know he had dug up something. The sound of several voices drifted toward him. Whoever arrived in the cars was coming this way.

Lander could do nothing about the mess at his feet. He grabbed the box and sprinted deeper into the woods. He moved the way Pop-pop had taught him; shadow-like, leaving no trace of his passing.

As he ran, his thoughts jumbled over each other. *What now?*

The outline of a plan came to him. He circled back through the woods toward town and the public library where he would check maps to find the Greensburg due east of Sheridan. Once he knew where he was heading, he'd catch a bus to the station near City Line Hospital. He knew the way there now. He'd buy a ticket for Greensburg by way of Camden and Sheridan. For the first time since finding Pop-pop Ian's note, the tension gripping Lander's shoulders relaxed its hold.

CHAPTER 3

It took some time to find Bethel on the map. Pop-pop had been right; after a long trip north to Sheridan then east to Greensburg, Lander would be close to the tiny town of Bethel.

"Why're you sittin' here instead of in school, Lander Devlin?" Mrs. Morrison the part-time librarian assistant asked, suspicion evident in the squint of her small dark eyes. "You cuttin' school again?"

"No, ma'am." Lander squirmed on his chair. "I'm here on a special assignment. You don't think I'd be here in the library if I was ditching school, do you, Mrs. Morrison?"

Suspicion still lurking in the set of her shoulders, Mrs. Morrison sighed. "Well, I guess not. Knowing you, you'd be out in the woods somewhere. But if I find out you're lyin' to me young man, your grandfather 'll hear about it."

"Yes, ma'am."

Several moms with preschoolers walked in, drawing Mrs. Morrison's attention from Lander. Breathing a sigh of relief as the gossip-prone woman scuttled toward the children's section, he returned the map book to its shelf and trotted out the door, dropping the old metal box in the trash can on his way.

Five hours later—and three-hundred forty-eight dollars and seventy-five cents poorer—Lander leaned back into the blue plastic chair in the waiting room of the City Line bus station.

After arriving at the Springfield Station and purchasing a ticket for Camden, he had learned he had an hour and forty-five minutes before the bus left. Pocketing the ticket, he headed back out to Graingers, the local department store, bought toiletries, extra clothing, and, most especially, a new jacket with deep, secure pockets before returning to the bus depot where he now waited.

Lander settled back into his seat on the bus bound for Camden, his backpack resting on the spot between him and the aisle. The muscles across his back that had knotted over the last day unclenched. Curiosity about the journal churned his thoughts. Looking around he decided he needed to wait a bit longer. Though he was impatient to read it, there were too many people sitting near him to chance pulling it from his pack.

He closed his eyes, hoping to make up for lost sleep. After a few minutes, his lids popped back open. He was too wound up. So much had happened that his brain wouldn't stop sprinting from one thing to another. Giving up on the idea of sleep, Lander watched the countryside slide by as the bus sped along the two-lane highway.

Without thought to what he was doing, he pulled one of the stones from his jacket pocket and began to rub his fingers over the rough surface. It warmed in his hand and the repetitive movement of his fingers over the uneven surface soothed his spirit. As he rubbed the coarse, pitted surface, it changed, growing smooth, like glass.

Looking down, a thrill ran through him. No longer a rough, plain, brown stone, the thing resting in his palm had become something beautiful. As the sunlight filtering in through the window hit the surface, it sparked deep within, shimmering in shades of blue and green, as if it was alive.

With a start, Lander dropped the glowing object into his lap. Instantly, its appearance reverted back to that of a plain, pitted, ordinary stone.

"Owl scat," Lander whispered. He picked the stone up, intending to return it to his pocket, but curiosity overrode common sense. Scanning the people sitting around him, he began to stroke the stone again, this time paying close attention to the transformation.

Within seconds, the stone was smooth, hot, and glowing in the sunlight. Again, Lander dropped it and it returned to its ordinary appearance. He plucked it from his lap, searching once again to see if anyone had noticed what had happened, then returned the stone to his pocket.

Eyes glued to the moving landscape; Lander struggled against his rising irritation. *Pop-pop Ian, if you were here now, I'd strangle you.*

Over the next couple hours, the bus stopped several times. Each time, as more people got on with no one getting off, Lander despaired of ever getting a chance to open the journal. He would have to wait until they arrived at the next major bus terminal where he would switch buses to continue his journey north.

The day began to wind down into evening and Lander's stomach growled as if he hadn't eaten in a month when the driver announced a twenty-minute rest stop. The bus ground to a halt and Lander joined the group of people getting off to use the facilities or grab something to eat.

By the time he got out of the men's room, the line for food was long. But, after his shopping trip this morning and paying for his bus ticket, he only had thirty-five cents in change and the one-hundred dollar bills. He couldn't use the vending machines; everything cost more than thirty-five cents. He would need to wait in line and hope he got his food before the bus left.

The cashier snarled at him when he handed her the hundred-dollar bill to pay for a cheese sandwich and lemonade.

"Ain't ya got nuthin' smaller?" she asked as she popped her gum, frowned, and with a sigh, reached for a marker to run across the bill. "I'm not supposed to take anythin' larger than a twenty. You're gonna have ta wait fer the manager."

"Please ma'am. It's all I've got, and I can't miss the bus."

Lander shuffled and twisted the money with an awkward movement. Grumbling about the delay trickled to him from behind. He turned to apologize when a man several positions back stepped forward.

"Here," the stranger said to the clerk, holding out a ten. "I think this should cover it."

Lander almost choked. The man, a good four inches taller than he, with broad shoulders, buzzed brown hair and piercing brown eyes, wore a black a suit.

He's one of the men from the hospital. How …

"T-th-thanks," Lander stammered. "But I can pay for my own food." He waved the wrinkled, sweat-dampened hundred-dollar bill at the clerk. "Please, ma'am, just take it."

Frowning, the woman plucked the bill from Lander's hand, swiped her marker over it, then, with slow, exaggerated movements, counted back his change while the people behind continued to complain.

Grabbing his food and change, Lander ran from the station. He pulled to a stop, debating whether to sprint from the parking lot or return to the bus, and almost dropped his food when strong, long fingers wrapped around his elbow in a bone-crushing grip. He looked up into the cold, dark eyes of the stranger. "Here, son, let me help you back to your seat."

By the time the bus started again, night had fallen. Lander watched intermittent lights flash then vanish as they rode through the town and into the dark countryside.

His hands twitching, Lander shifted his backpack to the floor at his feet when the man moved to sit next to him; imposing, silent, eyes roaming over the other passengers. They rode like that for miles; the man studying the people around him; Lander pretending to watch the dark landscape through the reflections on the window.

This man was big trouble, that much was obvious, but Lander had no idea why the man wanted him. So many unanswered questions jumbled and shifted through his mind. *So what if I'm different? I've never hurt anyone. Never stolen or cheated. Except those times I ditched school to be outside.*

He looked over at the stranger's profile in the half-light of an overhead lamp across the aisle.

"Don't even think it. I know what you are, you little freak. I have a gun and I won't hesitate to use it."

Lander groaned and ran trembling fingers through his greasy hair. "What do you think I am? I'm just a kid."

The man's eyes shifted to Lander and he huffed. "Sure. You keep up the lie; you're just a kid. A normal kid. *Right.* You can't fool me. I've seen what your kind can do. Keep your mouth shut, sit there, and behave yourself Mr. Normal Kid and we won't have any problems."

Tears burned the backs of Lander's eyes and he blinked to keep them there. This stranger knew more about him than he knew about himself. Would the man tell him anything if he asked? Glancing back over, Lander watched him scan the other passengers once again. *I have to try.*

"What am I?" Lander asked, his voice soft and unsure.

"Don't play games with me, kid."

"No, really. I don't know anything about myself except that I'm a junior at Wharton High School. I've lived with my grandfather my whole life and never left Wharton until yesterday when my grandfather died in the hospital. You were there, weren't you?"

Disgust wrinkled the man's nose as if he smelled spoiled meat.

"How did you do it, get into the room without us seeing you? I know the door bounced at one point, but we never saw you go in. And, when I looked, you weren't there. The only person in that room was the old guy we were sent to retrieve. Then, there you were. That nurse never even saw you, did she?"

"No." Lander's reply ghosted on a puff of air. "But I'm not lying. I know there are things I can do that others can't, but I don't know why. Pop-pop Ian never told me."

Lander turned. The man stared at him through narrowed eyes, brow furrowed, as if studying him. He wondered what the man was seeing. Just a normal, rather average, gray-eyed, sandy-haired, teen who loved the woods and was in desperate need of a haircut? Who avoided attention and yet could do inexplicable things? Or something else, something dangerous, something Lander knew nothing about.

"What's your name, kid?"

"Lander."

"Tell me, Lander, how did you do it?"

Lander pulled in a deep breath, looked out the window, and said nothing. *Trust no one.* Lander sniffled.

"You're not going to start crying on me or something, are you kid?" The man scowled, his voice a low-pitched promise of violence.

Lander stared at the darkness outside his window through his reflection on the glass. He shoved his backpack under his seat with his foot and determined he would find a way off this bus. Alone.

Several stops and a day later, Lander woke from a fitful sleep. The bus had pulled into a vast terminal while Lander slept. Dozens of other buses surrounded them, the deafening noise of multiple engines and the smell of diesel set Lander's teeth on edge.

High-intensity lights illuminated the entire area, including the interior of the bus where Lander sat, turning the night into day. Lander glanced to his side. The seat was empty. Alert to this opportunity for escape, he pulled his backpack from under the seat, slung it on his shoulder, and shoved his way to the front of the bus. Stopping in the doorway, he scanned the area for the stranger. The man was just a few feet away, watching the steps while he talked on a cell phone.

Grabbing the bar alongside the door, Lander swung off, past the people descending the steps in front of him, to the dark pavement below. He rushed toward the back of the bus. The man's familiar, deep voice yelled something as Lander rounded the back of the bus, turned up the other side, and slid to a stop. He focused. *He can't see me. Can't see me.*

Lander held his breath as he stood—still, frozen, balanced like on his rock—and watched as the tall stranger searched for him, swearing, shoving people. After circling the bus several times, the man released an oath, then jogged away. Lander suspected he was heading to the terminal office. He'd give the security people some kind of story and ask to see surveillance videos of the area around the bus.

Lander needed to move. Now. Focused on remaining unseen, he walked at a slow, steady pace toward one of the exit doors. The cool night air met the sweat on his brow, chilling his skin. He jogged across a parking lot then a dim, empty street. Only after he crossed several more streets and turned right and left a few times did he stop and pull in gulps of air that reeked of exhaust fumes and garbage.

This must be Camden. Now what do I do?

The streets called up images from the newspapers and comics he had read. Inner city images. Drug addicts, street crime, prostitutes, murderers. Indecision paralyzed him.

Loud voices set his heart to racing as a group of young people rounded the corner. He focused again. But he was growing weary. The stress of the last few days and the need to remain unseen in this strange environment drained him. He pulled the hood of his jacket over his head and backed into the crumbling old bricks of a building that sprouted right out of the sidewalk.

The sweet voice of an angel arose from the teenagers as they passed. The fresh feminine voice sang the first line of a song Lander recognized. Others joined in and Lander released a breath in relief. He had sung this song with Pop-pop many times at church.

"Be still and know that I am God." The words began to fade as the group moved away.

"Forgive me Pop-pop," Lander whispered. "I know you said to trust no one. But you also said church people are good people. I can't do this on my own. I have to trust someone."

Lander dropped his focus and, sprinting after the group of young men and women, shouted, "Please, please can you help me?"

CHAPTER 4

The singing stopped and a dozen curious faces turned toward Lander. The group looked to be made up of teenagers: white, black, Hispanic, an inner city mix of youth.

Two of the bigger guys stepped out from the group, both covered in tattoos and piercings, and one asked, "What do you want?"

Lander stopped in front of the two, his breathing labored by uncertainty as he blinked back tears of frustration. "I'm lost. Can you help me?"

The entire group responded. They moved in around Lander; exclamations of surprise filled the air. "Hoo boy! What's someone like you doing alone in this neighborhood after dark?" "You lookin' to get mugged?" "Ain't you got no sense?" "Look how he's dressed." "Of course we'll help you." "What do you need?"

A pretty girl with skin the color of milk chocolate, the one whose voice had first drawn Lander, moved to stand in front of him. A shy smile surfaced, and she grabbed his hand.

"Crossways Mission isn't far. We're heading back there now. You're welcome to join us if you want. I'm sure someone there can help you."

One of the girls started singing again. The others joined in as the group strode up the sidewalk. The pretty girl kept hold of Lander's hand. For the first time since finding the scribbled note saying his grandfather was at City Line Hospital, Lander felt at peace.

"I'm Becky," the girl holding Lander's hand said as they walked up several steps into a brightly lit room filled with a scattering of mismatched tables and chairs. "What's your name?"

"Lander."

"You're not from around here. Are you?"

"You can tell, huh?" A lopsided grin materialized on Lander's face.

Becky chuckled, deep and soft. "Yeah, kinda. Your clothes have country hick written all over them. And, besides, guys from around here don't ask for help. Just doesn't happen. We usually have to push them to let us help."

"What kind of help?"

"Oh, you know, the usual. Give them a sandwich, warm blankets, offer them a bed for the night. And, of course, there's the soup kitchen in the back. And tell them about Jesus, if they're interested."

Becky looked up at Lander, her dark eyes like rich turned earth. Her hair was dark too, almost black. Pulled back then divided into small braids that fell past her shoulders. Little beads at the ends of the braids jingled softly when she moved her head. Lander fisted his hands at his sides, resisting the urge to reach up and touch them.

Lander never got to meet Pastor Stevens that night, but he was given a cot with blankets.

"You'll be okay here," Becky said. "Pastor Stevens is just

really busy now. Problems with a local gang." She paused; her eyes focused on the middle of Lander's chest as she chewed her lower lip. "Our youth group helps out here every second Saturday. If you're still here when we come back, maybe we can talk."

"Sure," Lander said, planning to leave in the morning.

When Lander got in line for breakfast the next morning, he came face to face with Pastor Stevens; he was serving eggs.

"You must be Lander. I'm Pastor Stevens. We need to talk."

After getting an older woman to fill in for him, he motioned for Lander to join him at a table near the big windows at the front of the building.

"The kids from Trinity told me you asked for help last night. That you're lost. This area of the city isn't a good place for a country kid like you to be lost in." Pastor Stevens's eyes bored into Lander. "So, how can I help you?"

Lander stared down at his eggs as he poked at the pale-yellow lumps and pushed them around with a bent fork. He knew he needed help but was unsure how much to tell this man who stared at him as if he could read his thoughts.

"The day before yesterday I was on a bus, minding my own business, when some man tried to kidnap me."

Oh yeah! That sounds really believable. But he was into it now, so he kept going. "I was really scared and didn't know what to do. So, when we got to the terminal and I got the chance, I ran from him. I ended up on that street where Becky and her friends found me, and I asked them for help. That's all there is to it."

Pastor Stevens stirred his coffee, watching as it swirled in the heavy mug, silent, the knuckles of his other hand pressed into his lips.

Lander started to fidget in the silence. It reminded him too much of being in the principal's office after he had been caught ditching school. The principal did the same thing, sat quietly, waiting for Lander to crack and admit his crime.

Lander poked at the eggs again.

"I see," Pastor Stevens finally said. "I guess we ought to call the police and fill out a report. Make sure people know this man is trying to …"

"No!" Lander cringed as several people turned at his outburst.

Pastor Stevens's eyes narrowed, his lips flattening into a hard line. "Now, son, why don't you tell me the truth."

Lander stared out the window at a graffiti covered building across the street. Mixed messages sprayed in red, blue, and black marring the old red bricks; breakfast forgotten. The pastor waited, sipping his coffee from time to time as minutes ticked by.

"Four days ago, my grandfather died." Lander began again. "He was my only family. That's why I was on the bus." He breathed in, his focus shifting to his hands on the table, his fingers interlacing and twisting.

"And some man did try to take me off the bus. That's true. I don't know why he's after me, but he was outside my grandfather's hospital room and … well … now he's following me. I need to get to this town called Bethel. There are friends there who'll help me."

"I see." Pastor Stevens's eyes flicked up from studying his coffee to meet Lander's. "You're sure you don't know why this man would try to kidnap you? Perhaps you don't want me calling the police because the man following you is the police. I'd like to help, but I won't help someone running from the law. It'd be best if you just turned yourself in."

"No, sir." A potent mix of anger and frustration threatened to pour forth from Lander. All that had happened the last few days pressed against his already frayed nerves, pressure building like steam in a kettle ready to whistle. But he capped the rising tide. He needed help, and anger wouldn't do anything... except maybe get him thrown out of the one place he might find help. "It's not the law. But, honestly, I don't know who they are."

"They?"

"There were two of them outside my grandfather's hospital room. Then more at my home. I ran away, but the tall man from the hospital found me."

"Why you?" Pastor Stevens asked. "What do these people want with you?"

Lander sniffed and looked around. "Can we talk somewhere private?"

"My office."

"Okay." Lander swallowed hard, hoping he wasn't making a big mistake. "I've got to get something first."

"Meet me up there in ten minutes."

With his internal voice screaming *no*, Lander grabbed his backpack from the floor next to the cot where he had slept, and climbed the steps to Pastor Stevens's second story office. *Please God, Pop-pop always said you help people. I don't know if that's true. But ... could you please help me now.* He stifled the urge to turn and run as he knocked on the door.

"Come in."

The office was small. An old wooden desk with a ragged, well-worn rolling chair behind and two hard-backed chairs in front took up most of the room. Every wall was lined with shelves and every shelf was stuffed with books. Piles of books occupied every empty space on the floor.

A comforting warmth filled the place. Patches of bright yellow paint peeked from between the books where the walls could be seen. Looking around, Lander's suspicion evaporated. He didn't know how he knew, but Pastor Stevens was someone he could trust.

Lander pulled the door in behind him, shutting it with a quiet click.

"Have a seat." Pastor Stevens waved him to one of the chairs set before the desk. "Okay, son, why don't you start from the beginning."

"As far back as I can remember, I've been able to … well …" Heat rose up Lander's neck suffusing his cheeks. "When I … I … focus … I can go … invisible."

Lander's eyes flicked to the pastor's, but the man just sat still and silent, his expression closed. "And … I've healed things. Like a bird with a broken wing and Pop-pop when he fell from a ladder."

For the first time in his life, Lander spoke to someone other than his grandfather about the unusual things he could do .

As Lander talked, Pastor Stevens's expression hardened. "I think you've read one too many comic books, young man. What you're telling me is impossible. Why don't you try one more time? And this time, I want the truth."

"It is the truth." Lander focused and disappeared and reappeared a couple times. Pastor Stevens pushed his rolling chair back into a pile of books, scattering them across the floor, his mouth hanging open. Lander chuckled then, just for the heck of it, flicked fire with his fingertips.

"It's true. You weren't lying. Do that again."

Lander flicked fire on his fingertips then held it on the palm of his hand before snuffing it out by making a fist.

The pastor's eyes grew even wider. "And these people who are after you, they know about this?"

"I guess," Lander said. "At least I think that's what they know."

"And you have no idea where you got these special ... talents?"

"No, sir. Pop-pop always said I was different. But I never knew why. I always thought I was just a little unusual. But before he died, he told me to find a box."

Lander dragged his pack in front of him and pulled out the rocks and the journal. "These were in the box."

He placed the journal on the desk. Holding one of the stones in his hand, he began to rub it with soft even strokes. Within seconds its appearance altered from pitted brown to smooth, gleaming, bluish green.

"Whoa!" Pastor Stevens breathed out. "Does it do anything else?"

Lander shrugged. "I don't know. I just found it the other day and I haven't had a chance to see."

Setting the stone down, he watched it revert back to plain brown. Then picking up the journal, he ran his fingers over the tooling then handed it to the pastor. "I think this belonged to my mom. At least that's what Pop-pop's note said. I can't read the first pages; I don't know the language they're written in. But I was hoping to have some time today to begin reading what's written in English. You wouldn't happen to recognize the language there at the beginning? Can you figure out what it says?"

After scanning several pages, Pastor Stevens shook his head. "I'm sorry, son. I don't recognize this language." He paused, picked up Pop-pop Ian's note again, and read it for the second time. "You have me at a loss. I've never heard of anything like this before except maybe in the movies or a science fiction book.

"I want to believe you. In one respect, I have to believe you. But before I make a decision to help you, I'm going to have to pray about this. Can you give me the rest of the morning? I'll meet you at lunch and we can talk then. Okay?"

Nodding, Lander put the stones and journal back into his pack. "Sounds fair."

"The room next to my office is set aside for quiet study. It usually sits empty. Go ahead and use it. Take some time to be alone and read. I'll make sure nobody bothers you."

"Thank you, sir." After closing the office door behind him, Lander scanned the hallway and headed to the study.

Pastor Stevens and Lander both grabbed baloney and cheese sandwiches, juice boxes, and chips, then made their way to the same table where they had eaten breakfast.

After taking a large bite of his sandwich and chewing, Pastor Stevens said, "Okay Lander, I believe you. But even more, I believe you're meant to be here for now. You can stay as long as you need to. And when you're ready to head to Bethel, I'll see what I can do to help you get there. I don't think you should travel by bus though. I have an idea. When you're ready, we can talk about it."

Over the next several days, Lander worked around the mission. He cleaned, helped prepare meals, and even helped one of the volunteers, an older lady named Nancy, do the grocery shopping. But he spent most of his time up in the quiet room, studying the journal. Every evening, when things settled down for the night, Lander joined Pastor Stevens in his office where the two discussed what Lander had read that day.

Though Lander was frustrated by his inability to read the earlier entries in the journal, he began piecing together some of the story from the later entries that were written in English.

"So," Pastor Stevens said, summing up what he and Lander had discussed so far. "You think your people actually came from within the earth itself."

"I know it sounds crazy, but I think so. The journal refers to Surface Dwellers and Core Dwellers. Core Dwellers, like my mom and dad, can do things that Surface Dwellers can't. That's why I can do the things I do."

"And," Pastor Stevens continued, "At some point, a small group of Surface Dwellers led by a man named Aurelius Hunt penetrated the shield that surrounds and protects the core at the center of the earth. This Aurelius Hunt convinced several families to return to the surface with him, including your parents and grandfather."

"Yeah. My mom was pregnant with me.

"Once they were on the surface, something went wrong. Aurelius Hunt betrayed my people. Pop-pop Ian really hated that man. Said he was responsible for my mom's and dad's deaths."

Lander stopped for a moment, drawing in slow even breaths, struggling to calm his raging emotions. "Pop-pop wrote that Aurelius Hunt wanted to study us like some kind of science experiment because of what we could do. That's how my parents died. They wouldn't let him take me. They confronted his security people while the rest of the Core Dwellers escaped, including Pop-pop Ian and me. That's why Pop-pop Ian raised me the way he did and warned me to trust no one."

"That's quite a story." Pastor Stevens rose and paced in the small area behind his desk. "Aurelius Hunt is a powerful man. He owns companies all over the world. If he could duplicate what you do, it could be worth billions. It explains why those men wanted you and your grandfather. This whole thing is incredible. If you hadn't shown me the things you can do, I'd think you were just some messed up druggie with a burned-out brain."

They stared at each other for a minute, Lander still trying to wrap his mind around all he was learning.

"It's a shame you can't read your mother's journal entries."

"Yeah," Lander swiped at his nose. A growing sense of emptiness triggered a burning at the back of his throat. There was so much he didn't understand. "It would be great to read about the Core and Core Dwellers. If we could translate the earlier writing, we might be able to find out a lot about my people and what happened."

CHAPTER 5

The following Saturday, the Trinity Youth Group arrived as usual. By that time, Lander had finished reading Pop-pop's journal entries. He sat at the battered old metal table in the quiet room, his mind spinning as he scanned his grandfather's entries once again, hoping to find something he missed reading through the first time.

Set into an alcove surrounded by three tall, narrow windows with transoms above, the scruffy table seemed out of place. The stained-glass depiction of flowers and vines in the center transom cast the early afternoon light in a pattern of broken shadows across the golden wood of the floor.

Bent, with his nose almost touching the journal and his back heated by the sunlight, Lander struggled to read a particular entry. A cough from the doorway broke his concentration and he jumped up, his heart racing, knocking over his chair.

Becky stood there; her arms crossed. A grin that threatened to erupt into a full laugh crinkled the soft chocolate skin around her eyes.

"Nice jump, country boy." She sauntered into the room her focus shifting from Lander to the journal.

Lander slammed it shut.

"Must be pretty interesting stuff." Becky reached out to touch the leather cover.

"It's nothing." Lander shifted to block the journal.

"Sorry." A hurt expression surfaced on her face as she stepped past the table and looked out the windows. "Didn't mean to pry." She turned back to Lander and a hesitant half-smile broke through. "I'm glad you're still here though. I wasn't sure you would be."

"No. I'm sorry. I guess I'm just jumpy. But I'm glad to see you too, Becky."

"Really? I thought you might have forgotten me by now."

Lander willed his stiff posture to relax and smiled. Today Becky wore her hair pulled back into a long ponytail. A gray graphic tee with the word *faith* written down the front and snug jeans showed her curves to perfection. Lander swallowed hard as her smile brightened, illuminating the room and warming his heart. "No way. You aren't easy to forget."

"That's right. And you'd better not forget it country boy. Come on; everyone's here. It's time to hit the streets. And today, you're going to help."

The group welcomed Lander as if he was an old friend. Within a half-hour they were out on the streets. Lander hung to the back, his hands twitching as he fought zinging nerves at the thought of talking to strangers, while the others handed out sandwiches and pamphlets, and told anyone who was interested about Jesus. By the time they returned to help make supper, his stomach had stopped clenching, but he didn't think he ever wanted to participate in evangelism again.

When they sat down to eat, Lander watched Becky from the corner of his eye, marveling at her easy manner. She smiled and joked with those around her. She was so pretty and outgoing;

a comfortable peace filled Lander when she was near. Heat climbed his neck into his ears when she got up to get more water and his eyes scanned her curves again. He had always kept his distance from girls, too complicated. But with Becky it was different.

Working with Michael, one of the tattooed boys, and Becky, wiping tables after the meal, Lander scanned the area to make certain no one was near then approached Michael. "Michael, can you help me not look so different?"

"What?" Becky interrupted, her focus shifting in a nano-second from the table she ran a cloth over to the boys. "I think you look cute, country geek."

"I'd rather look more like everyone else."

"Why?" Curiosity scrunched Becky's brow. "I think it's refreshing that you dress different. Like you don't care what everyone else thinks."

"But that's the point." Lander pulled in a deep breath then released it in a huff. "I do care. I'd prefer to just fit in rather than stand out."

"Ohhhh," Becky stretched out the word. "I get it. You want to impress some girl. Who is she?"

Michael groaned. "Hey Becks, give the country geek a break.

"Don't mind her, Lander. She just likes drama. If you're really serious about changing your looks, I can help with that."

Zane, the muscular boy who had confronted Lander the night they met called out, "Hey, Mike, catch." He threw an object to Mike and ignited another in his hand. Light Sabers. Though Lander had never used one, he had watched others mock-battle with them.

The two young men maneuvered around tables and clusters of people, swinging their glowing swords and shouting at each other until Pastor Stevens stalked into the room and shouted, "Stop! How many times do I have to tell you two this is not a gym or a field? If you must use those things, go outside to the parking lot with them."

In under a minute the place emptied as everyone rushed to observe the Light Saber battle between Mike and Zane.

A part of Lander wanted to try wielding one; it looked like fun. But he backed into the shadows away from the overhead lights and watched as several young people took turns and battled. Once everyone who wanted to battle had a chance, they moved back inside for some warm drinks.

"Thanksgiving's only a couple weeks away." Mike slapped Lander on the shoulder and grabbed a Styrofoam cup of hot chocolate. "If you're going to do something about your look, we should do it before then. I can come by next Saturday if you want. We can go to the thrift shop. You can find good, cheap stuff there." He squinted one eye and gave Lander an appraising look. "Yeah. We need to do something about that hair. And what do you think about a tat? You've got some money, right? If you got some money you gotta get a tat."

"Wait just a minute." Becky stepped in front of him, looking very petite and pretty, as she stood toe to toe with the six-foot plus, muscular Michael. "You're not doing anything without my approval. Don't you even think about going shopping without me."

Lander ran a hand over his hair for the hundredth time, patting the net covering as he dished mashed potatoes to the long line of people who had come to Crossways Mission for Thanksgiving dinner. It was short, very short—on the sides. Long on top—long enough to tie into a tail. And dark, almost black. By the time Michael and Becky were done, not only did he have new hair, he had spent more money than he thought possible to purchase three outfits at an upscale shop Becky insisted had the best new styles. Though they were expensive, she pronounced them practical as he could mix and match.

When he questioned the wisdom of buying ripped jeans, his two consultants insisted he absolutely needed at least one pair with holes. But when Michael had tried to pull him into a tattoo shop, Lander drew the line. He wasn't ready to let some stranger stick needles into him.

He smiled at Becky, standing next to him, ladling thick, creamy gravy over turkey and mashed potatoes. Becky smiled and leaned close, her perfume drifting to Lander and smelling oh so nice. "You look really good, Lander. Nobody'd recognize you now."

He hoped she was right.

"Of course," she added, her eyes sparkling. "It's the hair net that really makes the outfit."

A sputtered laugh shook her as Lander's mouth hung open. "You do realize I'm kidding, don't you? You know you're really weird."

"Yeah, yeah, I know." Lander ran his fingers over his hair once again. He suppressed the urge to bounce on his toes as a grin threatened to slip past his lips; the world looked brighter than it had for weeks. The day he spent with Becky and Michael had been wonderful and Lander sighed in contentment. Michael walked toward them; his heavy muscles visible through his tight tee-shirt as he carried a steaming pot of mashed potatoes.

Living here at Crossways was helping Lander learn to accept other people. *Pop-pop, you were wrong. There are good people, people I can trust.*

Michael plopped the heavy pot onto the table to the right of the almost empty one. One of the many Thanksgiving volunteers scraped the remains from the empty pot to the top of the fresh mound and handed Michael the dirty pot.

Becky rocked into Lander's side and his feet shuffled from the impact. He sent her a questioning look. She looked up at him, chewing her lower lip, then sent him a wink that shot flutters through his stomach.

"Hey you two, no PDAs! This is a family friendly zone, you know." Michael's deep voice next to Lander's left ear startled him.

"PDA?" Lander's brows drew down. "What's that?"

Michael and the volunteer both huffed out aborted laughs.

Becky reached past Lander to punch Michael's arm, but he backed away. "Oh no, Becks. Not this time. These muscles are needed to carry the heavy loads. See?" He swung the empty pot up and around as he turned back to the kitchen. "Besides. You need to explain what a PDA is to your innocent new friend."

"Public Display of Affection," Becky mumbled, her eyes narrowed at Michael's retreating back.

Lander's mouth rounded as he dished out a portion of turkey over a mound of the fresh potatoes. *Oh … is that what we were doing?*

Becky's ladle hit the side of her pan with an extra loud clank. She stirred the gravy with exaggerated movements as the scruffy, bearded man Lander had just served reached out his plate for gravy. After plopping a healthy dollop of gravy on his mashed potatoes, Becky turned to face Lander. "We were just talking, country boy, so don't read anything into what Mike said. He's such a jerk sometimes."

Lander's gaze lowered to the tray of meat before him and his shoulders rolled forward. He continued dishing up turkey with automatic movements. *She's angry? With me? What did I do wrong? I thought she liked me. Girls … too complicated.*

Lander's thoughts bumped against each other, sliding around in his mind, while he continued to serve out turkey in a distracted manner. Until raised voices at the door drew his attention.

Four members of the gang Pastor Stevens had banned

from the mission stood inside the doorway. Sudden silence filled the room as all eyes shifted to the four. Dressed in gray hoodies with orange crossed daggers over their hearts, baggie jeans, combat boots, and orange and gray checked bandanas, they stood for a moment, smiles emerging, apparently pleased at the response their presence was triggering.

An arrogant grin spread across the face of a well-muscled young man with a shaved head. He strode forward with a confident swagger, waving for the others to follow as he crossed the room. Lander recognized him Ash, the gang's leader. As those in the line backed away, the gang members stepped in at the front of the line.

CHAPTER 6

everal people already eating got up and, leaving their half-eaten meals behind, walked out. Those who had been in line moved farther away, watching, eyes wide. Pastor Stevens must have been alerted. He strode out of the kitchen, wiping his hands on a damp dish towel.

"Ash, Troy, what are you guys doing here?"

Ash shrugged and turned to face Pastor Stevens. Crossing his arms over his chest, he tilted his head and a confident smirk slipped across his face. "Whada you think? We're here for the free food. There's free food here, ain't there? This is supposed to be a mission. Don't your God want you to help the poor underprivileged? Right now, my boys and me are needy. We're hungry."

"The last time I let you eat here, we had to call the cops. People ended up in the hospital. If you can behave, sit and eat quietly without any problems, fine. If not, leave now."

"You ain't the boss of us." Troy, a thin, wiry boy with a sprinkling of pale beard hairs and a reputation in the neighborhood as a sociopath, pulled a gun from the waistband of his oversized jeans and waved it at Pastor Stevens. "Right now, preacher man, it looks like I'm the boss. Whadda ya gonna do about it?"

"Put that away," Ash towered over the diminutive Troy, anger sparking in his eyes. "I said, put that away. We came in for food, not trouble."

Troy backed away from Ash, turning the gun on him. "I'm sick of you. Always lording it over the rest of us." His hazel eyes flashing, Troy laughed. "See, you ain't so big when I'm holdin'. Now, I'm in charge." The other two gang members faded into the crowd who had backed against the wall when the gang members entered, leaving the open area in front of the tables to Troy and Ash.

Raising his hands, palms out, Pastor Stevens spoke, his voice calm and steady. "Sure, Troy, you're in charge. Ash knows it. Everybody knows it. Why don't you put the gun away, find a seat, and I'll bring you a nice hot plate of food. Serve you myself, just like the man in charge deserves."

Troy swung the gun back toward Pastor Stevens. Whether he meant to shoot or not was unclear to Lander, but the thing went off.

Time slowed. Lander's eyes widened as he saw the trajectory of the bullet with clear certainty. His heart raced and adrenaline surged. But his panic faded as time remained frozen in the millisecond it took for the bullet to speed right for Becky. Her mouth opened in a round circle of shock.

Without thought, Lander grabbed the stones he always kept with him from the pockets of his jeans. He held one in each hand, arms stretched out before him, as he flung his body between the bullet and Becky. The stones flared, hot and potent against the palms of his hands. Immense energy surged from them creating a crystalline shield as if reading Lander's mind. The bullet hit the shield, slowed like it was moving through thick paste and dropped to the ground.

Time resumed.

Within seconds, several men pinned Troy on the ground as he cursed and struggled against them. With the threat neutralized, all eyes turned to Lander. The explosive release of energy left him drained and confused. Fear seized him; fear of discovery, fear of his difference, fear at needing to run again.

He glanced at Becky; she stood frozen, her eyes unseeing, her mouth agape. She shook her head and took a step back, away from Lander.

He wanted to cry, but instead a hysterical laugh broke from him, filled with pain and sorrow. He was different. He was dangerous.

"Lander. Lander. It's okay." Pastor Stevens's voice broke through Lander's haze, awareness of the pastor's hand on his arm drew his attention. Then Pastor Stevens was propelling him back through the kitchen. "Lander. It's okay. You did a good thing, you saved Becky's life. Nobody here will say anything. You don't have to worry."

"I have to leave, don't I?" Lander fisted his hands, attempting to control the trembling that threatened to spread through his body as the truth of what he had just revealed pummeled him.

Regret flowed across the pastor's features and he nodded. "Tomorrow. Tomorrow we'll get you on your way. For now, I think it best if you went up to the quiet room and stayed there. Don't worry, nobody whose here now will talk to the cops." The pastor's eyes shifted back toward the dining room. "But rumors will start. I can't stop it. And Ash won't forget what happened; neither will Troy. Staying here isn't an option."

"Sure. I understand." Lander swallowed hard past the burning lump in his throat. He had known all along he couldn't stay at Crossways for long, knew a time would come when he would have to get to Bethel. But he had been happy here, had made friends. Lander had hoped to stay at least until Christmas. Now he couldn't.

Becky brought a plate of food up to Lander a short while later, setting it on the metal table.

"The cops are here," she said, avoiding eye contact. "Nobody's telling them anything except Troy. But they think he's high so they're not paying him any mind." She paused, swallowed, and lifted her eyes to Lander's. "Thanks, Lander. Thank you. You saved my life." A sob broke through. She stumbled forward, flung her arms around Lander, and hugged him hard, repeating "thank you" over and over as she sobbed into his shoulder.

Lander lay awake on the loveseat in the study room later that night wondering if he should have kept his abilities to himself and avoided the whole mess. But if he had, Becky might be in the hospital … maybe even dead. That thought made his blood run cold. Though he had known her for a short time, unexpected feelings for her settled deep within him.

The following morning, Lander yawned and fought to keep his scratchy eyes open as he watched rain spatter against the windows in the quiet room. Pastor Stevens brought up a tray with eggs, bacon, toast, and two mugs of coffee. Lander's stomach rebelled at the thought of eating, so he refused the food but downed several mugs of coffee to combat the residual foggy haze resulting from all that had happened the day before and the sleepless night. The afternoon continued cold and rainy. Lander shivered as he waited with Pastor Stevens at the kitchen door.

"Right now, you probably feel like you can't ever come back here," Pastor Stevens said as a silver Kenworth towing a matching trailer pulled up in the alley behind Crossways Mission. "But, if you ever want to, know you're welcome here. Anytime." He grabbed Lander in a gentle hug and whispered,

"I'll keep you in my prayers. The Flemings are good people. They'll get you as close to Bethel as they can."

Lander hoisted his backpack to his shoulder, tumbled out the door, and dashed toward the truck, beads of heavy rain beating on the top of his backpack and head. A petite, older woman with short blonde hair gelled into spikes, jumped down and helped Lander up into the impressive cab of the rumbling, vibrating vehicle. She swung up after him, pulling the door shut behind her.

"Crummy weather," she exclaimed as she bounced droplets of water from her short hair. She turned to face Lander, who backed between the bucket seats, tripped over his feet, and landed on his backside on the bed.

Lander attempted to rise but, with a soft chuckle and wide smile, the lady waved him to stay then reached out a hand. "Hi. I'm Julie. This is my husband, Jason. You must be Lander. Pastor tells me you're a good kid with an urgent need to get to Bethel. Well, we're not going that far east up there—that would mess up our schedule so we can't take you all the way. But we've got to make a stop in Greensburg, so we can get you that far. You can catch a bus to Bethel from there. That work for you?"

"Yes, ma'am," Lander said, shaking Julie's hand as pent-up tension bled from his muscles.

The Flemings were a unique couple; Jason reminded Lander of a bear, large and weighty, while Julie was so tiny, she barely reached to Lander's chest when standing next to him. And riding with them was nothing like what Lander had expected when Pastor Stevens first told him about the couple. Julie talked—nonstop—Jason listened, grunting from time to time—whether in agreement or opposition, Lander couldn't tell. They had known Pastor Stevens since he was a child and Julie saw it as her duty to regale Lander with every story she could remember from the pastor's younger years. Julie also liked country music; she liked it loud.

"We decided to get satellite radio a few years ago. Best move ever. Now, instead of playing around, always needing to search out good stations, we get to listen to the music we like all the time. Right, Jason?"

Grunt.

Listening to Julie talk helped Lander forget his troubles for a time. She smiled and always had a ready laugh. No matter the topic, she talked with a level of knowledge that stretched Lander's brain. Even when she drove while Jason took a break and slept, her ongoing, one-sided dialogue never stopped. The only time the cab was quiet was when she napped. Once her soft snores laced the air and Jason turned off the radio, Lander, sitting in the other front seat, zoned out to the hum of the engine, the steady sound of the road, and Julie's rhythmic snoring.

Near noon the next day, they pulled into an industrial park where they backed up to one of the loading docks of an immense warehouse. While men unloaded the trailer, Jason, Julie, and Lander trekked to a diner not far from the industrial complex. Though the temperature remained in the thirties, the wet, cloudy weather had broken, and the sun was shining in a cloudless blue expanse. Lander stretched out his legs and pulled in deep breaths of the crisp air as they walked.

"Get whatever you want, Lander." Julie buried her nose in the over-sized, laminated menu. Jason got a burger, rare and loaded with everything, a large order of fries, and a Coke. Julie's order was the same except she got a diet Coke. "I'm watching my weight."

Lander gobbled up his cheese steak and fries, enjoying every bite of the tender meat, onions, and peppers dripping with cheddar cheese and slathered in ketchup. By the time they returned, the trailer had been emptied and packed with a new load. Soon after pulling back onto the highway, Lander settled into the back berth and, with Julie's voice a pleasant drone in the background and a full belly, slept.

The next morning, the Flemings dropped Lander at the bus terminal in Greensburg, about five hours west of Bethel.

"Wish you all the best, young man. It was a pleasure having your company these last few days." Julie hopped down next to Lander and grabbed him in a soft hug. "You ever need a ride again, if we're goin' that way, we'd be happy to help. Just let Pastor Stevens know. You got his number, right?"

"Yes, ma'am."

Lander's eyes nearly popped when Jason climbed down from the rig. The large trucker grunted and extended a hand. Taking Lander's in a crushing grip, he shook hands like they had been best pals for ages. He grunted again, turned and climbed back into his truck, followed by Julie.

"Take care, now." Julie waved out the window, her smile lighting Lander's insides. He watched them drive away and once they disappeared around a corner, headed into the bus station.

Lander set his ball cap low over his eyes, pulled his sweatshirt hood over the cap, and sauntered into the crowded station as if he didn't have a care in the world, though his eyes scanned the station without stop. He moved with confidence, purchased his ticket and headed to the bus. He was still different from other people, but now he knew more about blending in.

The rain had turned to snow by the time Lander stepped off the bus in Bethel, a light coating covered the grass and trees. The town was small, old, like Wharton, and he had no problems getting directions to the Elm Farm. Twenty minutes later he stopped on the gravel drive, scanning a large rambling, stone farmhouse. The snow drifted down like light seed puffs and in the crisp air, voices carried from inside.

Several lights were lit on the porch and inside the house, casting a warm, golden glow that reminded Lander of the light in his stones.

Then he saw the girl. It felt like a dream he had dreamed many times before. She was swinging on an old wooden swing hung from an oak tree with heavy ropes. Blonde curls poured out beneath a cap of orange wool. Her pink jacket was open, exposing pink and blue embroidery on the front of her white dress. She stood and smiled as the snow swirled around her.

Her curls bouncing, she turned, ran to the porch and yelled into the house, "Daddy, he's here."

CHAPTER 7

Desma stared unseeing at the kaleidoscope of warm colors; reds, oranges, golds, and browns splashed in varied abandon across the trees bordering the field beyond her kitchen window. The peaks of the mountains beyond seemed to float above the lower slopes now shrouded in misty fog. She washed another dish with a lethargic grace, immune to the allure of the autumn glories.

For sixteen years, she had struggled to embrace the beauties of the Surface; for sixteen years, she had ached for the irretrievable splendor of her home. She sighed. After so many years, she was still an alien in a strange land she refused to accept. She rinsed the dish, placing it in the drainer with the others. She stopped caring a long time ago. Depression had engulfed her regret along with the memories of her home, turning her life into an empty gray nothingness. The only thing that kept Desma from complete uncaring was the infinitesimal hope that one day she and her family could return home. That, and her bitter anger, sustained her.

Looking up at the clock, Desma grumbled under her breath. Violet would be home from school in a half hour. Desma's sons would arrive home a few hours later. *Twenty minutes. Just twenty minutes. A short nap. Oblivion.*

"Auntie Des." Violet's voice shattered the silence. The backdoor slammed pulling Desma to full alert.

"Auntie Des. I'm home."

Desma groaned, throwing her right arm over her eyes, striving to block out the reality of her life.

"Auntie Des, look what I made today!" With the youthful enthusiasm of a six-year old child, Violet swept into the room like a miniature tornado. "We talked about leaves and I made a tree picture with all kinds of colored paper leaves. I cut them out myself. Isn't it pretty, Auntie Des? Just like the trees in the woods. So pretty!"

Violet began to dance around the large living room, swinging her paper tree as if it was blowing in the wind."

Desma tried to ignore the child, but when she almost tripped over the mahogany and leather ottoman in front of the fireplace, scraping it on the oriental rug, Desma sat up, anger churning in her belly. "Stop it! Stop this foolery this instant before you break something. If you must prance about like a wild animal, go outside and do it."

She spoke in the old language of her people and Violet stared at her for a moment with furrowed brow. The girl dropped her gaze to the floor and chewed her lower lip. "I'm sorry." A second later, a smile broke out and her face brightened. "Then is it okay if I go outside now?"

"Go!" Desma waved toward the back door.

Violet ran out, laughing.

Desma's eyes roved the exposed-beam ceiling. By Surface Dweller standards, her house was luxurious. Two stories tall, it boasted a large, wraparound porch with tables and rocking chairs scattered across the expanse. A true stone building, with two-foot thick walls surrounding a well-insulated framework. Castor had it built sparing no expense.

In the great room where Desma now sprawled across a couch, a massive native stone fireplace filled the wall opposite the open kitchen. Specialty glass windows with heavy wood trim were set into the adjacent wall. Immense, stained timber beams framed the twenty-foot high, vaulted ceiling. Exotic hand-tied oriental rugs in muted shades of brown, green, and gray covered most of the dark mahogany floor. The furniture spoke of wealth and luxury in soft leather and brocades of complementary tones of tans and muted burgundy. Castor worked hard to help Desma adjust. But it was never enough.

Groaning with the effort, Desma pulled up from the couch. She meandered to the fireplace, her fingers brushing the heavy rock face before moving to caress the polished, dark wood of the mantle. Nearly two dozen precious stones were scattered along the heavy wooden mantle; just a small fraction of the wealth she and the other Core Dwellers had brought to the surface with them. Several had been used to purchase the farm, tear down the existing farmhouse, and build the house Desma had desired. Others had been used to purchase new identities.

Lifting one of the large gemstones from the mantle, she leaned her head against the grainy wood and gazed into the depths of the gem she cupped in both hands as she pulled in and released several deep breaths. Longing surfaced and she allowed it to stoke the bitterness within. At least it was something. Bitter anger was better than the gray nothingness she lived with day in and day out. Enjoying her descent into the acrid brew and well-stoked anger, she cried out when unexpected pain swept through her.

The gem tumbled from her numb fingers to the ground and Desma dropped to her knees. She had felt this distinctive sensation of tearing pain only a few times before. The first had been sixteen years ago when Cyanne and Jerod died protecting everyone else, giving their lives to secure freedom for the rest of the Core Dwellers who had journeyed to the surface with them four months earlier.

The high beams from Castor's jeep bounced against the darkened side of the barn as he drove up the stone drive later that evening. Desma watched as he parked the jeep next to the two vehicles already there. The lights went off and the jeep sat, still and silent for several minutes, before the door opened and Castor's large frame emerged.

He felt it. Castor will know who we lost. Desma watched from the kitchen window as her husband climbed the three wooden steps to the porch, stopping at each as if to catch his breath. Heavy steps plodded across the porch and Castor stood quiet and still at the door for several more minutes before entering the house.

Parker and Parrish looked up from the table, their faces pale.

"Who?" Desma asked without preamble.

Castor raised bloodshot eyes to his wife. "English, Desma."

Desma huffed her frustration. "We've lost someone and all you can think of is what language I choose to use? What if some Surface Dweller has learned the truth?"

"Don't Desma," Naara, Desma's closest friend, said, her voice soft and calm. "Give Castor a chance. We're all concerned."

"Mom, please." Twenty-six-year-old Parker rose from the table, his shaggy dark brown hair falling into his deep-set, gray eyes as he paced across to the fireplace. "Now's not the time."

Castor shook his head and waved his hands as if warding off Desma's bitter anger as he strode past. He sluffed off his gray woolen coat and stepped back into the mudroom to hang it before returning. Without a word he crossed the kitchen and trod down the hallway to his study. Emerging a minute later, he cradled a plain brown, pitted stone in his large, square hands.

"I'm no psychic," he mumbled as he pulled a chair from the end of the farmhouse table while Parker slid in on the bench next to his brother, exchanging looks with Naara and her husband Kenan who sat on the bench opposite.

Castor looked up at Desma, waiting.

Clicking her teeth, she sat in the other chair at the far end of the table. "Well, Castor. Are you going to keep us in suspense, or what?"

"Woman." Castor shook his head. "Your concern touches my heart." He scanned the kitchen and great room then asked, "Where's Violet?"

"I sent her up to her room," Naara said, her eyes shifting to glance at the stairs. "She's playing with one of those silly devices Parrish bought for her. Don't worry, Castor, we'll hear her if she comes down. That child doesn't know how to move without making a racket."

After a final glance at Desma, Castor focused on the stone in his hand. With a gentle touch for hands so large, he brushed the stone with his fingertips. It began to glow and grow warm, in seconds it morphed into a smooth gemstone, light amber in color with smoky dark carnelian swirling within its depths and black flecks near the surface.

Even from where she sat across the table, the hair on Desma's arms rose as energy coalesced around the glowing gemstone, the light reflecting off the faces of those gathered at the table, casting her husband in wavering bands of golden illumination and shadows.

Castor's eyes sought the depths of the shimmering stone as he focused. Desma almost reached out across the table to lay a hand on Castor's but refused the call of the Stone of Power. She hadn't touched one in years and wouldn't do so now.

Of the twenty-five people who had journeyed to the surface,

four died in the escape. Another two died in the sixteen years since. Castor's and Desma's extended family of six now sat safe at this table, protected by secure, well-established identities. *One of the thirteen original Core Dwellers not accounted for died today. Or ... perhaps ... the Devlin boy. But who?*

Castor raised tired eyes to Desma. "Ian," he said. "Ian Devlin is no longer living." He looked over at Kenan and his wife Naara, then at his sons, before lowering his eyes to his fisted hands.

Desma huffed and, grabbing a washcloth from the sink began to wipe down the already spotless table. "Well good riddance to the fool who convinced us to give up everything for a lie." She folded the cloth, returning it to the sink and settled into the routine of getting supper on the table.

Castor shook his head, his eyes still glued to his clenched hands. "It wasn't Ian's fault. He was lied to as well. And lost his son and daughter-in-law as a result. You need to forgive him, Desma."

"Ha!" Desma snorted. "As if that's going to happen. You just wait. I'll bet that Devlin boy is on his way here even as we speak. The old goat probably told him to come here if anything happened to him. Well, I'm not taking care of him. He can just find someone else. He's not welcome here."

Castor rose, anger lighting his eyes. "He will be welcome here. I gave Ian my word I'd take care of Lander if anything happened to him. My word Desma. Like it or not we will take in Ian's grandson if—no, when—he comes.

"It's been almost seventeen years! It's past time you let go of your anger and bitterness. Don't you see what it's doing to our family? To us?

"Desma, please, let it go already. We're here and here is a good place to be. The boys like it on the Surface and so do I. Our stones have bought us a good life here. Let go of the past and live in the present."

62

He raised his eyes to Desma and the lines of his face hardened. "You *will* show Lander kindness and Core Dweller hospitality when he comes."

"Who's Lander?" Violet's young voice dispelled the rising anger. She sat on the bottom step; her knees pulled up under her chin.

The adults looked around at each other. "I'll explain," Kenan huffed out a breath and rose from his seat next to Naara. "It's time Violet learned the truth."

"But she ... she ... was born on the Surface." Concern etched a line between Naara's brows as she pushed up to her feet as well and wrung her hands. "Are you sure she should know?"

Kenan glanced between Castor and Naara, then said, "She may have been born on the Surface, but she's our daughter, Naara, and she's smart. She'll understand. I'll talk to her in her room. Do you want to join us, Naara?"

An understanding smile spread across Naara's face. "No, dear. I trust you. You're better at things like this than I am." Her gaze flicked to her daughter, still sitting on the bottom step, looking even younger than her seven years. "Honey, Daddy has something important to tell you. Why don't you go up to your room with him?"

Violet hopped onto her feet and sprinted up the stairs, her voice drifting down behind her. "I knew it. I knew you guys were keeping some big secret all along. It's about time you told me. I'm not a little kid, you know. Come on Daddy." Violet turned and scrambled back down the stairs, grabbed Kenan's hand, and pulled him up the stairs.

The clenched muscles in Castor's back relaxed when he heard Desma chuckling. The rare sound brought back memories of happier days. And, he hoped, a promise for better days to come.

CHAPTER 8

Castor sighed as he patted his very full stomach. Desma's and Naara's hard work over the last week had borne fruit in a bountiful feast for the eyes and the stomach. For the first time since arriving on the Surface, Desma relented and took part in celebrating the holiday. Large arrangements of autumn flowers, grasses, and seed pods brought nature inside in various shades of gold, orange, pale yellow, and burgundy.

In addition to the traditional roast turkey of their adopted home, other saliva-inducing aromas had permeated the air throughout the morning, including Desma's specialty braised short ribs and Naara's Balsamic glazed Brussels sprouts. They rounded out the meal with a selection of side dishes that included sage stuffing and pumpkin soufflé.

Castor's contentment surfaced in the form of a smile as he looked around the table.

Even Violet contributed to the festivities. Before they ate, she talked about the Pilgrims and the Indians. She handed each person a few corn kernels and then talked about how the

Indians helped the Pilgrims. "Now we all need to say something we are thankful for. I'll start. I'm thankful for Mom and Dad, for Uncle Castor and Auntie Desma, and for my cousins, Parker and Parrish. Oh! Yes! I'm also thankful that Parker finally has a girlfriend. Welcome to the family, Kendra!"

An awkward moment of silence followed Violet's words, then Castor laughed and everyone else chimed in as well. Even Desma chuckled.

Violet bowed. "Now it's your turn Uncle Castor."

Castor read a psalm about thanksgiving from the Bible.

Desma had been better the last month, more open, less acerbic. As a result, Parker invited his young lady friend Kendra for Thanksgiving dinner. She arrived with a light-up-a-room smile and a tray of home-baked cookies. Desma received the offering with surprising grace, easing the tension that had been building in Castor's shoulders ever since he learned Kendra would be coming. He sighed in satisfaction once again as he watched the conversation flow between Parrish and Kendra, while Violet broke chunks off what had to be her sixth cookie, examining each piece before eating it.

Though Desma initially resisted the idea of Ian's grandson, Lander, living with them, she had, in time, come to terms with the situation. Watching her now, talking with Naara, Castor hoped this was a sign that Desma had at last let go of at least some of her bitter anger. Brief smiles came and went across her face as she and Naara whispered at the other end of the table. But then, Naara had always been able to bring out the best in Desma.

"Daddy," Violet mumbled around the cookie in her mouth as she looked across the table at Kenan. "Daddy, can I go outside and swing?"

Kenan glanced up, his eyes scanning the darkening sky through the large windows in the great room. "I don't know honey. It's pretty cold out there and it's growing dark."

"Awe, Daddy. Please."

"We can turn on the porch lights and go out with her." Parker looked at Kendra. "What do you think?"

"Sure," she responded, her bright smile appearing. "Come on, Violet. I'll push you."

Grabbing coats and boots from the mudroom, Violet gusted out the back door with Parker and Kendra on her heels.

"Kendra's really nice." Naara's eyes followed the two as they disappeared through the door. She turned toward Castor. "I'm glad you relented and gave Parker and Parrish permission to develop serious relationships with Surface Dwellers."

"Well." Castor let the word linger on the air. "It's Desma you need to thank for that. It was her idea for Parker to invite Kendra today." He smiled at his wife. "Thank you, Desma. It was a great idea.

"What do you think, Parrish? Christmas will be here before we know. Is there a special young lady you've wanted to have over?"

Parrish looked at his mother, a frown creasing his forehead. "Well ... actually, yes Dad. Sure. There's been someone special for a while now. It's just ... complicated."

Castor watched Desma, trying to gauge her reaction. He released a puff of air in relief when she smiled at Parrish. "Of course, Parrish. Your father's right. I've held onto harsh feelings for far too long." She nodded as if affirming her words to herself, her eyes unfocused. "You know, I have to admit, it feels good to finally let it go." Casting her gaze to catch Castor's her eyes softened. "Yes. This is our life now. I need to let go of the past." She rose, slapping her hands together. "Well, if you all will excuse me. There's cleanup to be done."

"Sit, Desma," Castor pushed up onto his feet. "You ladies did the cooking. And it was an amazing meal. Parrish, Kenan, and I will do the cleanup." He turned to face Parrish.

"Why don't you stoke the fire first. Kenan and I will get started in the kitchen."

Once Desma and Naara were settled in front of a well-stoked fire, sipping cups of brandy-laced coffee, Kenan glanced at the two before speaking quietly to Castor. "What happened? Desma's changed since the last time we were home. Don't get me wrong, it's a good change. But, don't you think it's a little unexpected?"

Castor rubbed his forehead with his lower arm, keeping his suds encased hand from his eyes. "Maybe. Maybe not. "She's been different ever since we learned that Ian died. We still don't know how he died and I'm getting worried about Lander. He should have been here by now.

"But, you're right, the change in Desma is a real relief, if an unexpected consequence. Maybe the brunt of her anger was defused with Ian's death. She always blamed him and Cyanna for what happened. I don't know."

"It sure makes being home a lot more pleasant," Parrish said. "I hope she doesn't revert. I'd hate to have it go back to the way she was before, always either hopeless or angry all the time. I like the new mom. She's like I remember her before…"

"Yeah," Kenan said. "Back—before—your mom was quite the hostess. She and Naara were noted for their extravagant parties and I know Naara enjoyed working with Desma to pull off this Thanksgiving dinner. She said it was like the old days." Turning to Castor, as he grabbed another dish from the drainer and started to wipe, Kenan asked, "Have you talked to her about Ian's grandson since the day Ian died?"

Shaking his head and grimacing, Castor replied, "Not yet. I'm sort of afraid to bring the subject up. She's been so much more contented lately I hate the thought of doing anything that might change that."

"Do you really think he's coming here?" Parker asked. "I mean, he doesn't know us. He probably has a good life where he's been living and won't even come. I wouldn't leave here; I have a life, a job, friends, family."

"Well, that's the point," Castor said. "Sixteen years ago, Ian took Lander and left. He insisted we split up saying it would be safer that way. And with his parents dead, and now Ian gone, he has no other family on the Surface. I don't think the boy had anyone except Ian."

"Yeah, you know how Ian was," Kenan said. "I wouldn't be surprised if he never even told the kid the truth about himself, where we come from, or our gifts. He was always quiet about things. Especially after Cyanne's and Jerod's deaths. He blamed himself and got even more reclusive than he was in the Core. Let's hope Parker's right and Lander never even shows up here. Because, honestly, I'm concerned that if he does come, he might lead Aurelius's people right to us. We've been safe for a long time now, we've established our identities, developed relationships. But we know nothing about this boy, Castor. Maybe he's even working for Aurelius."

Giving Kenan a look of disgust Castor said, "Like Ian would ever let that happen? He may have been eccentric, but he would never let his own grandson fall into Aurelius's hands. Of us all, he had the most reason to hate Aurelius. And, without his help … and Cyanne's and Jerod's sacrifices, we would never have escaped the island. Don't forget that."

As the men were finishing the clean-up, Violet, Parker, and Kendra stomped in the back door. "It's snowing!" Violet shouted, clomping into the kitchen in wet boots.

"Whoa," Parker exclaimed, grabbing the little girl under the arms and swinging her back into the mudroom. "You know the rules you little terror; no shoes past the mudroom."

"Ahhh!" Violet screeched with a huge grin. "The monster has me. Help Kendra. Save me!"

"Roar rhaawa," Parker roared as Kendra laughed. "I'm the tickle monster. Any little girls still wearing boots by the time I count to five will be tickled until they laugh so hard their eyes will pop."

Castor laughed at the antics of his son and Violet. Looking up, he caught Desma's eye. For a moment, he saw something there and feared the bitterness was returning, but then she smiled. His smile grew in response. Yes, it was a blessing to have the old Desma back.

CHAPTER 9

Darkness wrapped around the Elm Farm as muted mid-day light descended into late afternoon dusk. The last several days, ever since Thanksgiving, heavy gray clouds had blocked out the sun and deposited spits of rain at random intervals. Though warm for November, the air held a damp rawness that permeated the farmhouse despite a thermostat set at seventy-five degrees and a well-attended fire in the great room fireplace.

This evening, strong winds swept through setting the wind chimes to clanging and dropping the temperatures. Heavy flakes of snow supplanted the rain, coating tree limbs and collecting on the wet grass, turning the yard into a fuzzy white watercolor and muting all sounds.

"Violet is still out on that swing," Naara said to no one in particular. "I think we should call her in. Tomorrow is a school day and I don't want her catching a chill."

"She'll be fine, Naara." Kenan's calm voice filtered through the pages of the newspaper he had been reading for the last half hour. "She's enjoying herself and not rampaging through the house. Let her run off some energy while she can." He shook out, then folded the paper, before sitting up on the couch where he had been lounging. "How long until dinner is ready, Desma?"

Her head bent over a pot of potatoes, Desma said, "About twenty minutes. Everything else is ready and I'm keeping things warm, but these potatoes don't seem to want to get done."

Kenan rose and walked past Naara sitting at the kitchen counter, chopping peppers for the salad. He moved to the mudroom door and peered out the window. "Castor's home."

Desma looked over her shoulder and caught sight of Castor's headlights coming up the drive before Kenan turned on the outside floodlights, bathing the area in snow flecked brilliance.

"Why don't we give Violet until supper's ready, my dear," Kenan said, turning to face Naara. "It won't be that long, and she looks so happy out there."

"Does she look cold?" A note of worry tinged Naara's voice.

Kenan chuckled. "Not a bit. You know how she is. Likes the cold." At the sound of heavy footsteps thumping across the porch, he stepped back, allowing Castor to enter. After stomping to shake the wet snow and moisture from his boots, Castor sluffed off his coat, then sat on the bench to pull off his boots.

"I think your daughter is immune to the cold." Castor shivered and rubbed his hands together. "Not like us Core Dwellers, always cold away from the Core. She has the constitution of a Surface Dweller."

"What?" Kendra asked, leaning forward and peeking out past the arm of an overstuffed gray leather recliner in the great room.

Castor's mouth dropped open and his eyes bulged.

Parker jumped up from the other recliner and mouthed

sorry to his father before saying, "A family joke, Kennie. Because my mom is always so cold."

"Oh," Kendra's brow wrinkled, then a smile surfaced. "I get it. It's because she's cold at her core?"

"Right. Something like that." Parker spoke into the awkward silence that had followed on the heels of Kendra's question.

"Well." Kendra hopped up and reached out for Parker's hands. "Like Violet, I enjoy winter weather; and it looks so beautiful out there with the snow falling. Come on, Parker, let's join her."

"Not now," Desma said as a wave of relief at Parker's quick thinking battled with her frustration at needing to keep the meal warm while others rested. "By the time you two get ready, it'll be time to come back in. I can't keep this food warm all night."

"Sure, mom," Parker said. "Want us to set the table?"

"That would be a better use of your time than traipsing out in the dark and cold." Desma bent to check the roast in the oven, hoping it hadn't dried out.

Small footsteps pounded across the porch. Violet's voice echoed through the mudroom and kitchen. "Daddy, he's here. Lander's here."

Everyone froze. Desma looked up to see Parker's eyes meet Kendra's; a pained look suffused his face. "Kennie." He turned to Castor. "Dad?"

"What's wrong, Parker?" Kendra looked around at the panicked faces. "Parker? Parker? Who's Lander?"

Desma groaned and shook her head. After a quick glance at Naara, who stood, silent, staring at the counter, she turned to Kendra, and forced a laugh. "Just ignore them. It's another stupid family joke. Our family is just full of them. Lander's well … kind of … a black sheep. Haven't seen him in years. But nothing's wrong; we're all just a little surprised. That's all."

She turned to Parker. "You and Kendra go ahead and join Violet outside for a bit. I think supper is going to run even later now. And invite Lander to come in, why don't you?"

"Sure, Mom," Parker said after a moment's hesitation. "Come on Kennie."

The silence pervading the kitchen pressed down on Desma as Kendra walked out the mudroom door. Violet's voice filtered through the open doorway, then Kendra said 'hi' to someone on the porch.

Parker, who had stopped in the doorway, backed into the mudroom and held the door open. A thin young man wearing a short, dark brown, military-style jacket over a black hoodie with the snow-covered hood pulled up over a ballcap, slipped inside, nodding his thanks to Parker.

The boy stood without speaking, scanning the kitchen from the mudroom for what seemed like an eternity. Then, with a slow, controlled motion, he brushed the hood back, dropping melting snow to the floor at his feet.

Desma pulled in a sharp breath when he pulled off the ballcap to reveal long dark hair pulled into a short tail on the top of his head and shaved short stubble on the sides. Taking in the hair, clothing, and the posture, Desma was struck with the notion that this couldn't be Ian's grandson. This boy couldn't possible have been raised by the reclusive old man. He looked more like a model from the urban clothing website Parrish favored.

The tension in the room set Lander's teeth on edge. He couldn't mistake it for anything else and his stomach clenched as the awkward silence stretched. These people he had worked so hard to get to didn't want him here. He juggled the stones in his left pocket, attempting to calm his churning stomach as he lowered his hood and slipped off his cap with his right hand. He stood, still, silent, waiting. *Pop-pop, why did you send me here?*

A long minute passed before the large man standing in front of the others asked, "Lander?"

Nothing else. No, *hi*, or *come on in*, or any other greeting that would indicate to Lander that he was welcome.

"No." The word popped out as Lander took a step back toward the door and escape. "This was a mistake. I'm sorry."

He turned and reached for the doorknob. Like a miniature whirlwind, Violet flung the door open and rushed in with a blast of cold air, flinging snow in every direction as she threw off the orange wool cap and pink jacket, dropping both to the wet floor.

A huge smile highlighted dimples in her cheeks as she stepped up to Lander and wrapped thin arms around his waist. "I'm glad you're here. Everybody's been waiting for you."

She grabbed his hand and started dragging him into the kitchen before pulling to a stop. "Oh, no, no." She shook her head. "Come back. We need to take our boots off first. Can't track yucky stuff in the kitchen. That makes Auntie Desma angry."

Violet tugged Lander back into the mudroom just as Parker and Kendra walked in the back door. Suddenly the small mudroom was hot and alive with people. Lander's throat grew tight as an overwhelming sense of being trapped tunneled his vision.

"Violet." A deep voice boomed from behind Lander. The big man. "Violet, let Lander go. I think Aunt Desma will make an exception this time. You can't all fit in that room."

Parker reached past Kendra and opened the outer door again. "No problem, Dad. Kennie and I'll wait on the porch until Lander and Violet are done in the mudroom."

With a crooked grin and a wave, Kendra backed out the

door and Parker followed, leaving the tiny room to Violet and Lander.

"Well, don't just stand there." Violet pouted with her hands on her hips. "You need to get your shoes off. I'm hungry and we can't eat until Parker and Kendra get their boots off too."

Lander's hands twitched as the little girl plopped down on a bench and pulled off her furry snow boots. She smiled up at him and patted the bench next to her. "There's room here. You can sit with me."

His stomach still churning, Lander dropped his pack to the floor with a thud, took the seat next to the girl, and began untying his hiking boots.

The large man moved to the mudroom door and leaned against the jamb. "Sorry about the lack of greeting, Lander. We expected you sooner than this and then, when you didn't come, we thought you wouldn't. You took us by surprise is all. And, I must admit, you're not what I expected. The little girl who's taken you prisoner is Violet. I'm Castor. I'm sorry for your loss; I was an old friend of your grandfather's."

CHAPTER 10

A tremor crept up Lander's spine. "How? How do you know about Pop-pop?" A vision of Pop-pop's still form lying on the hospital bed as monitors sounded their alarm flashed in Lander's mind. "I mean ... you know he's..."

"We know." Castor's gaze dropped to the floor. He pulled in a breath, then returned his focus back to Lander. "We have a lot to talk about. But that'll come later. For now, what you need to know is that Kendra isn't one of us."

"Castor!" Several voices spoke at once. Lander's eyes darted across the room, noting the shocked expressions, staring at him.

"Castor, you don't know this boy!" the older of the two women protested.

Castor turned to face the others and shrugged. "It doesn't matter. He has to know." He shifted his attention back to Lander and raised his hands in a placating gesture. "Anyway, Kendra—Parker's girlfriend—doesn't know anything about us or the Core ... yet. We'll talk after she's gone. In the meantime, once Kendra and Parker are ready, I'll introduce everyone. To make things easier, we'll tell Kendra you're Parker and Parrish's cousin come for a visit."

Parker and Parrish? There are two? Are we really cousins? Do these people know me? Kendra doesn't know? Know what? Like all the things I don't know? A heavy sigh escaped as Lander's eyes scanned the puddled floor and he struggled to balance his roiling thoughts.

"That means you're my cousin too." Violet jumped up and down, drawing Lander's attention back to the little girl. She pulled the outside door open and poked her head out. "Parker. Kendra. We're done. It's your turn." Giggling, she sprinted into the kitchen and smiled up at the younger lady.

Parker and Kendra came in, took off their boots, and hung up their jackets. Kendra hung Violet's as well. Lander backed up against the wall next to the door and watched, clutching his jacket to his chest.

"Give me that and I'll hang it for you," Parker offered.

Lander shook his head. "I can do it myself." His connection to his stones grounded him and with them still resting in the coat pocket he'd not hand it over to a stranger.

"Sure, no problem." The tall, athletic young man offered a friendly smile then walked into the kitchen behind his girlfriend.

Lander slipped the stones from his jacket into the pocket of his jeans. A shiver ran through him; chilly air replacing the warmth of his coat as he hung it on one of several hooks set into the wall of the mudroom.

Castor called everyone to the table and made the promised introductions.

Naara and Desma began bringing over steaming plates of food. Lander followed Castor's direction and sat on a bench to Castor's left at a large, farm-house table.

"That's Parrish's seat but he won't be home for a couple hours yet. So, go ahead and sit there for now," Castor said.

Lander's nerves sparked and his hands trembled from time

to time. Though Castor and the others seemed to ignore the elephant in the room, they all cast glances at him when they thought he wasn't looking. It made him uncomfortable and he fought the urge to go invisible. That would only make things worse. For now, he would have to accept the situation and go with the flow.

He reviewed the introductions Castor had given, working to place the names with the faces of those around the table. *Castor: Pop-pop Ian's friend. Big man, muscular, strong; dark brown, gray-streaked hair; gray eyes; deep voice. Desma, his wife, cold, stiff, fancy hair, gray eyes… Oh wait, we all have gray eyes. Kenan and Naara: Violet's parents, younger than Castor and Desma but not by much. They seem old to have a child so young. Parker: twenty-something, shaggy, dark brown hair, nice build—must work out, spoiled. And Kendra: not one of us … whoever we are. Pretty. Dirty blonde hair cut really short, brown eyes. Violet: nice, has eyes the color of mountain violets. One of us but doesn't have gray eyes? Not one of us?*

Lander continued his internal dialogue as the conversation ebbed and flowed around him as if the others were avoiding talking to him. *It's because of Kendra. They're afraid I might say something in front of her.*

He looked over at Parker's girlfriend. Her eyes lit up as she laughed at something Parker had whispered.

Kenan's deep voice caught Lander's attention. He was talking about something that happened where he and Naara work. *Wait, not where they work. Where they were working. They travel.*

"I really hate when we have to travel those back roads in Chile." Naara closed her eyes and shuddered. "They're the worst roads in the world."

"But we got some great samples from that second site we stopped at. I think there's good potential for lithium carbonate there. We'll file those reports this week, Castor. I have to admit it, it was nice to take some time off this past week, but we need to get back to work. You know; no work, no paycheck."

By the time Parker left to take Kendra home, Lander had learned that Kenan and Naara were geologists who traveled all around the world. Desma never left the house. Castor owned at least two mines, one a copper mine in Chile where Naara and Kenan had stopped during their last trip. Parker worked for his dad and his brother Parrish did IT work for some big company and was away at a conference. Violet, who was named for the color of her eyes, was in the first grade and had a genius IQ.

Meals with Pop-pop had always been quiet, here in the Elm household, they were anything but. The conversations roamed topics and opinions and sometimes grew loud. He couldn't believe how much he had learned in so short a time. Still, he hadn't learned anything important. At least not yet.

After Parker and Kendra left, the others rose to clear the table and start the cleanup. Lander stood as well, but with a large hand on his shoulder Castor propelled him into the great room. "Sit, Lander. You're our guest. We'll be done here soon."

Lander sat on an expensive looking green and silver brocade couch. The fabric felt smooth and fine, unlike anything he had seen before. Afraid of snagging the material, he clasped his calloused hands on his lap.

As he scanned the large, warm room, a series of stones lined up in haphazard fashion on the heavy wood fireplace mantle caught his eye. They called to him.

Rising, he walked with a measured tread to stand before the fireplace and examined the first stone. It was gritty, gray and tan; similar to the ones in his pocket, but this one had a crystal shaped like a bubble oozing out from one side. The deep red crystal was as large as his hand and looked like a drop of giant's blood, still alive with motion. Fluid. Lander reached out to touch it.

"Don't." Desma's voice came loud and commanding. He looked over his shoulder where she stood, her face pinched into a frown. "That's rude, you know, touching someone else's treasures without asking permission."

Lander pulled his hand away and shoved it into his jeans pocket, then tucked his chin into his chest and hunched his shoulders. "Sorry. I didn't mean to offend. I didn't know."

"Apparently there's much you don't know." Desma narrowed her eyes as she stared at Lander, suspicion oozing from her like vapor from a hot road after a cool rain.

Castor came around the kitchen island and stood next to his wife. "It's okay, Desma. No harm done. The boy didn't know, that's all."

Then, shifting his attention to Lander, he said, "They're beautiful, aren't they?"

Turning back to gaze at the stones, Lander said, "They're amazing."

The hair on the back of Lander's neck rose as Desma said something in a language he didn't recognize. He dropped his eyes to stare at the flickering fire, mouth partly open, wondering if this was the language his mother had written the journal in.

After a moment, Desma snorted. "He doesn't even know our language, Castor. How can we be sure he's who he says he is and not some plant sent to trap us? You know we're playing a dangerous game letting a stranger into our house. And you want to talk to him about who we are as well?"

"Desma's right, Castor," Kenan's quiet voice preceded them as he and Naara moved into the great room. "We need to be certain he's really Ian's grandson before we say anything more."

"He needs to prove himself." Naara sat on one of the overstuffed recliners, pulling a pillow from the loveseat and hugging it to her chest. "As it is, we've already said too much. If he's an imposter, we have a situation here. I don't like it."

"Neither do I." Desma continued staring at Lander, a deep

line forming between her dark, wing-like brows. "From the moment you admitted that Kendra was not one of us, you put this boy's life on the line. If he's not who he says he is, what do you plan to do about him?"

"W-w-wait." Lander stumbled over the one word as fear began a tap dance up his spine. "I'm Lander Devlin. Really. I'm not lying. Pop-pop died. I found his box. He said I could trust Castor Elm. He said Castor Elm was the only person I could trust. I don't know what you're talking about, but I won't stay where I'm not wanted.

"I know I'm different. Pop-pop always told me I'm special. If that's why you're afraid of me, I'll leave. Really. I don't want any trouble. Please."

"Calm down, everyone," Castor rumbled. His mouth set in a firm line, he looked around the room, his focus sharpening near the fireplace. "Violet, honey, I think it's past your bedtime."

"Oh, my," Naara said, her eyes going wide at the sight of her daughter hiding on the other recliner. "Your Uncle Castor's right, Violet. You need to go up to your room. Now."

"Awww," the little girl moaned. "Just when it was getting interesting." She pulled her feet out from under her, stood, and stretched.

A sly smile worked its way onto Violet's face. She winked at Lander, then said something to him in the same language Desma had spoken.

Lander swallowed hard, wishing yet again that Pop-pop Ian had told him more about Castor and his family—more about who he was. "I'm sorry. I don't know what you're saying. Are you talking in the same language my mom and dad used? I have my mom's journal. Could you maybe take a look at it before I go? Please."

"Violet, upstairs. Now," Naara said.

Lander faced Castor, Desma, Naara, and Kenan wondering

if they were going to answer his question as Violet stomped up the stairs, mumbling to herself about life being unfair.

After her door slammed, Castor raised his hands, palms out toward Lander and said, "Okay, son, why don't you show me that journal."

"Hey, wait a minute." The thought that perhaps he was making a big mistake took hold of Lander again, pushing against the hope that had surfaced. Pop-pop's words circled in his head, *trust no one.*

"You all say you can't trust me, but maybe it's the other way around. How do I know I can trust you? I don't know any of you. Maybe you're working with those guys outside Pop-pop's hospital room, the guy who tried to kidnap me on the bus."

The faces before Lander shifted from expressions of doubt and mistrust to dread. These people feared the same men Pop-pop Ian had warned him about. *Unless they're just putting on an act to trick me.*

"What men?" Castor asked. But before the question was even out of his mouth, Lander focused. And Lander disappeared. Once again, he watched as expressions of fear morphed into expressions of surprise and wonder. But now he didn't know what to do; trust these strangers or flee the house. But if he left, where would he go? Back to Crossways Mission? At least he knew he could trust Pastor Stevens ... and he was welcome there.

"Wait. Wait." Castor turned in a circle, pleading. "You *are* one of us. We believe you. Show yourself, Lander. We believe you."

With cautious steps Lander made his way through the great room, avoiding Castor and Kenan who were now waving their arms, attempting to feel for him. *This is stupid. As soon as I pick up my things they'll know where I am. And, if I leave, who'll answer my questions?* He stopped, frozen in indecision. *Pop-pop said to trust Castor.*

Lander stood in the doorway to the mudroom and stopped focusing. The moment he appeared, Castor and Kenan stopped waving and Castor said, "I'm so sorry we didn't trust you. I know you're probably scared, and we only made it worse. Please come back in, sit down, and tell us what happened.

Glancing around, Lander swallowed, pulled in a deep breath and released it in a huff. He shuffled back through the kitchen, keeping his hands in his pockets, clutching his stones in a tight grip. Just in case.

CHAPTER 11

"Why don't we all sit down and hear what Lander has to say."
Castor waved Lander back toward the great room. Desma
sat in the puffy gray leather recliner where Violet had
been sitting. Naara joined Kenan on one of the two couches.

Still fidgety in the fancy surroundings, Lander moved past
Castor to the fireplace, sat on the raised hearth, and faced the
others.

Castor looked down at his hands and breathed out a puff
of air. With a shake of his head he turned and walked to the
fireplace. Lander stiffened. Castor was a large man; not fat,
muscular. He reminded Lander of superheroes he had read
about in the comics he hid from Ian—built like an athlete with
a well-trimmed, short beard and mustache, both light brown
and streaked with gray. Lander paid special attention to his
eyes. Lighter gray at the pupil shading to a dark charcoal gray
at the edges of the iris. Just like Lander's eyes; just like Pop-pop
Ian's.

Castor stepped to Lander's side and reached for the rock

Lander had been drawn to earlier. As his fingers came to rest on it, Desma said in a soft voice, "Oh, Castor, no. Don't do it."

Gently lifting the stone, Castor glanced back at Desma. "It's only right. We know the truth of the boy. Now, he needs to know the truth about us." He smiled at Desma. "It'll be all right."

Castor squatted, holding the stone out toward Lander on the palm of his hand. "This stone is from Myanmar. Watch." He closed his eyes and Lander felt a familiar pressure. The red crystal began to pulse and just like Lander had imagined, it began to flow within, as if alive.

"It isn't a Stone of Power, but a receptacle of wealth," Castor said. "I'm a Stone Worker. When I focus on what I see in the rock, the wealth within emerges."

The bubble of clear dark red grew. It moved slowly like thick syrup. Retaining its shape, it swelled outward as waves of energy moved within. After a few more seconds, Castor breathed in deeply, stopped the action in the stone and raised his eyes to Lander. "Our wealth. Sold on the open market, this uncut ruby will bring us thousands. But, once cut by Parker, it will be worth much, much more."

Looking back up at the remaining stones on the mantle, he waved at another. "The blue sapphire in that one will be worth even more." He pointed at a larger, dark gray rock with specks of clear green showing. "That one from Columbia contains an emerald. See the green. It's near perfect. When cut, it will add to our wealth. Like me, Parker is a Stone Worker, but his talents are more refined than mine. As a gem cutter, he is without equal."

Castor stood, gazing at the remaining stones. His eyes dropped to the one he held before returning it to the mantle. "We are alike, Lander. This is something neither you nor I can deny. Now, I need you to tell me. What happened? How did Ian die?"

Without another word, Castor moved to the empty recliner next to Desma and sat, eyes focused on Lander.

Struggling against the shivers skittering up his spine with so many eyes focused on him, Lander continued juggling the Stones of Power in his pockets as he took a few deep breaths.

Desma's glare caused his stomach to flip. *She* really *doesn't like me.*

Kenan and Naara seemed neutral, their thoughts hidden behind bland masks.

Seeking Castor's eyes once again Lander was relieved to see sympathy and encouragement.

"It's okay, son. Just start at the beginning," the big man said, his voice calm and friendly.

Pop-pop, I hope you're right. Keeping his attention fixed on Castor, pulling strength from the support he sensed in the man, Lander began to speak.

"Um … well… It was third period. Mr. Russell's U. S. History class. I got called to the principal's office. Mr. Bixler said something happened to Pop-pop Ian and I needed to get to City Line Hospital. Um … that's in Springfield. He said I had permission to leave school and go to the hospital right away.

Well … I stopped home to get some money and then headed to Springfield. It took me a long time to get there because I'd never done it before. Pop-pop … well … he was pretty protective. He never allowed me to go into the city and the bus routes were confusing."

Lander paused, looked up at Castor, grief tugging the sides of his mouth down. "Pop-pop always told me not to trust strangers wearing suits. I never thought much about it because we don't get any strangers in Wharton."

Lander paused, chewing the side of his lip. "When I got to Pop-pop's room I saw these two guys standing by the door, like they were guarding it or something. Government type strangers in dark suits. Just like Pop-pop warned me about. But I had to see him, so I went invisible.

"I got to talk to him for a bit before … before … you know…

"I don't know what killed him, but I think the doctor mentioned a stroke. I left before I could find out for sure. Before he … passed … he told me about a box that had all the answers. Then…" The memory of that moment set Lander to chewing his lip again as a burning lump grew in the back of his throat, setting his voice to cracking. "Then … well … then … he stopped breathing." Lander swallowed past the lump. "All these nurses and a doctor came running in. But before that— when everything started to go crazy—those guys burst in and saw me. But I focused and then they couldn't see me anymore. Nobody else saw me and … then … I left.

"Um … well … it was late when I got home and there were lights on and people all over the place, so I grabbed my gear and slept in the woods. The next morning all the people were gone. But they really trashed our house; it was a mess. So, then I dug up the box. It wasn't very big. I found a bunch of money, my mom's journal. Well, I guess it was Pop-pop's too, because all the later writing was his."

Lander stopped; a slight warmth seeped through his fingers wrapped around the two stones in his pockets. *Do I tell them about the stones? Do I need to tell them everything?*

He worried the side of his lower lip yet again, struggling with his internal monologue. He felt Castor's encouragement as he looked at the man and, with a deep, cleansing breath prepared to continue.

Desma rose, glaring at Lander, "And you came here knowing they were following you? Tell me, how did this man find you? You must have left some kind of trail.

"Castor, this foolish boy might have just led Aurelius Hunt directly to us. What are you going to do about this?"

"He didn't follow me." Lander's voice rose in protest, responding in kind to Desma's harsh tone. Anger and frustration boiled within him. "I lost him at the bus depot. Then I got lost. That's when I met Becky and her friends. That's how I met Pastor Stevens.

"Who's this Becky? And who's Pastor Stevens?" Naara asked.

After glancing up at Naara, Lander swung his eyes to the floor where he rubbed the toes of his right foot against the wood grain. "Just some people who helped me. Pastor Stevens runs a mission in Camden where Becky and her friends volunteer. He let me stay there for a while."

"Why?" Desma asked. "Why did he let you stay?"

"It's a shelter. And a soup kitchen. That's what they do; let people who have nowhere to go stay. I helped out while I was there, so he let me stay as long as I wanted."

"Why did you leave?" Castor asked.

Lander chewed on the truth, squashing down the need to tell all, before saying, "Pop-pop told me to find you. I stayed at Crossways for a while. When I didn't see the man after a few weeks I made my way here."

"Perhaps you did lose him at the bus station in Camden, but that doesn't explain how he found you in the first place," Kenan said, brow wrinkled in thought. "Maybe he just kept out of sight while you were at the mission so he could track you to us."

Lander thought Desma was having a heart attack or something, when she stopped pacing, grabbed her chest, and started sputtering. Finally, she spat out, "Kenan, you're right. We can't stay here. All these years we were safe and now ... this!" Her glare pierced Lander on a lance of guilt.

Resurging anger drove out the blossoming guilt. Lander planted his feet and pressed to stand. "No problem, lady. I'm leaving now. Okay?"

"No." Naara rose as well and shifted to stand in front of Lander. "If you've led them here, it's already too late to change that."

She offered Lander a reassuring smile, exposing dimples that evidenced her relationship to Violet, before she turned and paced to stand next to Desma.

Naara put her arm around the older woman's waist. "Don't panic, Desma. We don't know anything at this point. Perhaps Lander did lose Aurelius's men in Camden. Keep calm; we'll figure it out."

Everyone jumped as the mudroom door flung open and then slammed shut. "Hey there! Hi everyone! I'm home. What a mess at the airport. I thought I'd never get home."

"Parrish!" Desma released a sigh that bespoke her relief. "Oh, Parrish. I forgot you were coming home tonight."

"Nice greeting, Mom." A tall, young man, wearing a black cashmere coat walked into the kitchen, dropped a brown leather laptop bag and travel bag to the floor and stood staring at Lander while he tugged an olive-green, wool scarf from around his neck.

Lander stared back taking in the sandy blonde hair, long on top and shaved at the sides, similar to his own cut, and the deep gray eyes. Parrish looked like the polished version of his brother Parker. Both tall and well built, just like their father.

After a moment of sizing each other up, Parrish said, "Who're you?" Then looking up at the others continued, "Mom? Dad? What's going on here?"

CHAPTER 12

Rising from his seat, Castor cleared his throat. "Hi, Son. Come on in and meet our guest. You remember Ian Devlin, don't you?"

Parrish nodded. He slipped off his shoes and tossed them back into the mudroom before walking into the great room.

"This is his grandson, Lander."

"The baby that caused all the trouble?" A frown drew Parrish's lips into a firm line.

"So you do remember," Castor said. "Yes, Cyanne and Jerod's son. He's going to be staying with us for a bit."

"Because Ian died?" Parrish sloughed off his coat and threw it over the back of the empty couch.

"Parrish." Desma's eyes narrowed. "Hang up that coat."

"Aw come on, Mom." Parrish chuckled. "Give it a rest. I'll get the coat in a minute. I want to meet Lander."

Parrish walked up to Lander, holding out his hand in a friendly gesture. "You were too little at the time to remember, but I used to have fun making you laugh. You were a pretty happy baby." After shaking hands, Parrish studied Lander, his eyes roaming from feet to head. "Like your hair. That natural?"

Flipping the short tail at the back of his head with the fingers of his right hand, Lander said, "What? Oh, the color. Naw, got it done in Camden."

Parrish rubbed his hands together and grinned. "Sweet. Hey, Mom, got anything to eat? I was going to stop for something on my way home, but then didn't. I'm starving."

Desma stared at Parrish a moment, distracted, but then hustled into the kitchen saying, "Of course. We have lots of leftovers from supper. I'll fix you up a dish. Just give me a minute or two."

Parrish grinned and winked at Lander. "Best way to defuse Mom is to tell her you're hungry. She can't stand the idea of anyone being hungry. It's the way she's built." His eyes scanned the room. "But don't let me interrupt. Go on."

Everyone's eyes focused on Lander, setting his nerves to jumping again. Castor waved him to sit. "Please, sit down, relax. You don't have to make any decisions tonight. It's too late to go anywhere and I, personally, would like to hear more about Ian; and you haven't told us anything about yourself yet."

The rest of the evening went by in a kind of fog for Lander. He was beyond exhausted and struggled to keep his eyes open while maneuvering around questions he wasn't sure he wanted to answer.

After a bit, Desma cut through the discussion, a stern tone in her voice. "Castor, enough. Can't you see the boy can't even keep his eyes open. Come on, Lander, grab your things. Since you're staying, I suppose I need to show you to the guest room."

Parrish's gaze followed Lander and the muscles in his stomach tightened at the thought of how Ian's death and the young man's appearance were going to alter his family and their lives.

After the two disappeared down the second-story hallway, Kenan turned to Castor, the evidence of an internal storm brewing set in the lines on his face. "Why didn't you ask about the stones? You never even brought them up."

A thin smile of understanding curved Castor's lips. "Couldn't you see how he evaded answering certain questions? He's hiding something. I'm sure he knows more than he's saying. But what he's hiding I don't know."

He squinted his eyes in thought and pulled in several deep breaths, releasing them through his nose. "I think I'll take the day off tomorrow, stay home, talk to Lander some more. Parker can handle things at the office."

"If he has Ian's stones, they can open the Vortex." Desma's voice rose and her eyes glittered as she came back down the stairs. "Kenan is right, Castor. Ask him about the Stones of Power. We need to know where they are. The only way to get back through the Vortex is with those stones."

Parrish stifled the sigh that sought release. He was sick of the way his mother kept building up the Core as something special. *Why does she always moan about the stones and getting back to the Core? Can't she just let go of the past?*

"And what if he has the stones, Desma, but doesn't agree to help us, could you work them?" Castor arched a heavy eyebrow at her. When she pursed her lips in obvious frustration he smirked. "I didn't think so. The stones are worthless without the capacity of command to work them, access their power. Our family has never produced a Stone Sovereign. We are and have always been Stone Workers. And even if he has the stones, or knows where they are, the question becomes, can he command them; is he a Stone Sovereign? He needs to be handled carefully, like drawing a fragile gem from a resistant stone."

"What about the other families?" Kenan asked. "You've kept track of them. Could any of them have birthed a Stone Sovereign since we've been here?"

"We've been over this before, Kenan. The only family who traveled to the surface that possessed the sovereignty gene was Ian's. He had it, and so did Jerod. And Cyanne. Coming from two long lines of Stone Sovereigns, Lander is most likely one as well. We need to secure his trust and help. If he has the stones, and is willing, we might be able to navigate the Vortex and return home."

"That's all fine and good for you," Parrish said as he finished putting together a second sandwich at the kitchen counter and took a bite. He chewed then swallowed as everyone's attention reverted to him. "But I don't want to go back. Neither does Parker." He looked to his brother and they both nodded.

Parker pushed to his feet and walked over to stand next to his brother. "We like it here. We've talked about this. I want to propose to Kendra; marry her and start a family of my own. I don't want to leave."

Parrish picked up the line of reasoning again as Desma moved to stand on the other side of the island. "The Surface is what we've known most of our lives. We have no connection to the Core." He raised his brows and stared his father in the eye. "You know, maybe Lander feels the same way.

He shifted to face his mother. "The Core has nothing to offer that we don't have here. We have a good life now … all of us. Why do you insist on giving up all we've built here to cling to a past Parker and I don't remember, and that Violet never even knew?

He raised his hands in a pleading gesture, still focused on his mother. "Why can't you leave well enough alone and enjoy the life we have here. We'll lose everything if Aurelius Hunt finds us. Trying to return to the Core is a fool's errand, even if Lander has the stones."

Parrish looked from his mother to his father, willing them to understand. Parker wasn't the only one with a special someone on the Surface. Even if there was no way he would introduce his girlfriend to his parents as things stood now, he still hoped to find a way to resolve the issues in the future. If his parents insisted he accompany them back to the Core, he would have to refuse and that would be hard. His family had always been close. Circumstances forced them to be. The thought of losing not just his parents, but Kenan, Naara, and especially little Violet pierced his heart.

Castor shook his head. "I don't want to press the issue now. We don't even know if Lander has the stones or can help us. It's late and I can tell tempers are going to boil over if we continue this tonight."

"Castor." Desma drew out the name and Parrish knew that wasn't a good sign. He fisted his hand behind the counter.

"Desma. I said that's enough for tonight. We can continue this discussion tomorrow." Castor's tone caused Desma to back down, but Parrish could see the rebellion in his mother's eyes. He prayed the family wouldn't crumble under the pressure the next days would bring.

CHAPTER 13

Talen's gaze swept the mountains, misty and pale gray under wind-swept cloud tendrils, as his driver spoke with the security guard. The image of passing through the gateway to an ancient, fortified castle formed in his mind. Not many people were aware of the massive security surrounding the mountain-bordered complex, but Talen had been an employee here for well over a decade and knew every inch of the grounds intimately.

After a quick dialogue, the gate opened, and the midnight blue Escalade moved through, up the curved drive, and entered the circle fronting the two-story brick building flanked by palm trees and massive flower beds. The driver came to a stop and Talen stepped out onto the brick walkway. Tropical heat and humidity battered him.

Tucking his head, he ignored the droplets of sweat already forming and slithering down his face and spine. He climbed the two steps up into the shade of a portico that ran the full length of the welcome center that served as the gateway into Aurelius Hunt Industries Corporate Headquarters.

Heavy thunder rolled in the distance, vibrating the air.

The lobby, crafted to look like the entryway of an antebellum southern mansion but on a much larger scale, was filled with noise and children, setting Emmett Talen's nerves on edge. He didn't like children, especially noisy ones in large numbers.

Skirting the mass of grade school students and their accompanying adults, Talen headed toward the information center. Before taking more than a dozen steps, a woman's deep, husky voice called his name. Turning he spied Doris Beckman, Mr. Hunt's administrative assistant, beckoning him to a door set under one of the ornate curved staircases.

Closing the door behind them, smothering the noise of the lobby, Mrs. Beckman said, "Mr. Hunt is expecting you, Mr. Talen. With two school groups here to see the animal preserve and a storm imminent, I suspected you wouldn't want to be stuck in the welcome center."

Her heels clicking a quick staccato, Mrs. Beckman led Talen down a flight of stairs into a more utilitarian section of the welcome center; quiet, cooler, with concrete walls and floor. They moved swiftly down a hallway, to a half-filled parking garage where a golf cart purred near an oversized garage door.

She wasted no time sliding into the seat of the cart, her navy-blue pencil skirt riding up past her knees. "Quickly, Mr. Talen, I have no desire to get soaked."

She pulled the skirt down to cover her knees then tapped the driver on the shoulder. "The mansion, Tom."

Aurelius Hunt Industries Corporate Headquarters was a sprawling complex of buildings, manicured grounds, naturalized areas, and a large animal preserve. Past the public areas lay Aurelius Hunt's personal mansion. Beyond the mansion, the heavily guarded and walled Hunt Industries R&D Compound hugged the side of the largest mountain on the island. It was a twenty-minute ride from the Welcome Center to the mansion. *Cutting it close*, Talen thought as thunder rumbled, echoing through the mountains. Louder. Closer.

The first drops of rain spattered the pathway, leaving malformed dark patches on the pale brick as Mrs. Beckman slid from the golf cart seat, touched a toe to the pavement and sprinted to the mansion, a smaller version of the welcome center. Talen shook his head. He never understood why women insisted on wearing high heels and marveled at the assistant's ability to run in them.

The large center hall flashed. Luminous after images filled Talon's vision as vibrations of heavy kettle-drum thunder shook the ground and rumbled overhead. Talen glanced toward Mrs. Beckman.

She shivered and pulled her tan silk jacket closer around her waist. Shaking out her shoulder length golden hair, she said, "I hate the storms here." Regaining her professional demeanor, the fifty-something administrative assistant sent a cool gaze in Talen's direction. "Please, come this way; Mr. Hunt is waiting in the conservatory."

Aurelius Hunt stood under an elaborate dome of leaded glass, his back to the room, as he gazed out on the storm. Lightning flashed, as the tempest whipped the trees beyond into a frenzy of bouncing movement and plastered raindrops and leaves on the glass.

Talen stood with hands clasped behind his back, quiet, patient, as he waited for Aurelius Hunt to turn his attention from the storm to his employee.

Talen had worked for Aurelius Hunt Industries for sixteen years, ever since his uncle recruited him after his discharge from the army. 'Security work' his uncle had said. But it had been so much more. Mr. Hunt had been a surprise to Talen; the man was nothing like what he expected of the billionaire entrepreneur of the largest, privately-owned conglomeration of companies on the globe. A slight, soft-spoken, handsome gentleman with graying temples and a steel-trap mind.

Fifteen minutes later, the fury of the storm abated. Without turning from the wall of leaded glass, Aurelius spoke, his voice soft and cultured. "Well, what happened?"

"I lost him in Camden."

"How?"

"The tracking device glitched in the bus terminal. When it came back on, I found his pack at a donation center for some church." Talen grimaced and shook his head; his fists clenched at the thought of disappointing Hunt. "He had to have been there, but we'll need to track him the hard way now. Jack's working on it."

Silence. Displeasure flowed from Aurelius like a physical force. "First you kill the old man; then you lose the boy." Aurelius's voice had dropped to a whisper.

"The old man was weak, Sir. He tried to fight, but just killed himself with the effort."

"And you're certain you found no stones on him?"

"No, Sir."

"Jerod's son is the key. He must have the stones. Find him. Find him now, Mr. Talen, or I will be forced to replace you."

"Dad?" Olivia, Aurelius's daughter, bounced through the conservatory door. "Dad? Are you in there? Do you ever miss watching a storm?" Breezing past the grand piano, her presence lightened the heavy atmosphere of the room; the pink glow on her pixie face a sure sign she had been running.

"Hi, Dad." She rose up on her toes and planted a kiss on his cheek. "Missed you."

An adoring smile wiped the frustration lines from Aurelius's face as he pulled Olivia into a hug. Setting her away he scanned her with discerning eyes. "What are you doing home? Isn't school starting again? You should be there, not here."

"I know, I know. But I got back from Paris early and had a few more days before the next semester starts. And I really, really, really missed seeing you at Thanksgiving, so I decided to come home for a couple days. Hey, do you know there's a bunch of school kids in the welcome center?"

"Yes, my dear. I know. They were scheduled to tour the preserve, but the storm put that on hold. Those poor children are probably quite disappointed at being cooped up. But, no harm. I had Doris set them up with a free lunch while they waited. Storms always blow through quickly here; this one's already passed. They'll be out in the park within the hour.

"I was about to go and greet them, but with you here now, why don't you do it. I know you've always loved greeting the school tour groups."

"Do it with me, Dad. It'll be fun. Like old times." Olivia curled her arm around her father's elbow.

"Well … I do have to finish my business here first, but if you're willing to wait a few minutes my dear I'd love to join you. I'll meet you in the Welcome Center foyer in just a bit. Wait for me there." He kissed her forehead.

Smiling her delight, she ambled from the room. As she passed Talen, she gave him a friendly smile. "Hi, Mr. Talen. I hope you're taking good care of Dad?"

"Always, Miss."

Once the door latched behind her, Aurelius walked up to Talen, his smile replaced with a stern, flat-lipped frown. "We lost the last male you brought back two weeks ago, weak specimen.

"And though he didn't have the right gene or the power to open the Vortex, his blood samples have brought me very close to finishing the anti-aging formula I've struggled to perfect for the last sixteen years."

Aurelius's glacial blue eyes pierced Talen. Not for the first time, Talen was taken aback by the laser-like focus that resided beneath the surface of the normally reserved Aurelius Hunt; the intense drive that had made him the man he was.

"I will not fail." Aurelius ground out the words. "Do you understand? Your uncle died for this project; now I'm trusting you to get the job done. Find them."

Talen hesitated, his respect for Hunt warring with a growing sense of wrong. "Are you sure what we're doing is right. I mean, that kid didn't seem like a threat. He just seemed like a scared kid."

A look of disbelief crossed Aurelius's features. "If you don't have the stomach for this, I can find someone else who does. You're on borrowed time as it is. If not for your uncle's history with me, you would have been gone by now.

"That *kid* is no kid; you know that. He disappeared—right out in plain sight, he disappeared—didn't he? Tell me what normal kid can do that. These creatures may seem human, but they're not. Your uncle wasn't set on fire by a human; remember that. But, if you want out, despite what you know, tell me now."

"No, sir." Talen's right hand twitched. The memory of that stormy day sixteen years ago flooded his mind. How he stood by, helpless, as his uncle screamed in agony as the flames took his life. *No. Mr. Hunt is right. They're dangerous. Freaks.* "I'll see this through."

"Good man." Aurelius started out the door, then paused. "Stop in the kitchen. Have the cook get you something to eat before you leave. And keep me informed on your progress.

"At the moment, I need to greet some real kids—*human kids*—who deserve a better future; a future I can give them."

CHAPTER 14

When Lander woke the next morning, he lay still for a few minutes, hands behind his head, rehashing in his mind the events of the prior evening. Though the room was dark, his bio-clock insisted it was later than he realized.

Hopping from the bed, he grabbed the clothes he'd dropped in a pile on the floor last night and dressed, checking to be sure his stones were still in his jeans pockets. He stumbled across the room to a window and peeked around heavy, black, ceiling to floor curtains. Unprepared for the blindingly bright sunlight reflecting off a layer of glittering snow, he blinked, then squinted at the wonderland of fields and trees. *Much later than I thought.*

The house was quiet as he descended the stairs to the main level, scanning, wondering where everyone was. As he neared the bottom step, muted voices sounded from the kitchen nook. Castor and Desma were conversing in quiet tones.

"It's no coincidence we lost Duncan so soon after Ian," Desma said.

"I think you're reading too much into it," Castor replied.

"Reading into what?" Desma's harsh reply came in a hissing whisper. "We go for years not losing one and now two within one month. Castor, I'm just looking at the facts. Aurelius found Ian and he's dead; we know that much. Aurelius is probably behind Duncan's death as well."

"You don't know that."

"Tell me, Castor, are we safe? Isn't it more likely that we're living some kind of pipe dream fantasy because we can't accept the alternative? Will our identities really hold up if Aurelius decides to investigate the Elm and Burrow families? We must think of Parker and Parrish. Like they said last night, their life here is all they know. What happens if we're forced to run again; start over again? What will that do to the boys? To Violet?"

Castor sighed, a deep, heavy sound. "I don't know, Desma. I just don't know. But overreacting might be the worst thing to do. We need to be calm and continue with things as usual, trust the strength of our Surface identities. They were well made and have only gotten more secure over time. Don't panic, okay?"

Lander moved to the end of the hallway, pausing at the edge of the great room. Castor caught the movement and looking up, smiled. "Good morning, Lander. Did you sleep well?"

Lander nodded and slid around the kitchen island to stand near the breakfast nook. Desma rose from the table and waved to a chair. "Sit, Lander. I'll get you some breakfast. Bacon and eggs okay?"

"Yes, ma'am."

"Oh, so we've decided to be polite this morning? Last night I was 'lady'. At least now I'm ma'am. I guess your grandfather taught you manners after all."

Desma moved to the island to get Lander's breakfast.

Castor folded his hands and rested his chin on them, then he pursed his lips for a moment. "After you eat, why don't you bring your mother's journal down. We can look at it together and I'll see if I can help you with it."

Unexpected relief flooded through Lander at the thought of help, and for the first time since arriving at Elm Farm, he smiled. "Thanks, that would be great."

After wolfing down a large helping of over-easy eggs, crunchy bacon, and several pieces of buttered toast with lots of strawberry jam, Lander sprinted up to his room and retrieved the journal from his pack. Returning to the table, he sat next to Castor.

The man took some time to scan the contents, flipping pages, then nodded. "Yes. You're right. The earlier entries are in Corish and were written by your mother Cyanne. Later, Ian continued the journal, his first entries are in Corish, but then he switched to English."

Castor leaned back and stretched the muscles of his neck, before turning his attention to Lander. "Though Ian didn't tell you anything, he apparently wrote the later entries so you could read what was written there and understand at least in part."

Castor leaned forward and tapped the journal with his fingers. "According to what I see here, at some point Ian decided it was better if you didn't learn the truth of our past until you were older. That's why he never showed you the journal or taught you to speak or read Corish."

Lander reached out and touched the edge of a page. "Could you read me some? Something my Mom wrote early on?"

Sympathy drew down the corners of Castor's mouth and he nodded. "Of course. Here, let me read the first entry. She wrote this the day we left the Core with Aurelius Hunt."

As it has been deemed necessary by the Elders that those of us making this historic journey to the Surface keep a transcript of all that occurs during our travels, I, Cyanne, daughter of Amabilia, wife of Jerod, son of Ian, have committed to keep this journal. I will attempt to record to the best of my abilities so my brothers and sisters who have not joined us on this adventure may share in our experiences through my written words.

Aurelius Hunt, a Surface Dweller and friend who has traveled to the Core along with several of his men, has agreed to lead us back to the Surface once we have passed through the Avortex.

He has told us much about what we will find on the Surface. Everyone chosen by the Elders to go is excited to take part in this unique venture. For the first time since our descent at the time of the ancient flood, we will be able to join hands with our Surface Dwelling brothers and sisters.

The Elders have, after much deliberation, chosen twenty-five Core Dwellers to make the journey. We range in age from eight-year old Parrish and ten-year old Parker, Desma and Castor's young sons, to six hundred twenty-seven year old Materia, representing the Elders, and my husband's father Ian who will be seven hundred and fifty-eight years old tomorrow. I have placed a full list of travelers at the back of this journal.

Aurelius Hunt laughs at our recorded ages and tells us we count years differently from those on the Surface. But he seems impressed by our longevity nonetheless.

Jerod believes our reckoning of a year is probably close to Surface Dweller reckoning because we judge according to the changes in the Flux (what Aurelius Hunt refers to as the Outer Core) and that cycles with the turning of the earth, season to season on the Surface, fluxon to fluxon in the Core. I am curious to see if we can make the correlations while on the Surface. It should prove to be an interesting study.

Oh my! The son I carry within me is kicking hard. He must be aware of the excitement surrounding him as we make final preparations to leave the Core. I am certain he shares our zeal as his kicking has grown stronger. Almost as if he understands the path we are traveling.

Perhaps he can be a liaison between our ancient brethren and we of the Core as he will be the first Core Dweller born on the Surface since ancient days.

Aurelius Hunt tells me the Surface Dwellers call the solid surface land and the liquid surface water. In honor of this, Jerod and I have chosen the name Lander for our son for he will be born on the land. And in our language, Lander means sent.

I must end this entry here. Ian and Jerod are preparing to open the Avortex. If all goes as planned, we will see the Surface in two-day's time. Aurelius Hunt promises we will be awed by the sun and stars of the sky, something unknown to us who have lived always in the light of the Flux.

"I remember that day as if it was yesterday." Castor closed eyes framed by wrinkles birthed in sorrow.

"Our way of counting time was not that of Surface Dwellers, but Aurelius and his people kept track on their watches. He told us he had been with us for more than three months and he needed to return to his life on the Surface. In our reckoning, it had been a quarter of a cycle. Twelve months, one cycle; different names, but it was all the same.

"In the time he spent in the Core, he told us much about the wonders of the Surface. We trusted Aurelius; thought we knew him. We were wrong."

Lander hadn't heard Desma as she stepped in behind him with a silent tread. He turned in alarm when she spoke. She was weeping and speaking in Corish, the words jumbled and rapid. He now knew the language was the one his parents had spoken, the one Pop-pop Ian had never taught him. The language he wished he knew.

Castor rose and, moving to Desma, wrapped his arms around her as she quieted. Lander's leg bounced in the awkward silence.

"There was a time when I cursed Ian and your parents for convincing us to trust Aurelius Hunt," Desma said, then sniffed, blinking back threatening tears. She paused, swallowed a couple times, then, shaking her head, continued. "But it wasn't their fault. I know that now. Hearing Castor read Cyanne's words from that day—words filled with hope and excitement—reminded me that we were all eager to journey to the Surface. We wanted so much to connect with our brethren who had survived the ancient flood.

"I took pride in my family being chosen. Like Cyanne, I thought my boys could be ambassadors between the two peoples."

She shook her head. "It wasn't Jerod or Cyanne—or even Ian—who betrayed us, Lander. It was Aurelius. Whatever you learn from what's written in that journal, always remember your mother loved you.

"At the end, when she knew she was going to die, her thoughts were to keep you safe and out of Aurelius's hands. Your father, too … once we learned the truth."

"What happened? How did my parents die?" Lander's stomach twisted at Desma's words. He was finally learning the truth of what happened to his parents. "Please, tell me."

"Ian had gone up to study the writings in the ancient passages," Castor whispered. "He did that often, sometimes spending days in the tunnels before returning through the Vortex. I remember his story of meeting Aurelius so clearly. It's as if I just heard it yesterday."

CHAPTER 15

Ian stumbled out of the sparking green and rose coils of the Avortex. It had taken him almost eight hours to ride the energy field this time, the fury of the rising spirals propelling his body through at incredible speed; his only protection, his gifts, and his Stones of Power. At his age it was becoming more of a strain on his body to navigate the Flux.

Ian's life work had been studying the tunnels; the writings, the pictographs, the architecture. And the only way from the central Core to the outer rim and the maze of tunnels was through the Avortex. The only way back, the Vortex.

He returned one Stone of Power to the pocket of his jacket and readjusting the remaining Stone, he focused. A soft glow appeared, then exploded into a bright bluish-green radiance that bathed the surrounding walls and peeled back the darkness above. He dropped his pack to the ground. After a minute of rummaging, he found the map marking his most recent discovery. Checking his notes, Ian hoisted his pack and turned right to follow the corridor connecting the Vortex and Avortex to the warren of outer tunnels.

Ian quick-stepped, stirring up a cloud of ancient dust, as his heart raced with both the effort and his zipping thoughts. *Such an important discovery. If this is what I think it is … Take a breath Ian. It won't do to break a leg and die up here.*

Since his discovery, he had spent countless hours studying ancient texts. If the theory his studies birthed within him proved correct, a small tunnel exposed by an earth tremor a little over a cycle ago might be the gateway to a whole new series of Pre-Core, cut-stone tunnels.

Earthquakes did that; obscured or revealed passages in random abandon this close to the outer rim.

He hadn't gone far when he pulled to a stop. *Voices? No. It can't be.* He paused. Closing his eyes, he listened. The plunk, plunk of dripping water echoed down the corridor masking any other sounds. *Must be my imagination.* He chuckled. *I'm the only one scheduled to work the tunnels until Cyanne gives birth.*

But something nagged at him—a gut feeling that he was not alone. Ian changed direction at the next intersection and headed to the Highway. The longest and largest tunnel found to date, the Highway soared to a height of more than fifty feet and a width of nearly thirty. Built from worked rocks and covered in ancient writing, it was the most studied of the tunnels. Early inscriptions located along the portion closest to the outer rim dated from the Flood Era.

As Ian exited the smaller tunnel, he heard the sounds again. *Voices. No mistake.* He walked down the Highway, his Stone of Power clutched in his right hand. The voices and the sound of knocking grew louder with every step. At a bend, Ian pulled to a stop. *Language?* He tilted his head, a frown line forming between his brows. *Not Corish. Who …?*

Slow, soft steps brought him to the next bend. Hugging the wall, he peered around the rocky curve and scanned the Highway ahead. *What?* More than two-dozen people milled about in the tunnel. Lights and boxes of supplies stacked on wheeled carts lent an air of strangeness to the scene. Several of the men spoke but Ian couldn't make out the meaning of their curious words. *This near the outer rim? Surface Dwellers? Could there still be Surface Dwellers? Impossible.*

One stranger's eyes met Ian's and he said something to the man next to him. A shiver ran up Ian's spine as he became the center of attention. Though some of the men just stared, several pointed strange devices at him.

A tall man who appeared to be the leader of the group stepped forward and held his hand out to Ian. Ian took hold of the hand and the man pumped his arm up and down. Then, pointing to himself, the stranger said, "Aurelius. My name is Aurelius Hunt."

After a quick moment's thought, Ian smiled and pointed to himself. "Ian, son of Asael."

Within a few hours the two had shared a meal and were communicating at a rudimentary level. Ian walked Aurelius Hunt to a section of the Highway where writing covered the rocky wall. He hoped Aurelius Hunt would understand the words there. But after examining the writing, the man shrugged and shook his head.

Aurelius Hunt and his men camped in the Highway for the next four days as he and Ian worked on increasing their level of communication. A couple men from his group recorded the stuttering conversations as Ian and Aurelius grew to a better understanding of each other.

"I must return to the Core," Ian said, his speech slow and clear as Aurelius followed his words. "My family will worry if I don't return today."

"Can I join you?" Aurelius asked.

Ian pursed his lips and shook his head. He tried to get Aurelius to understand the dangers of traveling through the Vortex, but the man wouldn't be swayed. By the next morning, Ian had decided that he would allow Aurelius and a few of his men to accompany him back to the Core. The remainder of Aurelius's people returned to the Surface.

Castor paused and stared forward at empty air for several seconds as his final conversation with Ian flowed like a movie through his mind. He closed his eyes and lowered his head into his hands, elbows braced on the table. "Oh, Ian. You had no idea the harm our leaving the Core would cause." The secrets he kept weighed on him like a millstone tied around his neck. A moan worked its way up from the depths of his spirit, but he stifled it, unwilling to share his burden.

Desma snorted from the counter where she leaned on her elbows. "Well, you've told him this much, why not just go ahead and finish the story, Castor."

He glanced at his wife, trying to gauge her mental state, then turned to face Ian's grandson and tried to take a read on the boy as well. Lander reminded him of Cyanne; he had the same eyes and nose, now balanced by his father's bone structure. But when Castor looked at Lander, the one he reminded him of most was his grandfather. Ian had a way of concealing his thoughts. Though Lander's feelings had been easy to read earlier, his face now was a cold mask that Castor couldn't penetrate.

With an internal shrug, Castor continued. "Aurelius and his people lived with us for more than three months, studying the Core, learning all they could of Core Dwellers, our language, and our culture. They became friends. At least that was what we thought.

"When the time came for our visitors to return to the Surface, Aurelius suggested we send a chosen group of Core Dwellers to the Surface with him. He said we were family and wanted to share the wonders of the Surface with us. He and Ian had spoken much about the tunnel writings and Aurelius promised he would show Ian a book containing similar writing. He called it a Bible."

Castor stilled, staring into the cup of coffee he hadn't touched since he began the story. He pulled in a deep breath and released it with a huff. "Now that you've heard your mother's first entry, you can appreciate how excited we all were to see the Surface and meet our Surface dwelling brethren.

"We traveled up through the Avortex; pink, blue, and green spirals sparking and slipping past us. Ian, Jerod, and Cyanne used their Stones of Power to create a shield to protect us all. After leaving the Avortex, we made the two-day hike through the outer rim without incident." Castor paused, his mind focused yet again on his memories of that day. "Aurelius led us through a narrow crevice and out into an impossibly vast brightness. When we saw the sun for the first time, we thought it would blind us, the light was so intense. We had only ever experienced the muted light of the Core. It was all so green ... so overwhelming ... and beautiful."

"Until we learned the truth." Desma's voice, though soft, held a world of emotion. "But, at that moment, seeing the Surface for the first time, everything looked so beautiful and promising. We had no sooner walked out onto that spongy carpet of intense green with white and yellow flowers scattered through it, than Cyanne went into labor." Her eyes met Lander's. "It was almost as if you had purposefully chosen that moment to clamor to be released. We thought it a good omen; that we, like you, were being born into something new and wonderful." Desma sniffed.

Castor took a sip of his cold coffee. A shiver climbed his spine as he picked up the story. "Our delight was short lived. Within minutes we were hustled into the back of two enclosed trucks and whisked to an underground garage.

"Aurelius rushed Cyanne away while the rest of us—a very angry Jerod included—were taken to a large underground room with no windows, and locked in. It was very ... stark ... all white tile and metal, with a small sitting area and a row of metal bunk beds against the wall, bright florescent lights on the ceiling. We paced and complained to one another in our anger and confusion.

"But then Aurelius came. He explained that Cyanne had been taken to a facility where she would receive medical help. He calmed our fears, told us that our isolation was temporary and for our protection. To make certain we weren't infected with any Surface germs that we might not be equipped to survive. His words made sense at the time."

"But then days went by and nothing changed," Desma said, cutting off Castor's thoughts. "Fear that our *friend* had lied to us began to take hold." She walked over to the table, a cup of coffee in her hand, and sat next to Castor. "We should have seen the signs that something wasn't right. We still clung to our trust ... and then Cyanne and you were brought to the room. Aurelius told us we were now able to leave our quarantine."

"Things got better that day." Parrish stood in the doorway to the mud room.

Shedding his coat, he walked to the kitchen sink, grabbed a glass and filled it with water. "Just give me a moment and I'll tell you what I remember."

The thought that Parrish was old enough to remember his parents stung Lander. He had been a newborn and recalled nothing of that time or his parents. He wanted to hear more, but still his heart hurt at all Pop-pop Ian had kept from him.

Parrish downed his glass in one long gulp, then filled it

again before moving to sit across from Lander. "After we were released from quarantine—or what Aurelius called quarantine—we were permitted to go outside. Aurelius had his people take us places around the island. We saw so many things and learned so much. It was a good time. The island was an amazing place; diverse with life ... and these incredible storms that moved through almost every day.

"We even had a teacher. She was nice—young and pretty. And smart. Her name was Miss Claypoole. I really liked her. She played with Parker and me." An easy smile brightened Parrish's face and a light chuckle escaped his lips. "She actually ran around as if she too was a child like us."

"Until that last day." Weighty sorrow laced Desma's voice.

"The day she died." Parrish's whisper sounded loud and harsh in Lander's ears. "The day everything changed."

Castor shook his head as if coming out of water. "Enough for now, Lander. Enough for now." He stood, running his fingers through his beard, his breathing heavy. "I don't know about the rest of you, but I need a break. Talking about that time is ... just too disturbing. It was good to put it behind us. To dredge it back up now ..." He shook his head, his words faltering.

Castor looked up at the clock and back at Parrish. "Are you going to explain why you are home and not at work at this hour?"

"What I'm working on now I can do from home. And ... I needed to talk to you ... alone."

Lander stared at Castor before shifting his focus to Parrish; angry protest clamored for release, heating his blood. For the first time in his life someone was telling him what Pop-pop had always refused to talk about—what happened to his parents and the truth of who he was. And now he'd have to wait again. "But ... but. No! You can't just stop now. You still haven't told me about my parents ... how they died."

"Go, Castor." Desma pushed to her feet and stood in front of Castor, resting a hand on his chest. She gave him a soft push. "You too, Parrish. I'll finish the story for Lander. Though I don't appreciate his attitude, he needs to know. And it's not right to make him wait just because remembering what happened is hard for us."

CHAPTER 16

Lander followed Desma into the great room while Castor and Parrish went to Castor's office. Sitting on one of the couches, Desma patted the seat next to her. "Sit with me, Lander."

A lone tear dribbled a path from her right eye to her chin, unnoticed. Lander shifted his gaze to the fireplace. He swallowed back a sense of awkwardness in witnessing a stranger's sorrow.

Desma settled back into the couch, staring, her eyes focused on nothing visible in the physical world. Lander studied her features. Despite the anger lines etched around her mouth and between her eyebrows she possessed a classic beauty. Though Lander knew she must be much, much older, she looked to be in her mid-thirties with thick, shiny black curls pulled back on her head and finely arched eyebrows. Her focused expression reminded him of Ian, and Lander suspected she was immersing herself in a memory, seeing the events unfold in her mind.

When she spoke, her voice sounded like someone telling a story. It crackled with intensity. "Storm clouds built, dark and churning, over the mountains, spitting moisture into the already heavy-laden air. Surface heat leached sweat from my pores—so different from the heat of the Core.

"We had been on the Surface for almost six months and still hadn't traveled off Aurelius's island or been allowed to meet anyone except Aurelius and his staff. Tempers flared and we argued amongst ourselves. Everyone was tired of being treated more like prisoners than guests. Or, I should say, more like pin cushions. Aurelius's team of doctors were constantly taking blood samples or monitoring us while we used our gifts or worked stones."

Desma rose from the couch and began pacing in front of the still glowing embers in the fireplace. "They were all so interested in you, taking you from your mother for short periods of time almost every day. Cyanne had to step in and calm Jerod when a nurse took you for what must have been … oh, I don't know … maybe the twentieth time. A team of security people began accompanying the nurse whenever she came for you after that incident. We had believed Aurelius when he said he was our friend, trusted him. Though he still insisted everything his people did was for our protection, we were now certain that was not the case.

"Ian, your grandfather, and Materia, the elders' representative in the group, had asked that everyone come to the library after breakfast as a sign of our unity."

You see, the day before, we had all signed a petition. We either be allowed to travel off the island and meet with other Surface Dwellers, or we would return to the Core. We asked that Aurelius meet us in the library that next morning to discuss the details. Aurelius's reaction to our petition would answer the question of whether we were protected friends or prisoners. Though she scoffed at the idea that we were prisoners Nora,

Miss Claypoole, agreed with our decision and volunteered to present our request to Aurelius in person.

"She said she was glad we brought up the issue of leaving. She had been wanting to arrange a trip off the island for weeks and that it was about time we got to see more of the Surface. Nora was certain that Aurelius would understand our request and make time to meet with us. She told us that we had been very patient so far and Aurelius appreciated our patience. Then she left the library with our petition. We didn't hear anything or see her again until that, stormy, following morning."

The air conditioning in the library struggled against the hot, humid air of the island as thunder rumbled in the distance and the weak sun reflected feebly on the dark polished wood of the long study tables. It was late morning, almost an hour after the time of the requested meeting with Aurelius, and already the third storm of the day was brewing. Aurelius hadn't come. No one had come.

Desma sat near one of the large windows, her focus split between the ominous silence that pervaded the library and boiling, charcoal-gray clouds gathering in the gap between two hazy, blue mountains. She still mistrusted storms. Like everything else on the Surface, they were too much. Too much noise, too much light. And the force with which the rain pelted windows and walkways still scared her. The Surface was wild and unpredictable.

She glanced over her shoulder from time to time. Castor paced in an attempt to quell his nervous anxiety. Ian and Jerod sat at one of the three heavy wood tables, reading by the light of several desk lamps. Though they appeared calm, Desma couldn't miss Jerod's bouncing knee or Ian's absent-minded juggling of a Stone of Power.

The others were scattered throughout the library in small

groups or as individuals. Apprehension repressed the few attempts at conversation. Cyanne sat on one of the large red leather couches holding Lander. The baby laughed as he alternated between brandishing a rattle and twisting his searching fingers in tendrils of long, dark hair that had escaped Cyanne's ponytail.

Parker was trying to teach Parrish the game called Chess as Naara watched. Miss Claypoole had recently taught Parker the game and now he was determined to teach his brother. Desma caught the end of Parrish's sentence. "... never going to get this the way you teach."

"This is frustrating," Naara said, rising from her chair opposite Desma's to climb to the upper level and roam through shelves of books.

Shaking her head as her friend passed, Desma said in Corish, "Be patient, Naara. They'll come."

"Soon, I hope," Cyanne said, bouncing Lander. "And, Desma, remember. We're supposed to speak English."

Desma sighed and swallowed back the frustration that curled just beneath the surface. "I know. But I don't see the purpose. If all we're going to do is sit around here or walk about this island while silent, unfriendly security people watch us, then why even try. Maybe I'd enjoy it more if I could talk to someone other than just Miss Claypoole or the doctors. Right now, it all seems so meaningless. I just want to go home."

The oversized library door crashed open and Nora Claypoole stumbled through, her hair plastered to her head and her eyes round as full moons. "I'm sorry, so sorry." She pulled to a stop and stared at nothing, trembling. "This is all wrong." She swallowed and shook her head, as if clearing away cobwebs. A second later, she looked up, her eyes roaming over the Core Dwellers. "You have to get out of here! Now! It's Mr. Hunt."

She shook her head again and covered her face with her hands. After a couple deep breaths, she looked up.

Ian and Materia rose from their seats and Ian approached Nora. "My dear, what's wrong. Here, sit down and talk to us. Is Aurelius coming?"

Her eyes grew wild and Nora moaned. "No. He's not coming. He doesn't know that I know yet. We have to hurry. You were right to not trust him. He's not your friend."

She turned into the wall next to the door and punched it, then grimaced before turning back, a look of firm determination setting deep lines around her mouth.

"I forgot my phone in his office. I went back and Mrs. Beckman wasn't at her desk. The door to Mr. Hunt's office was ajar. I overheard ... oh God. I overheard him talking to the security chief. I didn't mean to spy on him but I'm glad I did."

She grabbed Ian's arm, and met his eyes with her own. "Aurelius thinks you're not human. Something came up in the bloodwork. Something about your DNA. He wants to keep you here as research subjects, especially you, Ian, and ... the baby."

"No." Jerod's shout echoed around the room as thunder rattled the window.

Nora's words sank in and Desma gasped. "We have to get out of here now."

"Get to the white room. Gather your stones and anything else you can grab." Castor huffed as he moved behind Jerod.

Ian stopped, breathing hard and leaning against the door jamb next to Nora.

Cyanne rose, cradling Lander to her chest as she moved toward the door.

"Everyone keep calm," Ian said. "We must remain calm if we're going to get out of here before Aurelius realizes we've learned the truth. We'll head to the tunnels."

"No." Nora's face drained of color. "He's already got strong security there. He's put in scanners and there's no way you could get near the cave. And as soon as he realizes you're running, it's the first place he'll expect you to go. No, our only chance is to sneak down to the dock and take a boat. Get off the island before he alerts security." She paused, looking around at everyone. "I didn't know. You have to believe me; I didn't know."

A tremble shook her small frame and she turned to face Ian again. "Is it true? What I've heard? That you can become invisible? If so, you're going to need that."

"Not all of us, but enough." Ian held the door ajar. "We can do this. But we must move slowly, like everything's normal."

They moved out of the library in small groups, reuniting in the white room.

"We waited until the storm passed, reduced to nothing more than a drizzle and a slight breeze," Desma said, lost in the memory. "Otherwise, our leaving would have been too obvious Nora said. While we waited, Nora demonstrated how to operate the controls of a speed boat to Ian, Castor, and Jerod. In case we got separated." She shook her head. "Who would have thought at that point that …

"By the time we approached the dock, Aurelius had figured out what was happening. I think he must have already sent most of his security to the tunnel entrance, so he didn't have that many guards with him when we saw him running toward the dock.

"Most of us were already on the boat when Nora … was … shot." Desma paused, swallowed back the pain of what happened that day, the memory that still haunted her dreams. "I'll never forget the look of shock on her face and the way the blood spread across her white shirt. She took one faltering step before stumbling and falling. She went still. I really don't think any of us understood how bad the situation was until that moment.

"Then Jerod pushed Ian onto the boat." A shiver raced up Desma's spine.

"Cyanne was beyond angry. I'd never seen her like that before. She handed you over the side of the boat to Ian and shouted, 'Take him. Disappear. Keep him safe.'

"Jerod handed Ian his own Stones of Power. He said, 'I love you Dad. Give these to Lander for me.' Ian hesitated for only a moment before shouting for the rest of us to disappear. He handed you to me and jumped back onto the dock with Jerod's stones. I think he wanted to help Jerod and Cyanne but it was already too late. Cyanne and Jerod shook their heads and pushed Ian back toward the boat. Then the two turned, striding toward Aurelius. Cyanne pulled out her Stones of Power and handed one to Jerod while Channer and Sarai helped Materia onto the boat.

"Everything beyond the boat went hazy, like I was looking at the world through a waterfall. Using their combined power, Cyanne and Jerod set a shield of protection around the boat, like the shield they had used to insulate us from the heat of the Flux when we traveled through the Avortex.

"Everything seemed to happen in slow motion from that point forward. Materia got on the boat. Ian stumbled on behind her. Then Castor scrambled to the controls. He turned a key and pushed the handle forward the way Nora had shown him. I remember clutching the back of a seat as the thing bounced forward. Once Castor knew he had control of the boat, he stopped it and waited for Jerod and Cyanne.

"Aurelius continued storming toward Jerod and Cyanne who now poured all their strength into holding the shield in place, keeping everyone else safe. Aurelius waved his arm, shouted. Then—I don't know how it happened—one of the security people appeared next to Jerod. He must have come up from under the dock. We heard three quick shots. The shield crumpled. Cyanne screamed. She went wild and flicked fire at the guard who had shot Jerod. The man screamed as fire flashed like lightning and overwhelmed him. She kept flicking fire, now at the remaining boats. She was so powerful they flared and exploded, sparks flying everywhere. By that time, with the shield down, the other guards . . ." Tears ran down Desma's face and her body trembled. She shook her head.

"You have to understand Lander. We had no choice. We took off. The last I saw your parents, they were lying in their own blood, Aurelius standing over them and watching us flee from his grasp. We feared they would follow us, but with the other boats gone, they couldn't.

"I'm so sorry, Lander. Cyanne and Jerod died so we could get away." Desma sniffed as more tears leaked from her closed eyes.

"How many?" Lander asked, his voice soft and shaky.

"How many?" Desma repeated, seeking to stem the confusion Lander's question stirred as she looked up at him. "How many what?"

"How many did they save?"

"Twenty-three. Everyone except Jerod and Cyanne made it to the safety of the mainland," Castor whispered from behind Lander.

"After that, at Ian's suggestion, we split up. He said we would draw less attention that way. During the next year, we lost Materia, Alora, and Danail. We don't know if Aurelius found them or they died some other way.

"Ten years later we lost Oria. We felt the loss of no one after that until Ian died. Then, two weeks ago, we lost Baruch. As far as we know everyone else is living in various locations, safe … for the moment."

The house was quiet for the next few minutes. Desma

worked her way back to the present, leaving the fog of memory behind. Lander rose from the couch, crossed to the stairs without a word, and climbed one step at a time to the second level. Desma's heart broke for him as she listened to his slow steps follow the hallway to the guest room. After the door closed. Silence again reigned.

Castor walked over to sit next to Desma and with warm fingers, took her hand. Then Parrish reached for her other hand from behind the couch.

A warm peace filtered through Desma. For so many years she had indulged her anger and fear. *I've been so wrapped up in myself and my feelings, I haven't considered how everyone else felt. The Surface has been good to us. My family loves it here. It is indeed time to let go of the past.*

CHAPTER 17

Lander closed the bedroom door behind him with a soft click, then leaned back into its strong support. He stood like that for a few minutes, just breathing, before moving to the bed. He lay down on the covers and rolled into a fetal position, numb. All that he heard, the things he learned today circled in his mind like a ring of vultures pecking at his sanity. Pop-pop hadn't told him any of this. Why?

Did you think I couldn't handle it? Did you think I'd be weak? Maybe you were right. I don't know if I can handle this.

Emotional pain roiled through him and he drew his knees in closer to his chest. And in the pain, anger was birthed. Anger at his parents for dying; anger at Pop-pop for not telling him anything about where they came from, for not telling him about his parents; anger at Castor and his family for surviving; anger at God for not protecting his parents and Pop-pop, for not protecting him; but, most of all, anger at Aurelius Hunt.

His breathing grew labored. The room seemed to shrink in on him and anxiety beat a rapid tattoo in his chest.

"Breathe." *I can't breathe. Outside.* The snowy woods called, offering open air and open space. A chance to recover from the emotional shock of learning the pain-laced truth.

With a quiet tread, he descended the stairs. Murmuring voices from the great room covered any sounds he made. He considered going invisible but shook his head. He could move with stealth but as soon as he picked up his boots and jacket, the others would know.

Keeping his head down, he slipped past the kitchen and into the mud room, grabbed his boots, hoodie, and jacket, then rushed out the door.

Moisture and cold crept up his stockinged feet as he jumped off the porch and sprinted across the yard into the beckoning woods beyond.

It had snowed again during the night, cloaking trees and bushes in heavy, white mantels. Wet clumps plopped onto the ground with mushy splats, scenting the air with wet pine and fir. Sunlight filtered through breaking clouds and glinted like diamonds on the wintry scene.

Lander sprinted a short distance into the trees looking for a place to sit and put on his boots. He shivered against the chill working up his feet. He considered returning to the house. *Stupid. Staying out here with wet feet.* But he needed solitude and time to work through his conflicting thoughts.

Finding a patch of dry leaves under a thick-limbed fir tree, he slithered under and sat on a layer of damp, brown needles. He tried to shove his feet into the boots, grimacing as the wet socks caught on the lining, tugging at his toes. Pulling his feet out, he jiggled around until he slipped his stones from his jeans pocket. Willing the two to warm, he set one in his lap and worked the other up and down his socks. The stone's heat soothed him, flowing through his whole body. Once his feet were nearly dry, he shoved them into his boots and worked his way back out from under the shelter of the fir. He slipped on his hoodie and jacket while scanning the area.

Hours later, long shadows crept across the pristine snow alerting Lander to the passage of time. He had roamed the woods for the better part of the day and dreaded the thought of returning to the house with anger still bubbling the blood in his veins. He worked his way back and was scanning the yard when the thought of Pop-pop Ian's Bible popped into his mind. Like a word planted within him. He needed to read the quote Ian had scribbled on the title page.

The family sat in the great room watching something on TV as Lander slipped into the back door, removed his boots, and hung his hoodie and jacket on a hook before softly tiptoeing his way up to his room.

He didn't turn on the light but fumbled in the darkened room.

The Bible still sat in the front zippered compartment of the new pack he had gotten at Crossways Mission. He hadn't touched it since putting it there. Now, he ran his fingers over the worn brown leather cover. Just feeling it, remembering the many times he had come home to find his grandfather sitting in the worn recliner, the purple and blue afghan one of the church ladies had crocheted for him covering his legs, reading.

Balancing the Bible on one palm, he reached into his jeans pocket and pulled out a Stone of Power. With a quick thought, the stone ignited, glowing with a soft blue light. He settled on the rumpled covers of the bed with a pillow propped behind his back, setting the stone next to him. Opening the Bible, he read Pop-pop's scrawling hand. "Greater love has no one than this, than to lay down one's life for his friends." John 15:13. Ian's favorite verse.

The story Lander heard today gave him a new perspective on why this verse had meant so much to his grandfather. Jerod had been Ian's son, Cyanne his daughter-in-law.

But could Lander forgive and accept the others as friends? Did he want to accept them? He didn't even know them, and he struggled with the anger still churning his stomach and burning his chest. *What about me? Mom? Dad? It wasn't my decision. You laid down your lives for them, but I needed you too and you left me.*

Lander closed the Bible and tossed it on the bed. He pulled up his feet and curled into a ball. His thoughts drove hunger and sleep from him.

At one point, Violet came to his door. "Lander, please come out and eat something. Everyone's worried about you. Please." Her voice broke, as if she fought back tears.

He turned his back to the door, still not ready to face the strangers who had taken his mom and dad from him. After a couple minutes, Violet's quiet steps moved away from his door.

Evening crept into night. The house grew quiet and Lander came to a decision. He needed to talk to Pastor Stevens and he wanted to see Becky. If Castor really meant what he said about helping Lander, he could do so by getting Lander to Camden to see his friends.

The next morning Lander skulked down to the kitchen, unsure about how his antisocial behavior yesterday had been received. Even if he was angry, he knew Ian would have given him heck for behaving like a spoiled baby. But Lander didn't care. These people were nothing to him. As far as he was concerned, once he learned what he could from them, he would leave and strike out on his own.

Castor, Desma, Violet, Parker, Parrish, and Naara were sitting at the large dining table, talking, passing around platters of pancakes, bacon, and fruit, butter, and a bottle of real maple syrup, while Kenan flipped pancakes at the cooktop on the island. As Lander approached, all conversation stopped. He tucked his chin. "I'm sorry I acted like that yesterday."

Castor rose and waved Lander to an empty seat. "We understand. It must have been hard with so much thrown at you in so short a time. But today's a new day. Kenan is making his world-famous blueberry pancakes. Sit. Join us."

Lander wanted to nurture his self-righteous anger, but it was hard. Surrounded by Castor and his family, listening to their easy-going banter, reminded him of the camaraderie he had experienced with Becky's youth group at Crossways. Something in him craved this feeling of belonging. These people could understand him in ways no others could.

But Lander refused to let his guard down. He didn't belong here, and he wouldn't let this sensation of kinship trick him into staying.

As the meal wound down, Desma and Naara rose to clear the dishes.

"I want to go to Camden." Lander set his focus on Castor as he spoke.

"Really?" Parrish asked. "I was hoping to get there week after next myself. Want to go with me?"

"Um … yeah … sure," Lander mumbled, his eyes flicking to the young man.

"Great. We can do it together and get to know each other better that way. It'll be good for both of us."

"What do you need to go to Camden for?" Castor's obvious curiosity creased his brow. "That's a ten-hour drive."

"Not a big deal, Dad," Parrish said. "I've wanted to visit a friend who goes to school there for a while now. So, if Lander wants to go, I can take him. I have vacation days coming that I need to use before the end of the year anyway."

"Camden? Week after next?" A smile brightened Naara's face and sparked in her gray eyes. "I think you boys will need some adult supervision on this trip. Camden has the best little clothing boutiques and a wonderful antique shop I've been wanting to get back to for a while now. And I do have Christmas shopping that needs to be done."

"Aren't we due in Caracas that week?" Kenan asked,

raking his hair with his fingers as he turned to face Naara. "We already have flights booked for that Monday."

"When were you planning to leave Parrish?" Naara frowned and shook her head at Kenan.

"Well, I need to be in the office all next week, but I could leave the following Tuesday. I do need to check with my friend though, make sure she'll be around."

"Do that," Naara said with finality. She set her eyes on Kenan. "I really do need to do Christmas shopping and Camden is just the best place for that … and … I haven't had quality time with my nephew in ages. Why don't you go ahead as planned? I'll book a later flight and meet you in Caracas later in the week."

"Later in the week?" Kenan chuckled. "I know you, Naara. If you plan to shop, you'll be there for at least a week. Parrish, how long were you planning to be in Camden? If Naara is going shopping, you'll need to plan on at least a week."

"I can only stay through Saturday; I'll need to be back at work the following Monday." Parrish said, "How about you, Lander. That okay with you?"

"Sure," Lander said, as plans to stay at the mission and not return solidified in his mind. "That actually works out really well."

A frown creased a line between Desma's brows. "I don't think this is a good idea, Parrish. Didn't Lander escape from that man in Camden? For all we know Aurelius Hunt could have people there looking for us right now."

"Don't be such a worrywart, Desma." Naara came up behind Desma and wrapped an arm around the older woman's shoulders. "Camden is a large place. Besides, Parrish is a big boy; he'll be just fine." Naara turned to face Parrish. "As long as your friend is agreeable, Parrish, let's plan on leaving Tuesday morning. We can take turns driving. If we leave early, we can be there late Tuesday night even if we stop for a nice lunch. I'll make reservations at that little sushi restaurant we ate at the last time we were there. Remember? They had the best Spicy Yellowtail Rolls. Oh, now I'm getting excited. Let's plan on it. See if your friend wants to join us. We can meet there for say, nine o'clock?"

The hint of a smile surfaced on Kenan's face. "'*She'll* be around' ... hum? So this friend of yours is of the female persuasion, Parrish?"

"You can ask." Parrish grinned. "And you can wonder, Uncle Kenan. But I'm not divulging anything."

Shaking his head, Kenan chuckled again. "I hope you know what you're getting yourself into, boys. Naara is a shop until you drop kind of girl." He turned to his wife. "I'll plan on you meeting me in Caracas the following week, my dear."

Naara gave him a broad smile. "Yes, darling. Thanks for going without me this time. I promise, I'll make it up to you when I get there. I'll bring that little kimono that gets you so ..."

"Ooh ooh, too much information," Castor interrupted, laughing and covering Violet's ears.

Fifteen minutes later, everyone had disbursed except Violet. "My bus comes in ten minutes," she said to Lander as she grabbed his hand. "Sit with me for a little and I'll read you some of that journal you brought."

"I don't think that's a good idea," Lander said.

"Oh, let her read," Desma said as she finished wiping down the counter. "She reads well. Let her read from the beginning of the journal. The earlier entries should be okay for her."

"She can read Corish?"

"Speak it and read it," Desma answered. "We all saw to that. We wanted her to grow up knowing her roots."

Lander's stomach churned. Once again, he was confronted by all he had missed out on because Pop-pop had chosen not to tell him about who or what he was. He wondered what it would have been like to grow up with a family, knowing a mother and father.

"Here." Violet, already dressed to leave, patted the seat next to her on the couch, pulling Lander back into the present. She looked like he had first seen her; white dress, pink jacket, orange wool hat. But now she wore pink and white flowered leggings under the dress. She speared him with her large, wise, violet eyes. "It's okay, Lander. You don't have to be afraid."

"Who says I'm afraid." The words came out harsher than Lander expected. "I'm not afraid of anything," he added in a softer voice.

She gifted him with a knowing smile, opened the large journal on her lap, and leafed through the first few pages. Violet lifted sad eyes to Lander. "Your mom wrote this, didn't she?"

"Yeah." Lander pulled in a deep breath and focused on his hands. This little girl seemed able to read his thoughts. He couldn't let her get too close.

"Cool."

She turned back to the first page.

"Castor read the first entry yesterday," Lander said, feeling useless as he scanned the strange writing.

"Okay." She ran her finger down the next entry. "Corish is pretty close to English. If I help you, I'll bet you could read this."

"Really?"

"You need to get going, Violet." Desma walked into the great room, wiping her hands on a towel. "I don't want you missing the bus again."

"Yes, Auntie Desma." She looked over to Lander again. "You know what? Aunt Desma could help you while I'm at school. She's a really good teacher."

Lander's face warmed when Violet leaned into him and planted a wet kiss on his cheek. "Hey! Why'd you do that?"

With a big, innocent smile and a wink, Violet sprang from the couch. "See you later."

She sprinted out the door slamming it behind her while Desma shouted, "And don't you slam that ... Oh, that child."

Lander fidgeted as Desma turned. A shiver ran through him at her cold expression. She huffed. "And now what am I going to do with you. You can't even speak Corish and I hate talking in English."

CHAPTER 18

Doris Beckman had been down to the Visitor Center twice in the last four hours greeting VIP guests and welcoming them to the island. The clacking of her heels echoed down the hallway as she strode into her office. Huffing, she grumbled as she struggled to straighten her now rather unruly, chin length, professionally dyed and styled hair. At forty-two years old, she cringed at the random strands of gray that appeared at the roots of her auburn tresses if left undyed. She loved working for Aurelius Hunt and his island was beautiful, but the humidity drove her to distraction when she needed to be outside for any length of time.

Pulling the hem of her orange silk jacket down, she pursed her lips as she stood in the doorway to her office and observed the secretary who had manned her desk while she was away. Legs crossed, her skirt riding up her thighs. Young and pretty, she tried to dress professionally—well, maybe. As far as Doris was concerned, the junior secretary wore her skirts way too short and was much too friendly with the new security guard who now hovered near Doris's desk.

"Hum, um," Doris cleared her throat, producing the desired result. The tall, dark-haired, security guard who looked to have come from middle eastern roots stumbled away from the antique cherry desk.

"Thanks for your help," he mumbled to the young secretary who tried to yank the hem of her skirt toward her knees. The security guard ducked his head in Doris's direction, and retreated from Mr. Hunt's outer office.

"Mrs. Beckman." The young lady slipped a strand of hair behind her left ear. "Was your trip to the Welcome Center successful?"

"Quite. Mr. Hunt's guests are now settled at the mansion. Anything come up that I need to address immediately? Calls that require my attention?"

"Well, Mrs. Beckman, most of the callers were okay with leaving voice mail. But there was one that was very strange. The caller sounded … weird … like he was using something to mask his identity."

"How so?"

"The voice was . . . deep, distorted and gritty, not normal. It sounded like the person was talking in a tunnel, his voice echoing around him. Anyway, he refused to leave a voice mail. Said the information he had was most important and personal to Mr. Hunt and that he would speak with no one else. He said he would call back later. Aside from that, everything was quiet."

"Thank you. You may return to your own desk now. I'll call you if I need you to cover again."

The girl pushed up onto her feet, once again pulling at her skirt. Doris frowned. "But, my dear, from now on, please dress more professionally. Otherwise, I'll replace you. Remember when you work for Aurelius Hunt Industries, you represent Mr. Hunt."

"Yes Mrs. Beckman." Aiming a quick nod in Doris's direction, the young woman scurried from the office.

Doris checked her desk to make sure everything was in order. She wondered about the strange call. It wasn't unusual for Mr. Hunt to get calls from peculiar people. Doris had fielded many such calls over the last twelve years. As Mr. Hunt's administrative assistant, she saw it as her duty to filter out any unwanted calls. But sometimes she couldn't tell if she should pass the call into Mr. Hunt or turn the caller away. Her first year on the island, she had refused to forward questionable calls several times. After missing an important call, Mr. Hunt had made it quite clear, let him deal with cryptic personal calls directly or he would find a new administrative assistant.

She had heard the rumors. Idle talk had been rampant her first years on the island. Hints about Mr. Hunt's eccentric behavior and why almost everyone employed on the island a few years earlier had been fired or disappeared. Reports of strange happenings surfaced from time to time. Whispered insinuations that some of what went on in the secure R&D compound behind the mansion was suspicious. Things the elite security guards and select scientists who worked beyond the inner gate wouldn't discuss.

But Doris liked Mr. Hunt; he had been good to her. He even paid for her husband's surgery after his motorcycle accident, though Doris had only been working on the island for a few weeks.

And Mr. Hunt was a noted philanthropist, always giving money to worthy charities. *Good grief, he even buys Girl Scout cookies from my niece. No.* Doris shook her head. *Those rumors are nothing more than the sour grapes of disgruntled ex-employees who want to damage Mr. Hunt's reputation.*

It was true that Mr. Hunt had fired a good number of employees before Doris came to work for him, but he had good reason. *He has a right to protect his research from industry spies.*

But she struggled against the rise of gooseflesh when she recalled the disturbing screams coming from the R&D compound several weeks ago. Though she usually left the island on the last public ferry of the day, at sundown, she had arranged for later transport to the mainland and stayed to finish some paperwork. Walking down the brick path back to her golf cart after leaving the necessary papers at the mansion, she heard the cries. *Just an animal from the preserve.* She reasoned with herself. *That's all. Some animal whose cries bounced off the surrounding mountains. It was dark. I let my imagination get away from me. They only sounded like they came from the inner compound, that's all.*

Pushing aside the disturbing thoughts, Doris began working on setting up interviews for some potential new employees. Human resources had already completed their interviews and now a couple of the more sensitive hires required Mr. Hunt's personal input.

Two hours later, Mr. Hunt breezed into the office, his face alight with his trademark broad smile. "Doris, thank you for settling our VIP guests in at the Mansion earlier. Did you make reservations at Le Cheri?"

"Yes, sir. As you requested, I reserved the small private dining room for nine o'clock. The *Mist of the Depths* is being readied for the trip to the mainland as we speak. As usual, George will captain the yacht and Roger will be your chauffeur this evening. The limo will be waiting at the mainland dock at eight thirty."

"Very good, Doris. Anything else?"

Doris pursed her lips, wondering if the earlier call was worth mentioning. *Probably best to allow Mr. Hunt to make the decision.* She told Aurelius of the call and the description the young secretary had given of the voice.

"Interesting." Aurelius's brows drew together over his straight nose as he rubbed his right hand over his chin. "I'll be here for about an hour, Doris. If he calls back, put him through. It might be worth my time to hear what he has to say."

"Yes, sir."

Aurelius vanished into his inner office. Doris finished scanning in several documents Mr. Hunt needed transferred to his laptop for his dinner meeting tonight. Completing the scans, she stretched, groaning at the release of tense muscles, before slipping out of her office for a quick trip to the Ladies Room and the expresso machine. As if on cue, the phone rang just as she rounded her desk, returning with cup in hand. Picking up the receiver Doris listened quietly for a minute. She immediately understood the young secretary's description. Buzzing the inner office Doris said, "Mr. Hunt, that caller we discussed is on line two."

After entering his office, Aurelius spent some time looking over the files Doris had left on his desk for the potential new hires. He leafed through most, scanning, then sat back to study the one file that piqued his interest. Aurelius had kept a close eye on this singular doctor's career for several years. Paul Eiger had doctorates in molecular genetics and chemistry as well as a medical degree but had run into some difficulties with questionable ethics in his prior employment. Aurelius read through the detailed report on the incident leading to the man's dismissal. *Perfect.*

Doris's voice penetrated his thoughts. "Mr. Hunt, that caller we discussed is on line two."

Aurelius set the folder aside and allowed a small smile to cross his face as he swung his tufted burgundy leather bankers chair to face the wall of windows overlooking the cliffs on the mainland side of his island. He took his time, making the caller wait, as he touched the controls to dim the lights and open the translucent blinds.

He scanned the shoreline in the distance beyond the wind-tossed, gray-green water. His eyes caught on two sailing yachts racing each other across the expanse, cutting through the water, tossing spray, sails dipping low as they turned to circle his island. *Beautiful. Someday I'll have the time to do that. Soon I'll have all the time I need.*

Once they disappeared beyond his sight, he pulled in a deep breath. "Back to the business at hand. He pressed the conference button on the phone. "This is Aurelius Hunt. I hear you have something of interest to me? I'm a very busy man. You have ten seconds to impress me before I hang up."

A distorted snort sounded from the other end. A grainy voice echoed as it ground out two words, "Lander Devlin."

Aurelius paused for a few seconds as the name pulled up images from the past. "Okay, you have my attention. I'm listening."

Five minutes later, he buzzed Doris. "Get Emmett Talon on the phone. Now."

CHAPTER 19

I don't get it." Lander allowed a growl of frustration to leak into his voice though he knew he shouldn't.

Desma released a huff, signaling her own irritation. "No wonder Ian never taught you to read Corish. You're hopeless. You're not even trying. Now, again, translate that line. It's similar to English. Just think."

Lander had been studying with Desma for over a week. Though she had worked through most of Cyanne's journal entries, reading and translating them into English as Lander wrote them into a spiral notebook, she insisted Lander do some of the translating himself. "Your heritage is Core Dweller," she had said last Monday when she brought the spiral notebook from Castor's office and handed it to Lander. "It's time you learned at least something of the language."

Difficult to work with, Desma rattled off in Corish frequently and berated Lander for not being studious enough if his thoughts drifted or he glanced out the window. He couldn't seem to please the woman no matter what he did. One moment she would mother him, make him a lavish lunch and tell him to take a break. Other times, without warning, she would storm away, slamming the office door while grumbling in Corish something that sounded like *idiot*. Lander figured it probably did mean idiot—or the equivalent—in Corish. It was a word he was coming to know intimately. At least he would be going to Camden Tuesday. He would get to see Becky and Pastor Stevens again.

He studied the journal entry again as Desma obsessively wiped the kitchen counter for what Lander thought must be the hundredth time. He was trying to sound out the words of the last segment written in Corish, his mother's last record, when something clicked. "The storm. She's writing about how the storms still unsettle … unsettle … Decima. You. She was writing about you."

"Finally." Desma grunted tossing the dishrag into the sink and coming to stand behind Lander. "Now, what else does she say?"

Scanning the page again, Lander translated, stumbling his way through the words. "'Though being on the Surface has been hard for us in many ways, I like it. Decima says it's too much; too much light of the sun, too much water around the island, too many bright colors, and too much noise and chaos during the storms that often rage across the island. Even now, she sits at the window watching, But I can see her trembling.'"

"Do you still hate storms?" Lander looked up at Desma.

The woman plopped down in the chair next to Lander's. "Idiot boy," she mumbled and slid the journal in front of her. A moment later, she began reading where Lander had left off.

"'I like the storms. They make me feel alive.' Of course she did. Your mother was always fearless." Silence pressed in on Lander until Desma continued reading. "They are wild and unpredictable. Sitting in the library, watching the rain—something we never experienced in the Core—beat against the glass of the large windows, I am caught up by the sound and the sight of it. The way the thunder rattles the glass, the way the water flows down in miniature streams.

"'In the Core, vapor seeps inward off the Sentinel Band that protects us from the heat of the Flux. The resulting mist blankets everything in its cycle, settling in droplets of moisture everywhere. And there are springs bubbling up from below and around us without ceasing, gentle and serene, never uncontrolled.

"'Everything is predictable in the Core, cyclical like the sun rising and setting on the Surface. Here many things are unpredictable, like the storms, which can be turbulent and frightening.

"'Our journey to the Surface has become like a wild storm, uncontrolled and unpredictable. It is because of Aurelius. We accepted his friendship, trusted him. And now I fear we have been trapped by his deceit. I have seen it in his eyes, he covets our gifts and our long lives. Yesterday we sent a petition asking to be allowed to leave Zephryn Island. We would like to learn more of the Surface; but if that's not possible, we want to return to the Core.

"'But I fear he will not allow this. It's strange even speaking of being *allowed*, like he's got control over us. But, if I was to be honest, he does. I don't know how we've come to this. And to make matters worse, he's taken immoderate interest in my son. Ian believes it's because Lander comes from two family lines of Stone Sovereigns and will most likely exhibit strong gifts with the stones and without.

"'If we are indeed prisoners here and the situation doesn't change soon, I fear the day will come when he will take Lander from me. I will not allow this to happen. I would die to protect my son.

"'Aurelius still hasn't responded to our request to meet this morning, but something has happened. Nora Claypoole just rushed into the library. I have never seen her so upset before. She is trembling with fear and fury. I fear what is to come. My brethren, if this journal somehow reaches you and I have not written in it again, please pray that my death was not wasted. I, myself, now pray for the safety of my friends and my family, Ian, Jerod, and little Lander. May God be with us all.'"

The older section of the journal ended with Cyanne's final words. Lander sniffled and rubbed his eyes with the heels of his hands, determined not to cry in front of Desma.

"It's what you said," he whispered. "The way you told it." He looked up, turning his face to scan the trees beyond the large plate-glass windows, blinking back the threatening tears.

"Ian must have taken the journal when we left the island." Desma's eyes squinted as she scrutinized the page before turning to the next. "Yes, the next entry is in English. Ian must have written it." After another moment, she huffed. "Judging by the date, he didn't start adding to the journal for several years."

Lander swallowed against the burn at the back of his throat. "Yeah, I noticed that Pop-pop's first entry was dated the day I turned twelve."

"Ah." Desma nodded. "That makes sense. The twelfth cycle is an important birthday among Core Dwellers. For it is then, that a child is first invited to join in community gatherings; not yet as a participant, but to observe. It is the first level of kinship. I guess continuing the journal was Ian's way of including you in our community."

"But he never showed it to me. Why not, if it was meant for me?"

"The second level of kinship happens on the child's twenty-first birthday, or as we would call it in the Core, his twenty-first cycle. Perhaps he planned to continue adding to it and give it to you then."

"Maybe." Lander chewed his lower lip. "But … he's dead now … so I guess I'll never know."

Desma's eyes met Lander's. Compassion and frustration warring for dominance on her features.

After several awkward minutes, Lander decided to face the divide Desma had established between them. She hadn't said so, but he couldn't miss the signs. "You want me to leave." It wasn't a question. Lander stated what he had felt from her ever since he arrived at Elm Farm.

Guilt overshadowed the other emotions and she turned away. But swinging back around to face Lander once again, she answered evenly, "Yes, I want you to leave. I don't trust you no matter whose son you are. And I fear for my family's safety. I worry that after all this time, your presence might bring us to Aurelius's attention.

"The first three years after we ran from Aurelius were hell. Constantly moving from place to place, staying one step ahead of that madman's searchers.

"We have a good life now, identities that have taken us years to establish. We have a life here. I may not like it; I've never felt comfortable on the Surface. But Castor and the boys, Naara, Kenan, and Violet wouldn't go back to the Core even if they could. This is their home now; the only home Violet's ever known.

"So, yes. For as harsh as it may seem to you, the protection of my own comes before anything else. Castor doesn't understand that. He wants you to stay here, become part of our family. He's a good man, but he's a fool. Your presence here puts our identities at risk.

"I'm truly sorry Ian died. And I'm sorry you're alone. But I think it best if you don't return from the trip to Camden. Do you understand?"

Lander's eyes focused back on the stand of trees beyond the window as he shuffled the stones in his pocket. "I understand. May I use Castor's computer. I'd like to e-mail Pastor Stevens and Becky, let them know I'm coming."

"You going to ask the pastor if you can stay there?"

"I'm planning on that, yeah."

"I'll get you logged on."

"Please understand, Lander. This is for the best. You'll see."

Lander took the stairs two at a time on his way to his room. After digging the paper with Pastor Stevens's and Becky's email addresses from his pack, he returned to the lower level and followed Desma into Castor's office.

The room reminded Lander of City Line Hospital, all metal, glass, and shades of gray. Sitting in Castor's charcoal colored leather swivel chair at the glass-topped desk with sculpted silver legs, Lander's knee bounced. The sterile surroundings intimidated him. Even the artwork was all black, white, and gray. His nerves settled a bit when he noticed several stones of various colors set on a white bookshelf. At least here was something natural.

Desma powered up the computer, clicked to a screen to set up new email accounts, and left Lander alone. Once he entered a fake name and a new email address, he emailed Pastor Stevens and Becky explaining that he was coming back to Camden next Tuesday and that he wanted to see them. He also told Pastor Stevens that he would like to stay at Crossways for a while if he could.

With the emails sent, Lander sat back, scanning Castor's office. Again, the stones caught his eye and with a quick glance to assure himself that Desma wasn't waiting outside the door, he strode to the shelf for a closer look.

All five were rough, unpolished, and a mottled gray color. Wondering if he could do anything with them, Lander picked up the first in line and held it in the palm of his hand, waiting to see if it would react to his touch. When nothing happened, he closed his eyes, felt the solid weight of the stone and focused as if preparing to disappear. He massaged it with the palm of his hand. The stone warmed and smoothed. Lander's eyes popped open. On his hand sat a shiny, polished, deep red stone with charcoal gray veins running through the red. As he flipped it over, marveling at its slick surface, he noticed a creamy white circle with red veining on the underside. While his stones were flattened like mini blue pancakes with green markings and black veins, Castor's stone was an oval, more like an egg.

Desma's approaching footsteps sounded a warning. Lander replaced the stone and sprinted back to the desk.

"Well, are you done yet?" Suspicion etched lines around her squinting eyes.

"Yes, ma'am," Lander mumbled as he slid past her to the safety of the hall.

He would leave on Tuesday just like he told Desma, but first, he would confront Castor. There was so much he didn't know about his gifts, his father's stones, and how to use them. He would learn what he could from Castor before Tuesday and hope it was enough.

CHAPTER 20

After supper, Lander sat in the great room playing checkers with Violet. It was their third game and she was unbeatable.

"I see Violet's found a new victim," Parker said as he and Kendra walked into the great room. The two had eaten at a local Italian restaurant and just returned.

Kendra sprinted to stand behind Violet. "Here, Lander, let me help you." She proceeded to tickle Violet eliciting high pitched squeals of delight from the girl. "Now, quick, switch sides."

"No, no, no," Violet panted out between squeals. "That's not fair. Stop." Releasing a high-pitched screech, the little girl turned around, reached out, and with a wicked grin, tickled Kendra.

"No you don't," Parker said, lifting Violet into the air away from the cringing Kendra. She shrieked, legs kicking out.

"Enough." Desma came around the island, a frown creasing her brow. "Why is it that every time you walk in the door, the play gets out of hand Parker? And you, young lady." She turned to Kendra. "You're of an age to know better than to encourage this kind of behavior."

Castor walked up the hall from his office and chuckled. "I don't know. It seems to me the only way anyone could win a checkers game against Violet is to cheat. Interesting approach, Kendra.

"Lander, instead of just sitting and staring, you should have made your move. Now, it's too late."

"That it is," Naara said, leaning over the island counter. "It is late. Time for bed, Violet."

"Aww, Mom. Lander was just about to crown me again. Can't we finish the game before I have to go to bed?"

"I think you've humbled him enough for one night. Bed. Now."

Still grumbling, Violet cleared the board and put the game away before skipping to Lander. "Thanks." She planted a noisy kiss on his cheek and smiled big. She flitted around the rooms and gave everyone else kisses before stomping with heavy steps up the stairs and down the hallway to her bedroom.

Lander rubbed his hands on his thighs, working up the courage to approach Castor with his questions. It was already Thursday and he only had four days left. *Now or never.*

Castor had walked into the kitchen and was pouring a cup of coffee when Lander stood and approached him.

"Castor." He hesitated, his gaze flicking to the floor as he ran a hand over the back of his neck. "I need to talk with you."

Opening the refrigerator, Castor reached in and pulled out a carton of creamer. Standing back up, he turned to face Lander. "Sure. What can I help you with?"

Nerves sent a wave of trembling through Lander's hands. He plunged them into his pockets, fisting his stones. "Um, can we … um … maybe … talk alone?"

"Let's talk in my office."

Sipping his coffee, Castor closed the door behind Lander and moved to sit at his desk. "Grab a seat, Lander." He waved at the black leather sofa with silver metallic legs that duplicated the ones on his desk. "Now, what do you need to talk about in private?"

Lander eased the Stones of Power from his pockets. "These. I need to know about these. I don't know much about what they can do or how to use them."

Castor's eyes grew large. "Are they what I think they are? Are they Jerod's Stones of Power?"

"I think so. I know they belonged to my dad. And I know they're really powerful."

"Have you used them?" Castor asked, eyebrows raised, concern wrinkling his forehead.

Lander nodded. "Just once. I didn't mean to; it just sort of … happened."

Castor rose, walked around his desk to stand in front of Lander. The stones began to glow in Lander's hand and Castor sucked in a breath. He reached out. "May I?"

Lander turned his hands to drop the stones onto Castor's open palms. No sooner did he release them than they went dark. Disappointment flitted across Castor's face. "It's as I thought. They will only respond to a Stone Sovereign."

"Please." Lander hated begging, but the need to know drove him. "Please … could you teach me."

Castor shook his head. "I can't. I don't know how they work. I'm not a Stone Sovereign." Sighing, he lowered his gaze to the floor and mumbled, "Ian, you old fool. You should have taught the boy."

Castor shifted his gaze back up to Lander. "I can't teach you much, but I'll share what I know. I can teach you about my own Stone of Power. It helps me keep track of our people on the surface. And, of course, I can pull wealth from stones where gems are present. But once you understand your gifts, you'll be able to use any Stone of Power. Stone Sovereigns can make use of all the gifts. As a Stone Worker, I'm limited."

Moving to sit on the edge of his glass desk, Castor faced Lander. He pulled in a deep breath and released it with a slow hiss, quiet, thinking for several minutes before speaking.

"Though our people have ever been few in number—most couples have only two or maybe three children—we are, as you now know, long-lived. I myself am 468 years old. Our longevity, like our gifts, dates back to the ancient days, when the world was shattered, and flood covered the Surface.

"Our fathers believed Noah's God led them to the cave and into the tunnel beneath the Surface before sealing it behind them, saving them from the destroying waters. They were a remnant; four families, twenty-seven people in all. Our ancestors.

"How they survived those first years in the tunnels, we don't know. But we do know that after a time, they began working the rough, rock walls and scratching their story onto them. A record for their descendants." Castor paused, raised his eyes to Lander, and motioned him back to his seat on the couch before sitting next to him.

"Ian had been studying the network of tunnels for years, always looking to find earlier records. His goal was to read all the wall writings. That was why he was in the tunnels that day. There had been a strong earthquake in the area a few weeks earlier that exposed the cave. Aurelius, interested in exploring the newly revealed cave on his island, led a team down into the tunnels. Aurelius and Ian met that day in the Highway. That was the name given to the largest of the tunnels, the one we now know was connected to the outer entrance. Aurelius's cave. I wish that meeting had never happened." Castor closed his eyes and shook his head. Rising from the couch, he began to pace in front of Lander. "But ... I digress."

"As our ancestors were creating the walls, they came across certain stones that were found to possess special powers. At first, only a few individuals could work the stones. Some stones gave light and heat, others grew plants even in the dark. There were stones that warmed to cook food while others protected their owners from harm. The most valuable stones, however, were the healing stones. But there were only two of those found until we entered the Core. The least valuable of gifts was the drawing forth of beauty in the form of gems. In a world where gems are readily found, it couldn't compare to the other gifts. Here on the Surface, however, this ability has made my family wealthy.

"Using stones of protection, the first of our people were able to brave the Vortex, traveling through the fierce heat of the Flux, through the barrier and into the innermost core. There they discovered a place of light and hope. Plants grew, water flowed, temperature remained constant. The Flux was the source of energy that surrounded and nurtured the small world. They realized they could live protected within the barrier that held the heat and energy of the Flux at levels where life could thrive.

"The people moved into the Core. More Stones of Power were found there than had been discovered in the tunnels. Our people prospered; our culture blossomed. For millennia, we lived in peace. In time, our families grew.

"Certain individuals began to develop gifts apart from the stones, gifts they could use without holding Stones of Power." Castor stopped pacing and faced Lander. "Why? You see, Lander, that was the question that spurred Ian into his study of the wall writing. Ian and a few of his friends who also carried the stoneless abilities began to travel the Vortex and the Avortex to learn what they could.

"It was an accident that led Ian to understand that those who possessed the stoneless gifts also had the ability to work any stone in any way and with a power unknown before. Without getting into the details of the accident, I must tell you Ian saved two of his friends and returned them to the Core using stones in ways unheard of before; not only bringing them through the Vortex safely, but transporting both while keeping them alive and comfortable at the same time. That was a tall order for anyone, even a Stone Sovereign like Ian.

"We began to study our gifts with more specific intent, each family working with a variety of stones. In the end, we traced two of the lines back to a time when there had been a rift between the clans—a little over two thousand years ago.

"Ian spent years studying the writings from that time. For some reason, the two families separated from the other clans and returned to life in the tunnels for several hundred years. We learned that only descendants of those who had sundered ties were able to work any stones. And, only descendants of those two lines displayed the ability to vanish, spark fire, and heal without Stones of Power. Not all the descendants exhibited the gifts, but all who did were direct descendants. We began calling those with these abilities Stone Sovereigns because all Stones of Power responded to them.

"Those two lines reside in you, Lander. Both Jerod, through Ian, and Cyanne, through her mother and father, were Stone Sovereigns. I am a simple Stone Worker. I see the beauty inherent in certain stones and the ability to bring it out. On the Surface, I have taken to calling this gift Wealth. But I do not know how your gifts work. Did Ian not teach you anything?"

Lander picked at a hole in the knee of his jeans as Castor's words sunk in. "To vanish, you already know that. I can spark fire, and I've done some healing. Nothing serious, cuts and scrapes mostly, one time a sprained ankle."

Castor nodded. "Well at least Ian taught you the basics. Lander, you know what you need to know. The Stones of Power, when used with your other gifts, will enhance your abilities, make you stronger. The only other thing I can tell you is that every Stone Sovereign works with two stones. I've mentioned stones of protection; those are the stones of creative power. Every Stone Sovereign is given one of those when he or she turns twenty-one. But the second stone is a stone of opposing power. Those a Stone Sovereign seeks out as he grows older. Your situation is unique for you have been given both at a young age. And, because they were your father's, I suspect they are quite powerful. I don't know much more than that. And the fact that every Stone Sovereign must choose wisely how he will balance the powers in the two stones."

"Choose to balance the powers? I did something when I was at Crossways. Something that I never learned from Ian. I think I did that protection thing without even trying."

Castor stood, looking down at Lander. Smiling he said, "Protection is a good thing. Well, son, I suspect with your family tree, you're a natural. I will enjoy working with you to see what you're capable of doing. But, I think I've overloaded you with enough information for one night. Besides, my coffee has gotten cold."

"One more question?" Lander asked.

Castor sighed deeply, but said, "Okay, Lander. Shoot."

"When Pop-pop was dying, he told me something I don't understand. He said to choose well. Not like my mother. Do you known what he meant? Do you know what happened to my mom's stones?"

Castor walked to the window and scanned the darkness. "I can't be sure, Lander. And I'm not even comfortable talking about this." He glanced back over his shoulder.

"I need to know whatever you can tell me."

Turning back to the dark window, Castor said softly, "After Jared was killed, Cyanne let go of her shield of protection. She began destroying Aurelius's boats, the dock, people. I think she chose destruction. She had always been a beautiful, kind, gentle soul. Never once can I recall her allowing destruction dominance. I can't be certain, but I believe something in Ian died in that moment. Not only had he lost his only son, his compassionate and caring daughter stopped protecting us to fling destruction and she died that way. In the end, she chose destruction over protection. I suspect that's the reason Ian didn't teach you more. He feared what you might become once you knew the whole story.

"If her stones weren't destroyed at the end, I suspect Hunt still has them."

The room got quiet after Castor stopped speaking. There were so many other questions Lander needed answered but he knew Castor wouldn't tell him anything more tonight. He wished he could stay longer, learn more from the man. Lander was tempted to tell Castor that he didn't plan to return from Camden, that they wouldn't get the chance to work together. But then, giving it a second thought, he decided Desma was right. It was best if he just left without saying anything.

CHAPTER 21

Naara rented a van for the trip to Camden. Though Castor had tried to talk her into taking the company jet, she refused. "Thank you, Castor. I appreciate the offer. But I plan to purchase several antiques and I prefer to bring them home myself rather than have them shipped. I don't want to deal with some irresponsible mover damaging a one-of-a-kind antique. It's happened before and I will not go through that again."

When Parrish saw the large white, utility rental van, he stomped back in the house. "Naara, this is ridiculous. Not all movers are careless. Please, let's take the jet or at least my BMW. I'll even pay to have your things specially shipped. I really don't want to ride ten hours in that *thing.*"

"It's your choice, Parrish," Naara replied, straightening her beige Armani lambskin jacket and grabbing her green Givenchy handbag from the counter. "I'm taking the van. You can ride with me or stay home."

She turned to Lander, who was still sitting at the counter drinking a glass of orange juice. "You coming?"

"Yes, ma'am." He jumped off the stool, threw on his hoodie and jacket, then hefted his pack to his shoulder and followed Naara out the door.

"Okay, okay," Parrish shouted. "Hold up. I'm coming. Just give me a few minutes."

"This is ridiculous," Parrish muttered again as he climbed into the front passenger seat. "This sucks. It smells like air freshener in here. Like something died and they're covering the stench with fake pine odor. Naara, what are you thinking? We could have used one of the company vans for nothing instead of renting this piece of crap."

He rolled down the window but then, shivering in the late autumn air, rolled it back up.

Lander hunched down on the bench seat behind Naara and Parrish. Naara floored the gas, fishtailing out the drive as Parrish grabbed the dash and moaned.

This is going to be a long trip. Lander groaned.

By the time they stopped for lunch, Lander was certain Naara had a death wish. She drove like a demon, fast, reckless, and with a complete lack of concern for safety. She used the horn often and swerved from lane to lane without warning.

"When we get back in that death-trap, I'm driving." Parrish glared at his aunt as they crossed the parking lot toward the exclusive restaurant where Naara insisted they eat.

Large sparkling chandeliers cast myriad pinpricks of light over the ornate dining room. Stark white, linen tablecloths covered tables surrounded by heavy wooden chairs with blue velvet cushions. Gold-trimmed dishes set on the tables reflected the light back up at the high ceiling.

Lander stuck his hands in his jacket pockets and hunched his shoulders. He'd never been in such a fancy place, not once in his life seen such ornate furnishings. Though Naara and Parrish seemed at ease in the surroundings, Lander's level of discomfort rose to new heights as the uniformed man who inclined his head in greeting, took notice of him with obvious disdain.

Glancing surreptitiously at Naara and Parrish, Lander realized how polished the two looked; both wore expensive clothing with confidence. Parrish's white shirt, black and white striped tie, fitted charcoal vest and tan cargo pants, topped by his thigh-length pea coat showed off his fine physique to advantage. His gray eyes practically glowed as they walked past several candelabras.

Lander hunched even more as he compared himself with the handsome, stylish man next to him. Intensely aware of the holes in his jeans and the hoodie peeking out from the collar of his military jacket, he scuffed his shoes on the polished wood floor. Becky may have called his clothes urban chic; here he felt more like urban bum.

Lander let Parrish order for him and was pleasantly surprised when the waiter brought the most delicious steak he had ever eaten. It came with a salad of organic specialty greens and tiny roasted potatoes that tasted of garlic and herbs. Parrish had ordered the same for himself and smiled his approval. Lander smiled back. "It's really good," he said.

"This place may be over the top, but Naara likes it. And as long as they serve food like this, I'll come back whenever I'm in the area."

Lander nodded as he chewed another bite of steak. Naara poked at her salad and complained the greens were limp. The waiter immediately removed the offending salad and, less than a minute later, slipped a new plate on the table.

Returning to the van, Naara and Parrish argued over who would drive. Lander breathed a sigh of relief when Parrish snatched the keys from Naara and sat in the driver's seat. Huffing her displeasure, Naara strode to the passenger side and took her seat.

With Parrish at the wheel the rest of the trip was uneventful.

As they got closer to Camden, Lander started to get nervous about seeing Pastor Stevens. Though his responding email had said Lander was always welcome at Crossways, Lander could sense a hesitation in the way it was worded. *Probably concerned about what happened on Thanksgiving. I'll have to be careful if those guys from the gang come around.*

Becky's latest email made Lander smile. It was so like her; upbeat and joyful. She told him about things that had happened since her last email. Michael had saved enough money for a new tattoo and when he heard Lander was coming, challenged him to join him and get one at the same time on Saturday. He even volunteered to make the appointment.

Watching the countryside slide by while the van covered the distance to Camden, Lander chuckled thinking how strange it would be to get a tattoo. He considered his options, what kind he would get. Maybe a sword or a dragon, definitely nothing lame.

His thoughts turned to Becky and he imagined what it would be like seeing her again Wednesday evening. Although the youth group wasn't scheduled to volunteer until the following Saturday, Becky and a few friends, including Michael, had committed to help with dinner Wednesday evening. Even better, Becky said she could spend the entire day with Lander on Saturday, if he wanted. "Especially if you get a tattoo," she had written with a smiley face after.

He tried to word his return email as if he didn't care but, in reality, he was excited to spend a day with Becky. They had emailed back and forth several times a day the last few days. He asked Desma to log him onto Castor's computer almost hourly. Desma grumbled, but Lander didn't care. It was worth putting up with her bad temper just to see if Becky had written.

Traffic in Camden was light by the time they entered the city limits. "Our reservation is for nine," Naara said. "So we have time to check into the hotel and freshen up before we head out. You did invite your lady friend, right, Parrish? I made the reservation for four people."

"I don't think this is a good idea." Parrish turned, avoiding eye contact with Naara. "I'd really like to talk with Livy some more before she meets the family. We haven't had a chance to get together lately. She was away and then got busy at school when she came back. Can't we just wait for another time?"

Naara grumbled about inconsiderate youth then turned in her seat to face Lander. "And I suppose you have some kind of excuse for not joining us as well?"

Lander shrugged. He had no desire to spend any more time than necessary with either Naara or Parrish. "I'd really like to get to Crossways and settle in there. They're probably serving dinner now and I can eat there."

Naara huffed and her eyes narrowed as she continued to stare at Lander. His muscles relaxed and he released a breath when, after a very long moment, she turned back to Parrish. "Well, I hope you at least will be joining me, Parrish?"

"Of course. Besides, Livy already said she'd join us. So, I guess you're going to meet her tonight."

Parrish turned in his seat and focused a pleading look at Lander. "Come with us. Please. We already have the reservation. You can meet Livy. And this place makes amazing sushi and sashimi. We can drop you at the mission after we eat."

"I don't think ..."

"Aren't your taste buds just longing for great sushi?"

"I don't know." Lander wrinkled his nose, unsure he wanted to try sushi. "I've never had sushi."

"What," Parrish exploded. "How can you have lived this long and not tasted sushi?"

"Oh, leave the boy alone," Naara said. "If he wants to eat mission food instead of sushi, that's his choice. Talking over her shoulder, Naara said, "We'll drop you off first. It's on the way to the hotel anyway. It'll just be easier."

Fifteen minutes later, Lander waved good-bye to Naara and Parrish, promising to keep the cell phone Parrish had given him several days ago charged.

"I'll call tomorrow." Parrish waved as he pulled away.

Hoisting his backpack onto his shoulder, Lander climbed the steps to the front door of Crossways Mission. He walked down the narrow hall to the soup kitchen, the familiar noises and smells welcoming him. Entering the brightly lit, yellow dining area, he caught sight of faces he recognized. Regulars, street people who came for supper most evenings. Within seconds he was noticed.

"Hey, look who's back," one grizzled old veteran said, grinning, his smile a mix of yellow teeth and dark empty spaces. "It's Lander."

Several people rose and came to greet him, pumping his hand or thumping him on the back. He smiled. Warmth spread through him … the warmth of welcome. Pastor Stevens bustled out from the kitchen. A broad smile lit his face when he saw Lander. Wiping his hands on his white chef's apron he approached.

"You made it I see. You're looking good. Someone's been feeding you well." Pastor Stevens thumped Lander's belly with the back of his hand. "Are you hungry? Come on, have a seat; I'll bring you a plate."

Lander swallowed and toed the floor. "That's okay, I can get in line. But, first, I need to know where I can put my stuff."

"If you want, we can lock your things in my office." Pastor Stevens pulled his keys from his pocket. "Drop your bag in there for now and then come back down. Things are slow here tonight. I'll take a break and eat with you."

Lander nodded. "Yeah, sure." He took the keys and climbed the steps to Pastor Stevens's office. After he returned to the dining area, Lander stood with his hands in his pockets waiting for the pastor to finish. A few minutes later he walked out of the kitchen no longer wearing his apron.

"Come on, kid, let's get something to eat."

They filled plates to heaping. Lander grabbed a soda while Pastor Stevens got coffee. They settled at an empty table and the pastor said grace.

"Now, Lander, you want to tell me what's going on?" Pastor Stevens watched Lander closely. The all too familiar feeling that the pastor knew more than he said flitted through Lander.

"I thought you weren't coming back; at least, not for a while. People here are still talking about what happened at Thanksgiving."

Lander frowned, poked at his food, and stared out the window. "They don't want me."

"Who?"

"The people Pop-pop Ian said would help me." Lander shoved his fork into a pile of mashed potatoes and sucked in a breath as he blinked back warm tears. He refused to admit the fear that stabbed holes in his shell of self-sufficiency but if he didn't get help from Pastor Stevens, he didn't know what he would do. "I have nowhere else to go."

Pastor Stevens shook his head and groaned, settling back in his chair. "I'm sorry. Of course, you're welcome here; I hope you know that. But, Lander, if you're going to stay, you're going to have to keep a low profile. Even now, your presence here could attract attention."

He shook his head again, his lips pressed into a thin line. "But we don't have to talk about this now." He paused and watched Lander push his food around the plate for a moment. "Stop poking at your food and eat already. Otherwise Becky is going to give me heck for not feeding you."

CHAPTER 22

Parrish showered and dressed. He looked with suspicion at the bed with the rather worn brown polyester bedspread where he had laid out his clothes for dinner. Naara had reserved rooms in a shabby hotel near the airport. *Not like her at all. What's up with this?* Usually it was only the best for Naara. *Why in the world would she ever book rooms at a place like this.* He shook his head while he walked to the cheap, flimsy desk and picked up his cell to call Livy.

"Parrish," Livy said, her voice raised with excitement. "Are you here? I'm almost ready. We're still on for supper with your aunt, right?"

Parrish hesitated for a couple breaths before speaking. "Of course. I wouldn't have asked you if I planned to back out. I just hope you're ready for this."

"I'll be fine. I'm more worried about you. The last couple times I brought up meeting your family, you were pretty emphatic about that not happening."

"Well, I suppose it had to happen at some point. Since

Naara invited herself on this trip, I guess we can start with her. Just remember, for now, don't tell her who your father is."

"Sooner or later, your family's going to find out you've been dating Aurelius Hunt's daughter. The paparazzi will see to that. I don't understand why you are making such a big deal of it. He's just my father; he's not some kind of ogre because he's rich. Your family isn't exactly poor either."

"I know. It's just ..." Parrish sighed. "I promise I'll explain it to you. Just not tonight, okay?"

"Yeah, yeah. I know. This deep, dark family secret. I'll let it go for now, Parrish. But you have to promise me that you'll tell me everything ... soon. We've been together two years now. It's time we took the next step. Unless ... you don't want to."

"You know I want to, Livy. I love you. It's just complicated. Please be patient with me?"

"I love you too." She grumbled meaningless growls, but then said, "Meet me outside my apartment in twenty?"

"Sure. At least as long as Naara is ready."

"Text me if it's going to be longer. Otherwise, I'll see you soon. Love ya. Bye"

"Bye."

Twenty-five minutes later, Parrish pulled up to the curb in front of the mansion that had recently been turned into luxury apartments. Four hundred Northrup Avenue had been one of Aurelius Hunt's private residences. But once Olivia chose to pursue her degree at the university in Camden, he had renovated the property. It now boasted three huge apartments; one was Olivia's, the other two were rented by select employees of the university.

Parrish had refused to take Livy out in the rental van and ignoring Naara's protests, had rented a series 7 BMW for the next week. The engine of the powerful BMW purred as the passenger door opened.

"Oh." Livy's eyes went wide as she took a step back. "I guess I'll ride in the back."

"Sorry," Parrish grunted. "Thanks.

Despite Parrish's fears for the evening, the meal went well. Naara was on her best behavior. She and Livy seemed to hit it off from the start and within the first half-hour, Parrish's nerves calmed enough for him to relax and enjoy the evening. Naara and Livy discussed a wide variety of topics from art history to the best places to get sushi. When their discussion moved on to the topic of travel, Parrish could barely get in a word.

"We're set for lunch tomorrow then?" Parrish asked when they dropped Livy at her apartment.

"What?" Livy asked with a smile cracking around her frown. "I thought you were going to pick me up early. You did promise me a *full day*, didn't you? I have plans you know, Parrish Elm."

A smile curled the sides of his lips. "You're right, I promised you the full day. What time do you want me here?"

Livy tilted her nose up into the air and sniffed. "Be here by seven-thirty. And be dressed to run."

"You got it." Parrish waved good-by.

"I like her," Naara said as they headed back to the hotel. "She's smart, beautiful. I can tell she likes you ... very much. I think she might just fit in with our family. You planning to bring her home to meet Castor and Desma soon?"

"I was thinking to. Now that you've met her and that went well, I'm going to see when Livy might be able to come up for a weekend."

"She's obviously well-travelled, and well-read. What do you know of her family?"

"I haven't met them, if that's what you meant. At least not yet. But, yes, she definitely isn't hurting for money."

"So, what's this about running?" Naara's gaze flicked to Parrish, one eyebrow arched.

He chuckled. "That's how we met. Running. We were both in a 5K fundraiser race a couple years ago."

"You've been seeing her for a couple years and this is the first we've heard of it? Isn't that some kind of record? Parker was only dating Kendra a few months when he insisted we meet her."

"Well, you know Parker is older than I am. He didn't have the luxury of waiting."

"Ha Ha. Very funny young man. But, honestly, why have you waited so long? Our life is here now, on the Surface. I know your mother still refuses to accept that, but you and Parker, and Castor, you've all adjusted. Living on the Surface has been good for us. I like it here and have no desire to return to the Core. I have buried the Core Dweller Naara El'shava; I am Surface Dweller Naara Burrows. Here we're wealthy and successful. Life is good. My daughter was born a Surface Dweller. No, I chose to put my past behind me. I think you feel the same. So why not bring Livy to meet your parents? They've accepted Kendra."

"It's complicated." Parrish kept his eyes focused on the road though he sensed Naara staring.

Wednesday evening Becky and Michael showed up with a couple other kids from the Trinity Youth Group.

"We have plenty of help." He waved toward the others as they began setting inserts into warming trays. "Why don't you two take the evening off." Pastor Stevens dropped his arm around Lander's shoulders. "Take Becky to that little burger place around the corner." A sly grin emerged as he drew his arm back and gave Lander a playful punch on the arm. "You two probably need some time to catch up." He turned to face Becky. "Go. Enjoy yourselves."

They headed toward the front door but pulled to a stop when it opened. A gorgeous young lady walked through, laughing. Parrish followed her in, his deep chuckle lacing the air. Lander stepped back, his mouth dropping open. "What are you doing here?"

"When I told Livy about this place, she insisted on coming by and seeing it for herself." Parrish moved to stand between Lander and Livy. "Livy, I'd like you to meet my ... what is it?" He wagged his eyebrows up and down, then shrugged. "Something like second cousin once removed, right? Anyway, Livy this is Lander; Lander, this is Livy."

Lander's mouth continued to hang lose as he stared at the petite young lady for a minute. She was beautiful. Long, strawberry-blonde hair curled over her shoulders, framing a heart-shaped face with large green eyes like brilliant gems. She looked physically fit and Lander remembered Parrish saying they both liked running. She was dressed in a double-breasted, black wool coat that fit snug at the waist and then flared out to just above her knees. The black made her green eyes look even brighter.

Holding out her hand Livy smiled. "Hi, Lander. It's nice to meet you. Parrish has been talking about you all day." She turned and looked pointedly at Becky.

"Um ... um." Lander blinked, then stumbled over his tongue. "Um, this is ... B-Becky, yeah." Pause. *Breathe!* "Yeah, Livy, this is Becky; Becky, this is Livy."

Becky reached out to Livy. "Nice to meet you. I love, love, love your coat. Where did you get it?"

Livy's bright, friendly smile lit up her face. "Thanks for noticing. This is the first time I'm wearing it and Parrish hasn't said a word. Typical male, right?"

Her smile growing, Becky nodded.

"Oh," Lander said, "And this is Parrish."

"Nice to meet you."

"Same here," Parrish replied. "So, where are you two

going? I thought you were volunteering here this evening. We thought we might help."

"Pastor Stevens said he has enough help, so we were going to a little diner not far from here for something to eat," Becky said. "Would you like to join us? They have the best burgers around."

"You wouldn't mind?" Livy asked. "I haven't had a hamburger in ages. What do you think, Parrish? We did run five miles earlier. And then we went to Martin's Walls and Rocks and I beat you climbing the wall. I think we could afford to eat greasy burgers tonight, don't you? And fries, right? Nice, messy, greasy fries?" She gave him a devilish grin and wiggled her perfectly sculpted eyebrows up and down. Come on. Please?"

Turning to open the door behind him, Parrish said, "Lead on."

They walked down the street and turned left at the corner, Livy and Becky in front, already exchanging information about where Livy had gotten her coat. Soon the two were comparing notes about best stores and boutiques in Camden.

Lander closed in on himself and remained quiet during the meal. He enjoyed listening to the others talk. The three kept up a lively conversation as if they had known each other for years. He liked sitting next to Becky, feeling her next to him. She laughed easily and when she did, little dimples formed in her cheeks and the beads in her black braids tinkled lightly. She was the opposite of Livy. Both were pretty, but Livy's light skin, blonde hair, and green eyes were a contrast to Becky's chocolate complexion, dark hair, and deep brown eyes. Lander loved the way the light played in her dark eyes when she smiled, which was often.

He felt more at ease with Becky than anyone else he had met since Pop-pop died. She had accepted him when he was alone, and he would never forget that. And—he had to admit—

there was something more. An attraction. He'd never had a girlfriend before. Pop-pop had forbidden him to make friends, and Lander had always been shy. But with Becky he felt comfortable, he felt right.

Eventually, Livy and Becky's conversation turned back to clothes and styles. Parrish grinned at Lander. "I think they'll be talking for a bit. How's it going?"

"Okay. You and Naara have a good time yesterday?"

"Good enough. Sometimes she can be so … weird. Usually she wants to stay in the best places." He chuckled. "I don't know what she was thinking, but she booked rooms in this sleazy hotel. Maybe there's a convention in town and all the better hotels are booked. I'm half tempted to stay at the mission with you tonight."

"You'd be welcome, but Crossways is full right now. With the colder weather, it's hard on a lot of street people. In fact, I don't even have a bed; I'm sleeping on the floor of the study."

"I have an idea," Parrish said. "After we're done here, we can pick up our things and you and I can get rooms at a better place."

"Naw, that's okay. I like staying in the study. I can read as late as I want, and nobody minds. Besides, this gives me a chance to talk to Pastor Stevens when he's not busy."

"Your choice, my friend."

After the meal, Parrish and Livy took off to go clubbing while Lander and Becky returned to Crossways Mission. They helped with cleanup before Becky left with her friends for home.

CHAPTER 23

Lander fought a losing battle with frustration Thursday; by late afternoon, his jaw ached from the number of times he had clenched his teeth. Every time it looked like he and Pastor Stevens would get to talk, something came up. Add to that his admonition that Lander avoid public areas, and Lander struggled against the pressure to do something ... anything.

The need to move drove him outdoors onto cold, wind-swept streets. The sun struggled to warm the frigid air, and Lander pulled his hood up close not only to shade his face from any curious passersby, but to block out the biting wind as well. After walking for two hours, he returned to the mission, chilled but calmer.

The aromas of fresh carrots and potatoes curled up into his nose as he spent the next hour helping with supper prep in the kitchen. He found a curious peace in focusing his mind on cutting vegetables for soup rather than his problems. Once the supper cleanup was done, Pastor Stevens called him to his office for a long talk.

"So, what do you want to do, Lander?" Pastor Stevens asked after Lander had told him about Desma and his promise to not return to Elm Farm.

"I don't know. I was, you know … sort of hoping … to stay here."

Pastor Stevens puffed out his cheeks then released a noisy breath of air. "I won't tell you not to. But if you do stay, you'll have to be careful." He shifted in his chair and the thing squeaked in protest. "Remember Ash? The guy who tried to stop Troy? Well, he's started coming to our Thursday evening Bible study. That's a miracle and I thank God for it. In the past, Ash shunned anything about God like the plague. And, given time, maybe others from the gang will start coming too. Ash is their leader. But I don't know how he'll respond if he sees you again. Like I said, though, if you want to stay, we can make it work."

Saturday morning, Lander took extra care to dress in his best outfit. Becky would be at the mission soon and he looked forward to spending the whole day with her. Parrish had also called yesterday and asked if Lander and Becky would like to join him and Livy for burgers again this evening. Livy had enjoyed their company and her burger so much on Wednesday, she begged Parrish to do a repeat.

After calling Becky and getting her approval, Lander set the plan with Parrish. He and Livy would meet Lander and Becky at the mission at six o'clock and they'd walk to the diner together.

Lander liked Parrish, his easy-going ways and sense of humor. Lander wished things could have been different. But he had promised; and Ian had drilled the importance of keeping his word into Lander since he was little. Lander wouldn't return to Bethel with Parrish and Naara on Sunday. He would keep his word.

But his return to Crossways Mission hadn't gone the way

he expected. *Why does everything have to be so complicated?* He almost came face to face with Ash yesterday when he headed back upstairs after supper. It seemed that no matter which way he turned he really didn't have any place he could stay without causing trouble. *Maybe Pastor Stevens could recommend another mission where I could do odd jobs for a bed.*

He put the dilemma aside for the time being. For now, he wanted to enjoy his day with Becky.

While he waited, he decided to spend some time practicing with his stones. He sparked fire several times, cupping small flames on first his right then his left palm, with and without his Stones of Power. He moved on to going invisible while flashing a protective barrier at the same time. Though he could maintain invisibility without a stone, he couldn't establish a decent barrier unless he used a stone. Each time he worked on the barrier while holding a stone, it grew stronger and faster. If he held both stones, a deep barrier flashed into place in a second.

At least that's going right. He considered cutting himself so he could practice healing, but then decided getting bloody with Becky due any minute probably wasn't a good idea.

Then another thought came to him. *I wonder what else I can do? Like ... maybe ... see Becky coming. Yeah! That'd be cool!*

He focused, but this time instead of seeking to vanish, he sought Becky. He envisioned her in his mind and sent his desire to see her into the stone as he rubbed his thumb over the warm, smooth surface. Nothing happened. *Am I doing this right? Is it possible to even do this? Awe, I wish I knew more about ... everything.*

Lander jumped when a knock sounded. He had been so focused, he hadn't heard anyone in the hall.

"Lander." Becky's voice came from the other side of the door. "Hey, Lander, you decent in there?"

Shaking his head in frustration, he said, "I'm coming out.

Just give me a minute." He replaced both stones in the pockets of his jeans and grabbed his hoodie and jacket.

"I have plans." Becky grabbed Lander's hand as soon as he stepped out the door.

"I have my mom's car so we can go wherever we want. We're going to the aquarium, first."

The Camden Aquarium was a short drive from the mission. Becky maneuvered the car into a tight spot in a parking garage then skipped ahead as Lander followed her into an elevator that deposited them on a sidewalk in front of the aquarium.

Lander stopped and stood, rooted like a statue, as he gaped up at the several stories high ceiling in the glass-walled main entryway.

"You've never been in an aquarium before have you?"

He shook his head, still staring at the vast expanse of glass ceiling.

"What? Did you grow up under a rock or something?"

He shrugged. "Yeah, something like that.

"Well, you're in for a treat, country boy. I'm going to be your tour guide. The Camden City Aquarium isn't very big, but it's impressive with habitats for a variety of sea life."

Becky's enthusiasm was contagious. He followed her from exhibit to exhibit. They both enjoyed watching the penguins as they jumped into the water and swam with incredible speed only to hop out again.

"The penguins are my favorite. I love watching them," Becky said. "It looks like they're having fun and they make me laugh."

But the biggest surprise for Lander was being able to stand on one side of a glass wall while a huge black and white whale shark swam by right next to him.

Jelly fish, sting rays, and fish of every color and size drew Lander forward. When they got to the Touching Pool, he joined right in with the little kids, checking out starfish, sea cucumbers, and crabs. His favorite was the Sea Urchin. He had never been in such an amazing place.

They stopped at a little creperie for lunch. Another first for Lander. Once again, Becky shook her head and commented on Lander's deficient upbringing. But then, getting serious she asked, "Is it because you're different?"

Lander stared at her open-mouthed, his heart dropping into his stomach.

Becky gave him a look that said 'don't play innocent with me.'

"I saw what you did on Thanksgiving. You saved my life. And ... the way you did it wasn't normal. What are you, Lander? Are you some kind of alien? Is that why you've never been to an aquarium or tried crepes?"

"I'm not an alien. Geeze, Becky, how could you think that. I grew up here on earth. It's just that in some ways I am different. And because of that, my grandfather was very protective."

"What about your parents?"

"They died when I was a baby. That's why Pop-pop raised me."

"Sorry." Sympathy creased lines around Becky's eyes.

Silence reigned as they ate for a few minutes.

"I'll understand if you don't want to talk about it. I don't care if you're different, I like you, Lander. I like you a lot. And I know you put yourself at risk when you saved my life. That was brave."

Joy at Becky's words filled Lander and he allowed a shy smile to surface. "I like you a lot too, Becky. This day has been amazing."

"Well, it's not over yet, my deprived friend. The next stop is the museum."

"A museum?" Lander grimaced. "Aren't they ... like, boring?"

"Not this one." Becky's large brown eyes sparkled. "It's a natural history museum. You like dinosaurs?"

The afternoon sped by as Lander and Becky moved from one exhibit to another, each more exciting than the last. Dioramas of various ecosystems including a pond, a meadow, and a rainforest caught Lander's attention; but the display showing human evolution from a stooping ape-like creature to homo erectus stopped him in his tracks.

"Do you believe this?" he asked Becky, his brow furrowed in thought.

"No." Her mouth flattened. "I believe God created us as humans. Sure, all created things change and adapt, that's micro-evolution. That's reasonable. But, as a Christian, I question macroevolution."

Their discussion of the pros and cons of the theory of evolution carried them through several more exhibits until they entered a huge room filled with fossils and the skeletons of full-sized dinosaurs including a Tyrannosaurus Rex and several different pterosaurs.

But, even more than the dinosaurs, Lander was drawn to the Minerals and Precious Stones Exhibit. Walls covered with gems, geodes, and uncut crystals pulled him forward. Becky circled the room, spending time gazing at the cut gems before returning to Lander. He hadn't moved more than a couple inches.

"Lander, come on. There's a lot more to see."

Her voice sounded from faraway. After witnessing Castor draw the ruby from the stone back at Elm Farm, Lander now understood. He saw what Castor saw, the precious locked within the mundane. The cut gems touched his spirit, but the uncut called to him.

He reached out to one ordinary looking black and gray stone from Australia, his fingers resting on the glass. The sign read Musgravite. He saw the perfected treasure within. Silvery gray with violet undertones. He knew instinctively how to draw the form out and what would need to be done to cut it into a faultless gem to display its glory. But one cautioning look from a security guard was enough to send him scurrying.

He looked around for Becky and found her sitting on a bench in the hallway beyond the exhibit.

She looked up at him and shook her head. "Do you realize how long you were in there? I've gone through several other exhibits, each time coming back here for you. And still you stood staring at those stones. What's with you and those things? Now we don't have time to see anything else."

Lander opened his mouth to say he was sorry, but nothing came out. Finally, he croaked, "Sorry."

Becky gave him a stern look and said nothing.

"I am; I'm really sorry," Lander said. "I didn't mean to stay so long. Are you mad? How long was I in there?"

Becky checked her cell. "No, I'm not mad. But do you realize that you were in there staring at those stones for more than an hour.?"

"Oh. Really?" Lander didn't know what else he could say. "I'm sorry."

"I guess I'll forgive you. This time," Becky narrowed her eyes at him. "But you owe me. Big time."

"Sure."

A smile replaced Becky's frown and she reached up. He grabbed her hand and pulled her to her feet. "Come on," she said. "We need to get back to Crossways if we're going to meet Parrish and Livy for six."

Becky parked in the back lot of Crossways Mission; Lander and she entered through the kitchen door. When they walked up the hallway to the front room a shiver rocked through Lander. *Why is she here?* Naara stood with Parrish and Livy, talking to Pastor Stevens.

"Here they are," Pastor Stevens said as they approached.

Parrish waved and Livy said, "hi, as a bright smile sparkled in her eyes."

Naara scowled and glanced at her watch. "We need to leave now if we want to eat anytime soon."

Livy chewed the side of her lower lip, obviously trying to suppress a grin as Lander and Becky walked up to the trio. "Yeah, some people are so irresponsible."

Parrish rolled his eyes.

Naara pinned Lander with a direct look, then took Parrish's arm. "My, look at the time. It's after seven. Let's go"

Without another word, Parrish waved for Lander and Becky to lead the way. "Lander," Naara said as they reached the front door.

Something in the way she said his name, set Lander's nerves on edge.

Naara turned and gave him a sweet smile. "I didn't expect you two to be so late, my boy. And as I missed lunch today, I'm quite famished. The pastor told us how popular this little diner is, so could you be a dear and run ahead and get us a table?"

Lander ducked his head at the sugar-coated rebuke. Naara had always been nice, if demanding, and he had no problem running ahead. However, a sense of danger flowed through him at her words. He shrugged off the sensation and mumbled, "Sure." He darted out the door and jumped to the sidewalk in one smooth move, then jogged toward the corner. Naara, Parrish, and Livy walked out to stand on the landing.

"Oh, darn," Naara called. "Wait for me. I left my purse inside."

Lander slowed and turned back at Naara's words, but she waved him on. "Not you. You keep going."

He turned on his heel and started off again until he caught sight of an SUV from the corner of his eye. *Black. Tinted windows. Run.*

He flung a quick glance back at the others coming down the steps, talking, laughing, unaware. Adrenaline pumped as he sucked in a deep breath. He pushed off the balls of his feet, pulling his arms in close to his side. A solid force slammed into back of his head, and hands grabbed him.

Lander stumbled, fighting to remain upright after the blow. A black hood appeared before his eyes and he tried to push it away. A prick on the side of his neck sent heat flooding outward from the point as the hood dropped over his head. Everything went blurry. He struggled for coordination. His fingers fumbled, unable to reach the stones in his pockets. His muscles refused to listen. Multiple hands seized him. His body collapsed. Movement. Hard, cold floor underneath. Oblivion.

CHAPTER 24

Livy's heart thundered in her ears and she clutched at Parrish's arm as four men jumped out of a black SUV with tinted windows and surrounded Lander. Her alarm morphed into confusion, churning her stomach. She recognized two of the men.

"Mr. Talen?" She whispered as Talen jammed a needle into the side of Lander's neck and another man threw a black hood over Lander's head. *What's he ...? Why ...?*

Becky's scream broke through Livy's daze.

"Hey! No! Stop! What are you doing? Stop! Police!" Becky bounded off the landing and sprinted down the sidewalk.

The four men threw Lander's limp body into the SUV and jumped in behind. Becky ran toward the vehicle, still shouting, her voice rising an octave. "No, no, no, no, no! Help. Somebody stop them. Help!"

The vehicle squealed away from the curb, taking the corner with tires screeching. Lander was gone. It was over in seconds.

Livy shook her head; shock spread through her, numbing her. *What did I just see?*

Parrish pulled his arm from Livy's grasp and sprinted down the sidewalk to Becky's side.

Naara walked after him, grabbed his arm and pulled him back. "Let it go Parrish. Just let it go. Forget you saw anything. It's for the best."

"What?" Parrish hissed as he turned furious eyes on Naara. "What's for the best, Naara? What did you do?"

She pulled to her full height, her back ramrod straight, her face a mask of haughty disdain, silent, staring. Parrish's eyes widened. "What have you done?"

Pastor Stevens stepped out next to Livy and stared at the corner where the SUV had just vanished. He took Livy's elbow, drawing her inside. "Everyone come inside quickly. Standing out here like this won't help. We'll call the police and wait inside."

Parrish had already pulled his cell phone out and was calling 9-1-1 when Naara grabbed it from his hand. "What are you doing?" She glared at him.

"Inside, now." Pastor Stevens's command was harsh. "Before you draw even more attention." He waved Naara and Parrish up the stairs as people began gathering and staring at them.

With a muttered oath, Naara turned and followed Pastor Stevens and Livy in. Parrish put an arm around a sniffling Becky and guided her up the steps. "We'll figure this out. It'll be okay. We'll get him back."

Pastor Stevens ushered everyone into the kitchen and closed the door. He grabbed the phone from Naara and shoved it at Parrish. "Now, Parrish, make that call." Then glaring at everyone, he said, "Is someone going to tell me what's going on here?"

"They took Lander." Becky sobbed, crumbling down into a chair. She looked up at Pastor Stevens, tears pooling in her eyes and running down her cheeks. "Some men put a thing over his head and put him into a van. And then he was gone."

"Not a van." Livy moved to stand next to Becky and put a hand on her shoulder. "It was an Escalade." She shifted her focus to Parrish. "I know who took Lander. Those men ... they work for my father."

Naara sputtered then hissed an oath. A look of horror crossed her face and her mouth sagged open as she stared at Livy. "What did you just say? Who is your father?" Naara shook her head. "No. It can't be."

Holding back tears as confusion fogged her mind and jumbled her thoughts, Livy said, "Aurelius Hunt. My father is Aurelius Hunt. But ... something's wrong. My dad's security people would never kidnap someone. My dad's not like that. Why? None of this makes any sense."

Parrish stumbled back into a worktable. It rose up on two legs before thumping back to the ground. He shook his head and met Livy's eyes, a look of pain in his own. "It wasn't supposed to happen this way. I wanted to introduce you after ... after ..." He turned his focus on Naara. Livy had never seen him so angry. "What did you do?"

Naara raised her chin in the air and flashed a cold look at Parrish. "I did what I had to do to keep my family safe. You should be thanking me Parrish Elm; I brokered a deal to purchase our safety, our ability to continue living as we have been without fear."

She narrowed her eyes and stalked up to Parrish. "But more to the point now, Parrish, is what were *you* thinking? Dating Aurelius Hunt's daughter? That monster's own daughter? You know what he did to us; how could you? I did what I had to do. But you ... what were *you* thinking? That he would forget who you are and just accept you because you fell in love with his daughter? That he would actually allow that relationship to continue? Don't make me laugh."

"Stop this!" Pastor Stevens's voice rose over Naara's rant. "You two need to set this aside and focus on what's important now." Turning to Livy, he said, "These men, you said they work for your father? You're sure about this?"

The tears Livy had worked to blink back flowed over her lower lashes and dribbled down her cheeks. "Yes. I'm certain. I recognized two of them. There's no mistake. I've seen both on Zephryn Island. Maurice Jackson I've seen only a few times recently; but Emmett Talen, I've known since I was a child. He's worked for Dad for a long time."

"And do you know why your father would send them to kidnap Lander?"

Catching Parrish's eyes and focusing on him, she answered Pastor Stevens's question. "No. You have to believe me. Please Parrish. I don't know. I didn't know."

Slipping past Naara, Parrish moved to stand in front of Livy, tilted her chin up, and looked into her eyes. "I believe you."

She pulled in a sob and clutched onto him. "I love you Parrish. You know that, don't you? I'd never do anything to hurt you."

"I know."

Naara slammed her fist on one of the tables and swore. "You're an idiot, Parrish. I'm not going to stand around and watch you screw up what I've done.

"Be reasonable. There are things you don't know, are too young to remember. Aurelius wanted Lander. From the beginning. He was obsessed with him from the time he was born. The son of two Stone Sovereigns? Wow! He was something special."

She shook her head and pinched her lips into a flat line. "You don't understand. Aurelius desired him for the power of his gifts. If Cyanne and Jared had just given him to Aurelius back then, everything would have been different. Now he'll leave the rest of us alone. But only if we let him have Lander.

"Think about it, Parrish. Never having to look over our shoulders again. Never needing to fear who might discover the truth."

"What truth?" Becky exclaimed. "Who are you people? I don't understand any of this. All I know is that my friend was just kidnapped right in front of my eyes." She pushed to her feet and walked over to Parrish and Livy. Looked Parrish in the eyes. "Please, help him."

"I agree with Becky," Pastor Stevens said. "I know little of this history, but I do know enough to realize that giving Lander to Aurelius Hunt isn't going to do anything to make the rest of you safe."

"You know nothing," Naara hissed as she spun to face him. She ran her gaze around the room, pointing a manicured finger at each one there. "This doesn't concern any of you. You think you know Lander Devlin? Ha! You don't know anything. He's not what you think. I'm warning you; leave it alone. Forget you ever met that boy." Her eyes dropped back to spear Parrish. "I'm going home, Parrish. Are you coming with me?"

Parrish shook his head, his brows drawn together in a frown of disgust. "No, Naara. I'm going to stay here and see if I can fix this mess you've made. I won't trade Lander for my freedom." He shook his head again. "I won't do that."

"You're a fool." She took a step and stood before Parrish. "I don't regret what I've done. Think about it. Think about your parents ... your brother ... Kenan ... Violet. You'll see. I'm right." She walked out.

Becky pounded her fist on a table with a loud bang. "Can someone tell me what's happening?"

"I don't understand either. Your aunt called my father a monster, Parrish." Livy struggled to digest what Naara said. "She doesn't know my father. If she did, she wouldn't talk about him like this. No. Wait." Her stomach knotted and a burning lump grew at the back of her throat. "Has our being together all been a lie, Parrish? Were you using me to get to my father?"

"No," Parrish said softly. "If anything, it would have been the other way around."

Confusion drew Livy's brows together, then anger stirred in her. "And what's that supposed to mean?"

Pastor Stevens stepped between the two. "I think we should move this conversation up to my office. It's more secure. And Parrish. Call the police."

They climbed the steps to Pastor Stevens's second floor office. Pastor Stevens plopped down in his worn chair behind his desk. Becky sat on the only other chair. Parrish sat near Livy on the floor, but she huffed and turned her back to him.

"Before I make this call," Parrish said. "Pastor Stevens, I need to ask, how much do you know about Lander and the rest of us? I know we're all worried about Lander and we want to help him, but before we can do anything, we need to know who knows what. And … how much we should tell the police."

Livy thought she would pass out as Pastor Stevens related what he had learned of the story while Lander stayed at Crossways Mission before. "This is a joke," she said, pulling away from Parrish, anger curling her lip. "People living in the center of the earth? That's just absurd. No one could possibly survive the heat even if it wasn't solid.

"And to attack my father like this? No." She shook her head. "I won't believe it. Special gifts? The whole thing is preposterous. It's like some awful, B-rated movie script. My father would never do the kinds of things you are accusing him of doing. He's a good man. He's kind and tender hearted. Everyone knows he's one of the world's leading philanthropists."

"I don't know about the other stuff," Becky said in a soft voice. "But I do know Lander saved my life on Thanksgiving.

I don't know how he did it, but he stopped a bullet. It was heading right for me when he jumped in front of me and then... it just ... stopped. Right in midair. It hung there for a second then dropped to the ground. A lot of people saw it."

"Livy." Parrish wrapped his fingers around Livy's shoulder and turned her to face him. He looked at her for a moment, then licked his lips. He squeezed his eyes shut then with a groan opened them. "I was eight years old when we followed Aurelius Hunt from the Core to the Surface. My parents, everyone who was with us, were all so excited to see the Surface, meet Surface Dwellers.

"We thought they had all died in the ancient flood. But then Aurelius came and told us amazing things about the Surface. We thought he was our friend.

"We had been living on Zephryn Island for over a month. I remember my parents were beginning to question why Aurelius wouldn't let us see anything more than his island.

"There was a lot I didn't understand; I was only eight and I was bored. There was so much I wanted to see, things I read about in the library. So, one afternoon, I snuck out and walked the beach past the main house. I shouldn't have been there; we weren't allowed. But I slipped past the guard and walked for a long time. That's when I saw you. You were with your nanny and even at five years old, when I saw you for the first time, I thought you were beautiful. You were friendly and greeted me like we'd always been friends. You asked me if I wanted to run on the beach with you. I did. Do you remember that? The day you ran on the beach with a strange boy?"

Livy's eyes rounded as memories of that day came to life in her mind, the warm breeze, the roaring surf, how her nanny had been so nervous. "That was you? I remember. I never saw that boy again."

"No." Parrish lowered his gaze to the wooden floor. "When your father heard about it, he doubled the guard around the inner compound. We weren't allowed beyond that perimeter unless we were accompanied by Miss Claypoole and several guards."

A groan escaped Parrish's lips. "Things got really bad after that. But Ian, Lander's grandfather, encouraged us to be patient. We ended up living cooped up like prisoners for five more months.

"Livy, I know this is hard for you to accept. But it's the truth. I know; I lived it. I remember the day my family and I escaped. I saw your father order his security guards to kill Miss Claypoole. The only reason we were able to get away was because Cyanne and Jerod, Lander's parents, stood between your father and the rest of us and called up a shield of protection.

"They were so brave. I can still see them as they fell, shot down by your father's security. They died to save us."

Parrish lifted his eyes back to meet Livy's and cupped her cheek with his right hand. A part of her wanted to pull away, deny every word he was saying. But another part felt the tug of the truth in his words.

Parrish's voice was soft when he continued. "The only reason I was able to run that 5K race and meet you again two years ago, was because I escaped from your father and Zephryn Island. Lander's parents did that for me. Now, it's my turn to help him."

"No," Livy whispered, pushing to her feet and backing away from Parrish. "This isn't true." Pain and confusion battled each other, sending chills through her body. Looking down to the floor she shook her head. "I can't listen to this anymore."

She whimpered, the need to find the truth pushing her to move. She turned and faced the bookshelves behind Pastor Stevens's desk and pulled in a shaky breath. "But ... I know what I saw. Mr. Talen and Mr. Jackson work for Father. And I watched them kidnap Lander. It happened right in front of me. I can't believe my father would give orders for them to kidnap someone like they did, but I saw it happen. They must have been following Father's orders."

She gritted her teeth and turned to face the others. "No! None of this makes any sense ... unless ... unless ... what you're telling me is the truth. And if what you're telling me is true, that means the man I know as Father . . ."

Livy shuddered and tears tracked down her cheeks. "I don't know my father at all."

CHAPTER 25

oices ... where ... am ... I?

Lander wrestled against the darkness that enveloped him like a moth in a cocoon. Consciousness called to him, drawing him up out of the void of shadows.

Voices—muted and fuzzy—echoed through his mind and drew him up to the surface of his foggy stupor. Without opening his eyes, he tried to move, but the muscles in his arms and legs wouldn't respond.

Paralyzed! Panicked thoughts flooded his mind. He struggled against the pull of the void, but he was too weak.

Sick ... so sick.

He slipped back into the black nothing.

Sometime later Lander woke again. Two seconds later or two weeks later, he didn't know. The voices were gone. The white noise of running equipment remained. He fought the gooey gunk that refused to allow his eyelids to open. One eye popped open. He groaned and squeezed it shut again. Bright, overhead lights thrust daggers behind his eye. Little by little, he opened them again. Lifting his head, his blurry sight revealed the reason he couldn't move. He wasn't paralyzed. Heavy leather straps around his legs and arms bound him to a metal table. He swallowed hard, the cotton of his mouth causing him to grimace.

O God, please help me! Help me! I'm … afraid.

He turned his head. He lay in a room of white and gray. It reminded him of the room in City Line Hospital where Pop-pop Ian had died. There was an IV in his left arm. He looked back up at the florescent lights and a tear tracked its way from the outer corner of his right eye into his ear.

A door opened and several sets of footsteps entered the room. Tied down as he was, Lander couldn't see who had walked in, but he heard voices.

"Yes," a man's deep rich voice said. "The technician was right."

A tall, unusually thin man with a receding hairline hovered on the edge of Lander's line of sight. He wore a white doctor's coat with a nametag that read Dr. Eiger. Looking back, he spoke to the others who had come in with him. "Give me a minute to check, but by now the drugs should be flushed out of his system."

Dr. Eiger walked to Lander's side and leaned over to shine a small flashlight into each of his eyes.

"Where am I?" Lander asked, his voice rough. He coughed. "Why am I here? What do you want with me? My name is Lander Devlin. I'm a senior at Wharton High School. You've made a mistake."

While Lander was speaking, two other men walked forward. One, a well-dressed older man of average height with a neatly trimmed blonde beard flecked with gray and intense blue eyes, moved with a confident stride to stand next to Dr. Eiger.

The other man sent Lander's heart into a panicked rhythm. He was the man from the bus, one of the men who had kidnapped him. The muscular man with wavy, dark brown hair and deep-set brown eyes skirted Lander's bed and walked across the room to lean against the far wall. He stared at Lander with flat eyes, his face an emotionless mask.

"No mistake has been made." The older man sniffed. "I know exactly what you are." Glancing toward the doctor, he said, "Well, Paul, can we draw the blood now? I've got a meeting this afternoon and I'd like to see him tested before then."

"Yes. Yes. Of course." Dr. Eiger waved for someone behind Lander to come forward. "Ms. Wilson, we'll need a pint. Quickly. Mr. Hunt is a very busy man."

Ms. Wilson walked into Lander's field of vision. She wore blue scrubs like some people Lander had seen at City Line Hospital. Her dark hair was pulled back into a tight bun. She didn't look older than mid-thirties, but her expression was stony.

Lander's pulse raced and he wrestled against the restraints. She ignored his struggle, turned off the IV, and moved to Lander's other side pushing a cart and another piece of equipment. A short, white thing. After checking a clear plastic bag set on it, she turned the machine on, and the bag began to tilt back and forth.

"Don't fight this," she said in a calm voice, then slid a gray band with gauges on it under Lander's upper arm, pulled it snug and pumped a bulb. It pinched his arm and Lander's fear climbed another notch.

With the gray band snug, she placed a soft, squishy tube on Lander's palm. "Squeeze. Once the blood begins to flow into the bag, you'll need to continue squeezing every few seconds."

Turning her back to him, she picked up a needle from the cart. It was attached to the bag by a clear tube. Nothing in Lander's experience had prepared him for this. Her eyes focused on Lander's arm and she examined the inside of his elbow, probing with her finger. Then apparently finding what she was looking for, she inserted the needle into the vein in his arm. He moaned. "Please, don't."

Ignoring him, she juggled the needle a bit and then removed a clamp from the tube. Dark, red blood began flowing through, collecting in the bag.

As Lander watched his blood filling the bag, Dr. Eiger walked over with the other man.

"Do you know who I am?" the older man asked.

Lander shook his head. But the truth sounded loud and clear in Lander's head. *He's Aurelius Hunt. The man who killed my parents.* All Pop-pop's warnings sounded in his mind and he blinked against the fear induced tears that threatened.

"Don't lie to me, Lander. I'll know." Hunt moved to stand by the side of the table, his cold blue eyes examining Lander as if he was a curiosity.

Lander shuddered. He looked up into eyes the color of a light blue summer sky. But there was no warmth in them, just a calculating look.

"Who are you?" Though he knew the answer, the dread that filled him wouldn't allow him to accept the truth.

"You already know, Lander Devlin. But to be sure there is no mistake, I'm Aurelius Hunt. I knew your parents."

Lander moaned and swallowed hard, but then anger swallowed up his fear. "You killed my parents." He closed his eyes, determined to find his focus and burn the man responsible for the deaths of his family.

Aurelius chuckled. "Mr. Talen."

A painful jolt coiled around Lander's ankle and sparked up through his body. His breath exploded from him. He gasped air back into his lungs and screamed.

"Don't do that now." Dr. Eiger's voice held a note of annoyance.

Aurelius waved a limp hand at Dr. Eiger. "Ms. Wilson, is the flow still steady?"

"Yes, Mr. Hunt. The shock had no effect on the blood flow."

"Good. You see Paul, no harm done," Aurelius said. "Now, Lander. What you just felt was simply a small sample of what you will experience if you try to use any of your so-called gifts. I've spent enough time around Core Dwellers to realize when they're trying to access their focus and I can't allow you to do that. Mr. Talen also is well versed with your tricks and, as one of your kind was responsible for his uncle's death, he is always most eager to inflict pain."

Aurelius shifted position to stand near Lander's feet. "I'm sure you're familiar with the ankle bracelets used to monitor a criminal's movements when under house arrest. You're wearing something similar, but this is an anklet of my own design. It has two probes. You just experienced the first one. The current, triggered by radio frequency, flows through your body sparking your nervous system. I hear the current can be quite painful.

"Mr. Talen, Dr. Eiger, and I each have a triggering device which we will not hesitate to use. Mr. Talen's piece is currently set at the lowest level." A calm smile flashed across his face. "There are nine more levels."

He raised his hand and held up two fingers. "The second probe contains a drug similar to the one used to incapacitate you earlier. In addition to the manual control, it's synced to the electric fence that surrounds this building. If you attempt to leave, you will be rendered unconscious.

"If not for the fact that I need your blood drug free at the time of collection—and that I need to observe what you are capable of—you would currently still be in a drugged state. Experience has taught me that keeping your kind ... *lethargic* ... is the safest way to handle you."

Ms. Wilson removed the needle from Lander's arm and pressed a cotton ball on the site of the draw. She held the ball tight to his arm for a moment before checking beneath it. She nodded in satisfaction and placed a band-aid on the cotton ball, then moved to the other side and extracted the IV.

"I'm done, Mr. Hunt." She gave him a quick nod then wheeled her equipment away from the table.

The door behind Lander opened. "We're ready Mr. Hunt," a voice called before the door clicked shut.

Aurelius rubbed his hands and a small smile spread across his lips. "Excellent. Perfect timing.

"Paul, I'm glad you're with us today. This demonstration will put to rest any concerns you may still harbor at experimenting on humans."

"I appreciate your concern, Aurelius. But I know you've read my file. So, you must realize that I've put stumbling blocks like outdated moral ethics behind me long ago. We do what others fear to do in the name of scientific research and the advancement of our species.

"I believe that's why you sought me out for your little project in the first place. I think we agree that evolution assisted by manipulating the gene pool is the cutting edge. And I'm excited to see what you've hinted at in our correspondence."

"From a purely scientific perspective I agree, Paul," Aurelius said. "However, as a humanitarian I must point out that we as humans are social beings. History has shown that civilizations grow best when like-minded individuals have banded together and accepted a general rule of ethics. Something that holds us together as a society. Please understand, I'm not advocating some religious code, just a secular rule for the betterment of our species.

"But I'm also a realist. Currently accepted ethics are still rather archaic. And we are bound to work within the constraints our society places on us. As such, we are forced to pursue our research in secret, even if that research is for the betterment of the human race.

"The average citizen would look at our subject and see another human, just a teenage high school student. He would call a halt to our work regardless of all we've achieved. But, be that as it may, you will witness for yourself just how *not* human these Core Dwellers really are.

"And it is for the improvement of our own species that I have spent these last sixteen years and millions of dollars studying these Core Dweller traits and abilities."

Aurelius turned to Talen. "It is time Emmett, release the subject and bring him to the testing chamber."

Aurelius walked out with Dr. Eiger, discussing those things that set humans apart from other species. Lander heard something about DNA as the door closed behind them.

Talen pushed off from the wall and walked to Lander's side. "Behave yourself now you little freak. I'm going to undo the straps and if you give me any trouble, I'll be more than happy to give you another demonstration of the Wasp. That's our pet name for Mr. Hunt's ankle bracelet. Fitting, don't you think?"

Lander lay still while Talen undid the straps around his arms and legs; he didn't want to give the man any excuse to use the Wasp again. When he didn't move after Talen stepped back, the man gave him a cold look and pulled a small black device from his pocket. He waved it in the air and wagged his thumb. "Get up."

Lander stumbled getting off the table. His face burned when the realization he was wearing nothing more than a thin gown that was open in the back hit him. He lifted his hand to rub the ache at the back of his neck. He grimaced. Short, stiff bristles covered his head.

"Here," Talen growled, throwing a light-cotton, button-front shirt and a pair of pants in the same material at him. "Get dressed."

With nowhere to hide and Talen glowering at him, Lander

slipped the pants on before removing the gown. After he threw on the shirt and buttoned the four buttons, he searched the counters for his stones. They were gone, along with his clothes.

Talen waved Lander toward the door.

"You won't find them," Talen said as they walked down a stark white, cinderblock hallway.

"What?"

"You're little weapons. Those innocent looking stones that, in the hands of a Core Dweller, can blow things up ... kill people."

"I wouldn't hurt anybody," Lander whispered. Talen ignored him.

After a short walk, Talen opened a heavy, reinforced metal door and directed Lander inside, closing it behind him.

The room was white. Ceiling, walls, and floor reflected the florescent lights set in the high ceiling, bathing the area in intense, bright illumination. The walls were bare, but the outlines of what looked like doors and windows could be seen in several places.

Turning around, Lander stumbled on numbed legs. The door he had just walked through was gone. Nothing more than the dark outline remained. No handle, no way out.

There were no furnishings, though cameras were set at intervals along the top of the twelve-foot high walls. Speakers broke the solid line of the ceiling in several places.

Lander pulled in a couple deep breaths and attempted to calm his acute panic. But his hands refused to stop trembling, He walked deeper into the room, his eyes scanning the walls before he returned to the now hidden door through which he had entered. He ran his hands along the outline and tried to pry it open.

Something clicked to his right, he turned. Another outline shifted, revealing a door. A man wearing black military fatigues walked through the back-lit opening. Lander didn't recognize him, but he acknowledged the threat inherent in the man's bearing and posture. Lander backed away.

The man smiled. It wasn't a friendly smile. It was the kind of superior expression that Lander had seen on the faces of bullies at school. It sent Lander's stomach into flips.

Aurelius Hunt's voice boomed through the room. "Welcome to my experimental laboratory, Lander. I designed this room to test Core Dweller abilities. You are not the first I've tested here but you are the prize I've sought. The only remaining Stone Sovereign on the Surface.

"The man now facing you wants to hurt you. Please believe that this is true. The device in his hand is a Taser, looks a little like a plastic gun, doesn't it? I assure you it will not kill; I have no desire to kill you. You're too valuable alive. But I do need to assess your capabilities. Unless you stop him, he will cause you intense pain. So, Lander, defend yourself. Let me see what the son of two Stone Sovereigns is capable of doing."

As soon as Aurelius stopped speaking, a popping sound filled the sudden silence. Unprepared for what was happening and unsure of what he could do without his stones, Lander stood still, his eyes on the man. Then the probes hit.

Pain, intense and irresistible, seared through his muscles, paralyzing them. Unable to break his fall, he hit the ground on his side, hard. The man smiled down at him as a scream tore from his throat. He didn't know how long the man stood over him, enjoying his pain, but finally it was over. Lander groaned as he turned over, lifted up onto hands and knees, muscles aching like he had just been pummeled by a jackhammer.

"I'm disappointed, Lander." Aurelius's voice came over the speakers again. "I did expect something more enlightening. Perhaps next time you'll be more willing to reveal what you can do. I'd like to stay and duplicate this experiment to see how you'll respond now that you understand what's happening, but I've another commitment this afternoon. Mr. Talen will return you to your room for now. Sleep well, Lander. We'll try again tomorrow."

CHAPTER 26

Enough, I've had enough talking." Becky covered her ears with her hands. "I'm calling the cops right now. We've already wasted too much time arguing." She pulled her cell phone from her back pocket but stopped as Parrish's hand dropped onto her arm.

She met his eyes, sad, filled with unspoken compassion. "You need to understand what might happen if you call the police, Becky. You've seen and heard enough to know we're not … normal. I agree we need to find Lander, make sure he's safe. But if you choose to get the police involved, others will learn the truth. Lander, all of us, my family, will be exposed. Not to mention all the crap that will come raining down on Livy's father and his reputation if this gets out. You open that door, and we can never go back."

Livy pressed up onto her feet and walked to stand next to Parrish, determination etched on her face. "Parrish, I'm going to put an end to the accusations against my dad once and for all. Confront him, give him a chance to defend himself."

She flicked her eyes to the darkened window for a moment and pulled in a deep breath before focusing again on Parrish. "My father keeps a company jet here in Camden. I'm going to arrange for the pilot to take me to Zephryn Island, to see my dad right now. Would you come with me? If Lander's there—and I doubt that—we'll find him and get to the bottom of what's really happening."

"Are you sure you want to do this? What if the truth you find is more than you can handle?"

"He's my father, Parrish. Good or bad, I need to learn the truth. I'm going. With you or without you. I can't pretend what just happened didn't happen and I need to look my father in the eye when I ask him why his people kidnapped an innocent teenage boy. Someone I know. A friend."

"Okaaay." Parrish drew out the word, his brow wrinkled in concentration. "I'm probably going to regret this, but I'll go with you.

"Naara was right about one thing." Parrish turned his back on the room and paced to stand in front of the window. "Your father's been hunting us for sixteen years. I want to help my friend … but if things get too crazy, I'm out of there. I won't risk my family's safety. I can't agree with what Naara did, but I can understand why she did it."

Parrish's phone rang. He pulled it from his back pocket and hunched over to take the call. While he was talking, Livy called to arrange for the jet.

"You knew about this?" Becky asked Pastor Stevens, her voice shaking. "Knew about Lander being one of those Core Dweller people?"

"Yes. I promised Lander I'd keep his secret. When he first came here, he didn't even know the truth himself. He was confused and scared. Those men were after him. He needed someone to confide in and I tried to help.

"When he saved you on Thanksgiving, I was just as surprised

as anyone else. Actually … so was Lander. But I read parts of his mother's journal with him and came to understand that he needed to find others like himself. We both thought once he got to Bethel everything would settle down. I guess we were wrong."

Livy cursed as she slammed her phone down on the table. The news that Talen and several other security personnel had, just moments ago, taken the jet, tied her stomach into a tight knot of misgiving. "I can't get the jet. It's on its way to Zephryn Island. Why is this happening?" She closed her eyes and gritted her teeth, a growl of frustration leaked past her lips as doubts about her father chipped a hole in her heart.

Parrish turned back to the others. "That was my brother, Parker. Naara called my mother and insisted she order me home. I explained things to Parker, and he wants to help. Did I hear you right, Livy? You can't get the jet?"

"Guess what?" she snarled. "What a surprise. Misters Talen and Jackson boarded it a short while ago with several guests they are escorting to Zephryn Island for a meeting with my father.

"I'll call the airport and see if I can line up a charter."

"Hold that thought," Parrish said. "Let me call Parker back. We have a contract with a charter service we use for the company. If one of their jets is available, he can arrange for it to pick us up and take us to the airport at Coral City. Of course, we might have a problem getting onto the island after."

"Don't worry about getting on the island." Her brows lowered. "I mean, really. Who's going to stop the bosses' daughter and her friends from spending a few days relaxing on daddy's private island?"

She leaned against Pastor Stevens's desk and drummed her fingers on the top, nurturing the idea that once she saw her father, she would look him in the eyes and see the truth of his innocence. He would laugh the deep belly rumble she loved and explain away all the accusations.

A crash sounded in the next room, startling everyone. Pastor Stevens rose and, holding his finger to his lips, strode out the door and over to the storeroom next to his office. Parrish, Livy, and Becky followed on his heels. The pastor paused in front of the door for a moment, then yanked it open. "Michael Traynor? What ... How long have you been there?"

Warmth spread through Becky at Michael's name, soothing the ache that had been growing in her since Lander's abduction. "Michael? What are you doing here?"

Michael tucked his head and slunk out into the hallway. "I came over hoping to find you and Lander. I wanted to try to convince him to go with me to get the tattoo. I even had a tentative appointment set.

"I got here just as those slime balls were stuffing him into their SUV. Boy, I'd like to get my hands on those jerks." He scuffed the floor with a sneaker and shrugged. "Whatever. Anyway, after that I just kept close to you guys hoping I might be able to help. Is it true? I mean, everything. Wow, surreal, huh? Whoa! Aliens. Aurelius Hunt. Conspiracies. This is awesome!"

"Awesome's not exactly the word I would use. Get in here!" Pastor Stevens said as he grabbed Michael's collar and dragged him into the office. After everyone else returned, he slammed the door behind them.

"You idiot," Becky snarled, punching Michael in the biceps.

"Ow, what'd you do that for?"

"Because you're an idiot, Michael."

"Gee, thanks. Nice to know what you really think of me."

"Stop." Pastor Stevens raised his hands as he barked the command. "Michael, do you understand how serious the things we've been discussing are?"

Michael's expression sobered. "Yeah, I do. It might not seem it, but I'm not an idiot. I want to help Lander too. I like the dude. He's a friend. And, when you go to that island, I'm with you."

"No." Parrish's cold eyes flicked to impale Michael's. "And we're not aliens. We're from this planet just as much as you are. We're just from a different … part."

"I'm going, too." Becky crossed her arms and prayed that neither Parrish nor her parents would try to stop her.

"And what are you going to tell your parents?" Pastor Stevens asked. "Oh, Dad. Mom. By the way, I'm going to be gone for an indefinite amount of time. I need to fly off with a couple other irresponsible young people to a private island owned by an evil billionaire philanthropist, to rescue a boy capable of stopping bullets. That's what you're going to tell your parents? Right!"

Becky clicked her tongue and rolled her eyes. "No. That sounds stupid when you say it that way. I liked Livy's idea. Mom and Dad, I've been invited by a wonderful new friend to spend a few days on her father's private island. It's a once in a lifetime opportunity. I promise I'll catch up with my school-work when I get back. Please. And they will, of course, say Becks, we trust you. Sure, you can go."

Two hours later, Parker was on his way. Livy and Becky took off to drop Becky's car off at her house then go shopping for toiletries and other necessaries. They were walking in the kitchen door as Parrish stepped out of a cab into the parking lot behind Crossways.

"You ready for this?" Livy asked as Parrish climbed the couple steps behind Livy and Becky.

Parrish huffed out a breath which smoked in the frigid, late night air. He nodded. "Are you?" He held the door for the two to walk through and pulled it in tight behind him.

Michael bounded into the kitchen, bouncing on the balls of his feet, he stopped with a lurch. "What took you guys so long? I've been waiting forever. Are you ready?"

"I just asked that," Parrish said.

"Yes. Yes." Livy gritted her teeth. "I'm committed to this and I'm ready for this. Stop asking me, okay?"

Michael shrugged and Parrish sighed.

Becky threw daggers at the two with her eyes and threw an arm around Livy's shoulders. "I'm with you Livy. We're going to seek the truth regardless of where it leads. I know you're worried about your dad but, like you said while we were shopping, he probably didn't even know what those men were doing. They were probably moonlighting. And if that's the case, he can help us find Lander."

"Right. Thanks Becky."

Becky hoped she was right as Livy turned to smile at her.

They gathered all the luggage in the kitchen and Pastor Stevens said a prayer, then everyone piled into Pastor Stevens's beat up old Ford Transit van and they headed to the airport.

"Are you sure you're okay with getting involved in this?" Parrish asked from the front passenger seat. He turned to look at the pastor's profile.

"Parrish, I told you. This is the least I can do." He snorted. "If I could get someone to run Crossways, I'd go with you."

Parrish nodded as he tapped his fingers on the phone sitting on his lap. "I know. But we have no idea what we're getting into or how long we'll be gone. We can't ask you to leave the mission for some unknown amount of time.

"I still can't believe Becky's and Michael's parents were okay with this."

"Well, Becky's parents trust her."

"Of course, what did you expect. I've never given my parents a reason to not trust me." Becky spoke up from behind Pastor Stevens

He shook his head. "Yes, Becky. They're both professionals. They work all the time and travel a lot, so you're used to staying alone. You've travelled around the world with friends and you're pretty independent." He flicked a quick look back over his shoulder at Becky. "You're a smart kid.

"As for Michael." He released a deep sigh. "Well … let's just say, he could do just about anything—as long as it doesn't land him in jail—and they wouldn't care."

They pulled into the gravel parking lot of a small independent airfield. Pastor Stevens kept the van running and the heat turned up. They waited for Parker.

CHAPTER 27

The Challenger 350 touched down with a short squeal then taxied to the broad blacktop area in front of the four hangars.

"Okay, that's it." Parrish stepped out then turned to open the back door. He reached in to help Livy out, but she ignored his hand and slipped past him before heading to the back of the van to help Pastor Stevens unload their bags.

Parrish huffed, responded to Becky's shrug with a crooked grin, and helped her step down.

"Nice goin' dude." Michael chuckled as he jumped through the door. "You've got some major 'splanin' to do to make things right with that girl."

Parrish slammed the door. "Yeah. Yeah. Don't I know it."

Livy made a point of ignoring him as everyone grabbed their bags. Though the silent treatment was expected, it still hurt. But Parrish knew Livy well enough to understand she needed time to process all that had been thrown at her, and he hoped that learning the full truth wouldn't crush her. She didn't know her father … just the image he presented to her and the world.

Parrish hefted the strap of his bag onto his shoulder, straightened up and moved around the van. Pastor Stevens stood at the driver's side door.

"Thanks Pastor. I appreciate all your help and the way you've been there for Lander. I hope we can continue to count on your silence about the things you've learned."

"Of course, Parrish. I'm sorry I can't do more to help you. But know I'll be keeping you all in my prayers."

They shook hands. "Thanks Pastor, that means a lot."

"You have my cell number, don't you?"

"Yea."

"Good. Keep me in the loop, okay?"

"Sure, Pastor Stevens. Will do."

Parrish waved goodbye, turned and lifted his eyes to scan the area for Parker. He stopped, gritted his teeth, and took a step back. "Oh, no. Parker … why did you bring them?" Shaking his head, he jogged past Livy, Michael, and Becky.

"Mom. Dad. What are you guys doing here?"

"Sorry," Parker said as he approached behind his parents. "Naara called. You can guess the rest."

Castor walked up to Parrish and pulled him into a hug. "We're so glad you're safe son."

Desma slowed a few paces away, her eyes focused like twin laser beams on Livy. Her mouth pursed, she moved to intercept the girl. "You're his daughter, aren't you? Did he send you? Is that why you're here? Is this some kind of a trap? Naara seemed to think so." Desma's nostrils flared and she took another step forward. Parrish feared his mother's temper; that she might lose it and slap Livy, but Desma halted and squeezed her eyes shut.

"Mom, stop! It's not like that." Parrish dropped his bag and slipped back to stand next to Livy."

Desma shook her head and held up her hand, her palm

facing Parrish. "Not now, Parrish. Don't talk to me." Opening her eyes, she glared at him. "I'm not ready to talk to you yet."

The sun broke over the horizon, sending skittering beams across the pavement and sparking ice crystals along the roofs of the hangars. Desma pointed a finger at Livy, Becky, and Michael. "Castor … tell your sons to help these *strangers* into the jet. Now. We need to talk, but not out here in the open."

Castor waved the young people forward. "Come on, Desma's right. We can't stand out here like this. He flashed Parrish a quick smile and the tension-wrapped muscles between Parrish's shoulder blades loosened a bit.

A few minutes later everyone claimed seats on the butter-soft, gray leather chairs and sofa. Desma and Castor took seats on the couch and as Parrish made to walk by them, his mother grabbed his arm and pulled him down onto the seat between the two. Livy sat across the aisle from Parker, while Becky and Michael moved into the seats behind them.

Shortly after, the pilot announced take off. Everyone fastened their seatbelts and in a matter of minutes, they were in the air.

No one spoke until they leveled off and belts were released. Sitting between his parents, Parrish winced when his mother turned to face him. Her eyebrows drawn low over her eyes; she gave him a level look. She started to speak but stuttered to a stop. The level of anger steaming off her set warning bells to clanging in Parrish's head. He raised his hands to ward off her anger. "Mom …"

"No!" she growled. "Don't Mom me! Not now. Not after what you've done. Did you think we wouldn't find out? Do you think this is some kind of a joke?" She sputtered again then began to rattle off in Corish.

"Desma. English." Castor leaned past Parrish and placed a gentle hand on Desma's arm. "Please. You need to calm down. This isn't helping anything. Okay?"

He shifted his focus to Parrish. "How did you meet … *Livy* is it?

The next fifteen minutes slid by as Parrish filled his family in on how he and Olivia met and their growing relationship.

Though Desma seemed to calm after a bit, Parrish squirmed when she rose and strode to stand before Livy.

"So … my son tells me he trusts you. I think he's a fool. Give me one good reason to trust you as well." Desma swung her arm in a dramatic pose, her eyes dark and glinting. "Convince me that you haven't been sent by that monster you call a father to search us out and deliver us to that man, trussed up like some kind of Christmas present.

She leaned in, her hands dropping to the arms of Livy's seat. "Is that what this is all about? Was Lander's kidnapping just a bit of cheese in the trap? How convenient. Look at us, all following you back to Zephryn Island."

"Mom. Stop." Seeing the tears in Livy's eyes, everything within Parrish rose up, prompting him to protect her. Shield her from his mother's anger. Parrish sprang up and, taking his mother's hands, stepped between the two. "I know you're angry, Mom. But don't take it out on Livy. She didn't do anything. She didn't even remember meeting me on the beach until I reminded her of it. You can't hold her responsible for her father's actions."

Parrish scanned the faces around him, attempting to gauge where the others stood. Livy's eyes were closed tight. Tear drops hung from her dark lashes and sparkled on her cheeks. Parker's head had fallen forward into his hands. Behind them, Becky and Michael just stared—like twin deer in headlights.

He pulled in a breath and lifted a quick prayer for guidance, then dropped to one knee in front of Livy. He squeezed her hand and whispered, "It's going to be okay, Liv. Just give my mom some time. Trust me."

Pushing back up to his feet, he guided Desma to her seat, grateful that she didn't resist him. His dad met Parrish's gaze and gave him a short nod. Castor shifted to the seat next to Desma and draped an arm around her shoulders.

"Mom." Parrish kept his voice soft and calm. "This isn't the way I meant for this to happen." *No. More like the farthest from it as possible.* "I wanted to take time and introduce Livy to you; let you get to know her before ... before I told you who her father is.

"She was as surprised by the kidnapping as I was. She's not part of some conspiracy by Aurelius Hunt to trap us. She didn't know. Just ... please ... give her a chance. If you do, you'll find out she's loving, caring, smart, and ... I know you'd like her if you just ..."

Desma raised flat eyes to Parrish. "I love you son, but we are not having this conversation now. You say I need to give Livy time; well, you need to give me time. I don't process surprises well. And this ..." She shook her head. "This day has been one big surprise after another." She fisted her hands together before her face and released a puff of air into them.

"I know you trust Livy. And because you trust her and I trust you, I'll ... well, I'm not going to make a promise I can't keep." She met Parrish's gaze. "I will reserve judgement for now." Desma looked to Livy. "For now, young lady. But ... if you do anything to hurt my son, I will end you."

"Desma." Castor pulled her closer to his side. "This whole thing is out of our control. You know it and I know it. And ... from what Parrish has told us, it's out of Livy's control as well. If she's willing to seek the truth about her father and what happened sixteen years ago without running away from it, I think that says a lot about her character. Let's trust Parrish and give the girl a chance."

Desma nodded and snuggled closer to Castor's side.

"Thanks Mom. Dad." Parrish breathed a sigh of relief. *Not the way I imagined introducing Livy to Mom, but ... all things considered ... it could have gone a lot worse.*

CHAPTER 28

L ander paced the small, padded room Talen had taken him to after the testing. It reminded him of being caught in a snow-storm two winters ago, nothing but white, white, and more white ... and cold.

Though the pain from the Taser ended as soon as the current stopped, his muscles continued to jerk, exacerbating the ache that seemed to permeate every bone in his body. The thought of facing that agony again drew tears to his eyes. He tried to blink back the wetness only to be forced to wipe it from his cheeks. He plopped, crossed-legged on the floor and chewed on the knuckle of his right thumb.

But what can I do without my stones? Disappear? Flick fire at the man? ... Yeah, right. Can I set a shield without them? I never tried. A mirthless chuckle slipped through his lips almost triggering another round of tears. *Pop-pop never told me I could do things like that. If it wasn't for those idiot gang members, I wouldn't even know that now.*

Setting aside the pain-filled memories of the Taser, Lander

closed his eyes to focus like he did on Thanksgiving. Even though his stones had called up the shield then, he hoped he could at least gain some protection without them.

He worked at building the barrier for what seemed like an hour before exhaustion drove him to take a break, but it was hard to focus with thirst and hunger chipping away at his concentration.

He swallowed and worked to gather some moisture in his parched mouth.

The room had no bed, just padding all around, even on the floor. A simple metal toilet, round and smooth, with no flushing mechanism, was fastened securely to the wall. White padding covered where it was anchored.

It's like they don't want me to hurt myself. Yeah, right. I wonder what that's about. He pondered why that might be, but the only answer he could come up with sent chills down his spine. He pushed the sickening thought from his mind as quickly as it had come. He wouldn't allow himself to go there. At least not yet.

He lay down on his back and tried to sleep. His eyelids drooped over scratchy eyes and exhaustion haunted him. But between the bright overhead lights he couldn't turn off, and his nerves jumping at every little noise, sleep was impossible. The overwhelming need for water drove him onto his feet and he paced.

As his desperation rose, he even checked the toilet to see if there was any water there. *Gross but … maybe.* But it was some kind of waterless system.

Lander examined the device strapped to his ankle and attempted to remove it with no success. He paced the room. Counted steps, stared at the ceiling, counted steps again. Banged against the padding on the walls, tried to tear it off.

Flopping down on the floor again, he threw an arm over his eyes. It didn't work. Sleep proved elusive. He wasn't sure which was worse, his thirst or those lights. Eventually, though, he drifted off.

Sometime later, he woke. Everything was the same. He counted the padded squares. Sixteen across on all four walls. Sixteen from ceiling to floor. The room was a square. The squares on the floor were larger, eight across both ways. The ceiling was a drop ceiling with four recessed florescent light fixtures. *Bright always bright.*

He practiced focusing again. *I can do this. I have to do this. Simple. Just a simple barrier.* This time he worked at it for what seemed like a long time. But here in this room, time lost all meaning.

He paced, he counted, he slept. Hunger and thirst continued to plague him. *How long has it been since I ate? Lunch with Becky at the museum. How long ago? Seems like forever.*

He fought the need to cry, sniffling but blinking the tears away until the feeling passed.

Then the door opened. Talen stepped into the doorway and smiled.

"Time for round two, boy."

"No, Please. Please."

Talen's smile grew wider. He pulled out his control, it looked like a TV remote control, and fixed his eyes on Lander's leg. He waved the device. "We can do this the hard way or the easy way. Your choice freak."

The Wasp. Lander wondered if he could handle another *sting.* What if Talen increased the power level? A shiver ran through him at the thought. His shoulders drooped and he shuffled along behind Talen to the testing lab. This time when he walked in, his eyes caught on a table set with a glass of liquid and a sandwich sitting on a plate.

"Good morning, Mr. Devlin." Aurelius's voice boomed from the speakers. "By now, I'm sure you're quite thirsty and hungry. This time I've added the incentive of food and water.

If you show me something worthy of my time, you will get both. If not, Mr. Talen will return you to your room without either. Do you understand?"

"I understand that you're insane. That's what I understand," Lander shouted up at one of the speakers. "Your Mr. Talen calls me a freak, but I'm not the one holding someone against his will and forcing him to perform before he can get food or water. Who's the real freak here, hum? It's not me."

"Feisty this morning are we Mr. Devlin? Very good. Show me what you can do."

Lander responded the second he heard the swoosh of a door opening, he turned to see the same man from yesterday, the Taser in his hand. Lander didn't wait, didn't give the man a chance to attack. He crouched and focused, going invisible while erecting a barrier.

He heard the click of the Taser, prayed that his barrier was strong enough, and gulped in a breath in relief as he watched the probes hit his invisible buffer, slow, stop, and then drop to the ground.

The man with the Taser cursed, scanned the room trying to locate Lander with no success. Seconds later, a hiss sounded, and a powdery mist filled the air. It covered Lander, revealing his position to his attacker. The man stalked toward him. Snarling, Lander threw himself at the man and tackled him to the ground.

Stupid, Lander berated himself as Taser man quickly flipped over, pinning Lander face-first to the floor, grinding his knee into Lander's backbone. Clapping and laughter came through the loudspeaker.

"Well that at least was something," Aurelius said. "Mr. Martin, you may release the subject. Mr. Talen allow him to enjoy his meal before bringing him to the medical wing. Dr. Eiger would like to see him before he's returned to his room. When you're done there, Mr. Talen, meet me at my office. I have another task for you.

"And you, Mr. Devlin, I look forward to seeing how you respond to a new challenge tomorrow."

"No, wait." Lander huffed, turning his head to speak around Martin, who still held him to the floor. "You don't have to do this. Please. I'll show you what you want. I never learned much more than what you've seen. Please, believe me. Pop-pop never told me anything, never taught me what I can do. But I'll show you what I know."

Lander lay still, breathing the dust from the floor, hoping Aurelius would agree. He choked back a sob when Aurelius said, "I think not. Tomorrow, Mr. Devlin."

Lander grunted as Martin's weight shifted. As soon as Taser man was off, he sprang to his feet, facing the man. The door to the hallway opened. *What do I do? What?* He debated attacking Martin flinging fire at him and then running. He'd have to get past Talen before the man activated his anklet though, he'd have to deal with Talen first.

By the time Talen walked through the door, Lander had gone invisible again, sprinted past Martin, and, with the force of momentum behind him, flung his shield at Talen. The man woofed out a breath as the barrier smashed into him, driving him back through the open doorway and into the opposite wall.

Lander was through, running down the hallway. *Stupid*, his mind shouted. *Where am I going?* It didn't matter where, just away. He knew he could stay invisible for a long time and unless they had the halls equipped with the white powder misters, they couldn't find him. *The anklet*, his mind shouted again. *They'll use it … catch you.*

He turned down different halls, trying to put the testing lab as far behind him as he could, wondering what the range was on the anklet. Right, right, left, another left into another hallway. This one ended in double doors. Lander plowed into them. Locked. He backtracked up the hall and turned, facing the double doors. Taking a deep breath, he focused and rebuilt his shield, then rammed it into the door the same way he had just attacked Talen. With a crunching noise, the doors slammed open, propelled into the walls beyond with bone-breaking force.

The plain white cinderblock walls Lander had passed through were replaced with dry-walled, cream-colored walls. Pictures showing racing yachts hung at intervals. And, thirty feet ahead, a glass door with heavy rain spattering against it showed a vista of mountains beyond.

Hope soared. His ankle prickled; the first indication the device had been activated. He ignored the sting and willed himself to keep running. One more step, another. He pushed through the pain that exploded through his nervous system and gained one more step before his muscles turned to jelly and he dropped to his knees. *No! No!* He struggled against the drug's irresistible command to let go. He was still conscious when Talen and Martin arrived, breathing hard. Then he knew no more.

Lander blinked his eyes open. An antiseptic smell reminding him of the hospital burned his nose. He was once again strapped to the metal table, the IV in his arm. His swollen tongue stuck to the roof of his mouth. He pried it down and ran it over his teeth.

"Water." His voice sounded like soft wind soughing through dried reeds.

"Ah, so you're awake."

Lander turned his head. Dr. Eiger stood at the long white counter. "I hope you realize how foolish your actions were."

The doctor moved to stand next to the table, looked down on Lander with a frown, and shook his head. "Foolish. But impressive."

He stepped out of Lander's range of vision then returned pushing a wheeled stool. He sat and rolled to a position next to Lander's head. "I've looked over your bloodwork. At least as much as I could in so short a time. It would appear that Mr. Hunt's theory is indeed correct. The blood tests human, normal white cells, red cells, etc. But the DNA … ah the DNA … is unique. I wouldn't have believed it unless I saw it myself. I look forward to spending much more time in study to be certain, but it appears that your DNA is significantly different from normal human DNA. An impressive variation I haven't seen before.

"And, on top of that, your telomeres are also dissimilar. Longer, stronger. That could be the key to understanding your longevity. It's all really quite exciting.

"Let me see, how can I explain this to someone like you?" He sighed and ran a finger along the side of his nose. "Imagine if you would, a small child playing with typical wooden blocks. He has standard square blocks with the letters A to D. But visualize his delight if he were to suddenly find a new set of blocks including a block with the letter Z. This block isn't just square, it's a hexagon, and, on top of that, the whole new set has a layer of protection rendering them more resistant to damage.

"In this, you see my euphoria. Known DNA is the child's original square blocks; your DNA consists of those same blocks now covered with a tough outer layer, and with the addition of the new hexagonal Z block as well. Imagine the implications!

"And after personally witnessing your demonstration this morning, I find the idea of studying you quite exhilarating."

Dr. Eiger stood and pushed the stool out of the way. "This brings us to the reason why I asked to have you brought here again this morning. I wanted to collect your DNA from sources other than your blood to rule out any contamination that might cause these abnormal readings. A cheek swab should do. I could have just asked Mr. Talen to obtain one, but, once again, I was concerned with contamination. And a few strands of hair…"

Dr. Eiger looked up and nodded. The nurse from the day before came forward with what looked like a gigantic Q-tip. "Ms. Wilson."

Exchanging positions with Dr. Eiger Ms. Wilson settled on the stool. "Open your mouth." When Lander complied, she swabbed the inside of his cheek. A look of frustration crossed her face. "Doctor, it appears he's dehydrated. I'm not sure this sample will suffice."

Eiger huffed and clicked his tongue against his teeth. "Here. Let me."

Lander tried to move his head away as Eiger rammed the swab into the side of his mouth. With a brisk motion, he ran the thing down the inside of Lander's cheek, then with a grunt handed it to the nurse.

Ms. Wilson sealed the sample in a plastic bag.

"Don't forget the hair."

"Of course, doctor."

Lander cringed as she yanked several strands of hair from his head and placed them in another bag. Then, before she left, he tried again. "Please, water."

"We're done here." Dr. Eiger spoke into an intercom on the desk as Ms. Wilson looked to him for permission.

"He does need water," she said.

With a nod from the doctor, Ms. Wilson brought over a paper cup of water. Holding Lander's head up, she helped him sip the lukewarm liquid. When it was gone, he asked, "More, please."

Without a word she filled the paper cup again and helped Lander drink that as well.

A couple minutes later Talen entered. One look at the

man's face and Lander knew he had made a big mistake trying to run earlier.

Before undoing Lander's restraints, Talen pulled out his control and held it so Lander could see the screen. He punched a button and the number on the display jumped several notches. "I don't like trouble, freak. As you can see, I've set this thing up several levels. You even look like you're going to try something, I'll hurt you. My head's still pounding from hitting the wall earlier."

He touched the control and Lander's body went rigid. Pain shot through him. Talen only held it for a second. He released it and smiled. "Remember freak, payback. There will always be consequences for your actions."

Talen followed Lander back to his room and Lander was careful to not give the man any reason to use his device. And then he was back in the padded room. He slumped to the floor, still hungry. His body trembled. If he had eaten anything, it would have landed on the floor at his feet as his stomach knotted. Though thoughts threatened to send him into panic mode, he refused to dwell on what the future would bring.

CHAPTER 29

Though Livy planned to keep emotional distance from Parrish, she found it a more challenging prospect than she'd expected. Just being near him stirred up feelings of want; and, after his mother's words, she needed Parrish's comfort more than ever. She wanted him to hold her, to keep her safe, to make the whole nightmare of what was happening go away.

She refused to accept the things Parrish and his family said about her father. They couldn't be true. But every time she closed her eyes, she saw Talen jabbing the needle into Lander's neck again and Maurice Jackson dropping a black hood over his head as he crumpled into their waiting arms. The images morphed into a nightmare and she woke sometime later, thrashing and sweating.

Parrish crouched next to her seat, worry creasing his brow. "Are you okay?"

She shook her head and clutched his biceps, then with a scowl released his arms and turned away from him to scan out the window. Fluffy white cumulus clouds marked with the darker swellings of building thunderheads flew past.

"It was just a dream." She pulled in a deep breath, still trying to cope with the remaining images and fear triggered by the nightmare.

"It was so vivid. I was the one who had a hood dropped over my head. The dust inside filled my nose and I couldn't breathe. The needle jabbed my neck, sharp and stinging. It was horrible."

She turned bleary eyes back to Parrish. "I'm sorry. I just don't know what to think. I know wherever Lander is, he's scared and alone. But I refuse to accept my father had anything to do with his kidnapping." She turned back to the window and sat without speaking for a minute before asking, "Where are we?"

"About an hour out from Coral City."

Parker walked up to stand behind his brother. "You two okay?"

Parrish nodded. "Yeah, we're fine. Just a nightmare."

Livy looked from Parrish to Parker. They were so alike. Both tall and athletic with chestnut hair and the same unique gray eyes. Light pearlescent silver gray near the pupil but dark charcoal gray around the edges of the irises. Just like Lander's. *They're the same. And Naara's too. Do all Core Dwellers have gray eyes?* She looked up toward the couch where Castor and Desma sat, deep in conversation.

"Do you …" she started to ask, but when Parrish and Parker focused on her, her tongue tied itself in a knot. *If I accept the truth of what they are … am I committed to accept the truth of what they say about my father?*

She shook her head and turned back to the window. "Nothing."

She wrapped her arms around her middle and once again retreated into herself to continue chasing the endless circle of her thoughts. Memories of the little boy she played with on the beach shifted into comparisons. *Were that boy's eyes gray? Oh …*

I don't know. I can't remember. She startled when Castor walked up and sat next to her a few minutes later.

"How are you holding up?" he asked.

What do you think? And for that matter … why are you even talking to me. Without a word she turned to scan out the window, uncertain what to say to the man. She struggled against the need to attack him for vilifying her father, but he was Parrish's father and confronting him would achieve nothing.

He chuckled and she turned irritated eyes on him. "And what could you possibly find funny in this situation?"

A crooked, sympathetic smile softened the lines of his broad face. "I know Desma was hard on you earlier. But that's her way. She is very protective of those she loves. And when she feels they are threatened … well … she has quite a temper."

His gray eyes snared her green orbs. "I know you have no reason to trust us and you're only going along with this because you care for Parrish. And, frankly, we have no reason to trust you … except that you care for Parrish."

He closed his eyes for a moment, stood and shuffled his feet as if working out pins and needles. He pulled in a deep breath through his nose and released it with a heavy sigh. "You're putting on a show of strength, but this thing about your father has got to be tearing you up inside. I want to believe you don't know much of what your father has done, that you didn't remember Parrish as the boy on the beach until yesterday. You were just a child when we escaped the island."

He dropped heavily into the seat across from her and turned to scan the clouds building in the distance, just as she had done earlier. His voice drifted to Livy though he continued to stare out the window. "According to Corish law, Aurelius should be held responsible for his actions and punished. Justice for Jerod and Cyanne demands he die. He turned our lives into a living hell when we trusted him."

Castor stopped speaking for several minutes. Livy wondered if he was going to continue or if he had fallen asleep, when he spoke up again.

"One of the most remarkable things we found on the Surface was the words of Noah's God written in a book for all to read—the book you call the Bible. After reading it, I've wrestled with the idea of forgiveness. The need to come to terms with what happened and let it go. Now I've ..." Castor's words faded, and a faraway look came to his eyes.

He shook off his daze and faced Livy again. "Despite what you might think, I have no desire to confront your father, or seek vengeance. My first priority is to see Lander safe and then make certain no harm comes to him or my family again.

"And yet, even if your father isn't behind Lander's kidnapping, he still needs to be held accountable for what he did sixteen years ago. Though I dread this confrontation, it's long overdue.

"Anyway, I wanted you to know that I will try to confront your father with dignity." He offered the same small, crooked smile from before. "I don't blame you for what happened and... I'm here to listen if you need someone to talk to."

She shifted her gaze back to the clouds now boiling below, presenting her back to Castor, hoping he would get the message. When he didn't move, she turned to face him and huffed. "I can't even talk to Parrish now and you think I'm going to melt and pour my heart out to his father. A total stranger ... my father's enemy. I'm sorry, Mr. Elm, I don't know what you're used to, but that's not going to happen."

He nodded. "You're right; I'm not Parrish. And I understand. But I have to think, considering the circumstances, you might just need someone who will listen with a more ... mature ... perspective."

Livy glanced back while running her hand over the fine gray leather of her seat. "And you really think you can be objective?

About my father? It seems to me, of all people, you'd be the last person to have a *balanced* perspective. No—I take that back—Mrs. Elm would be last."

He chuckled. "Yes, she does have a temper and can be quite protective. If things work out and you become part of this family, that protection would extend to you as well. And, please call me Castor."

She groaned and twisted in her seat, leaned against the cool glass of the window. "I don't know ... maybe. I do need to talk ... Castor." She settled in, looked up into his wise, gray eyes and decided to trust him ... at least for now.

"Before yesterday evening, everything was perfect. Daddy was this wonderful philanthropist. He donated to so many charities. He was named man of the year by various institutions and publications so many times I've lost count.

"I had my studies." She glanced over to meet Castor's gaze. "The most caring, handsome, brilliant boyfriend. I had dreams for the future. Now. I just don't know. I'm confused. Angry. And I don't even know who I'm angrier with ... Daddy for lying to me, or Parrish ... and you ... for exposing *his* lies. Or are you lying? I don't even know anymore. But I refuse to accept that my father is some kind of monster."

Castor's voice was so soft as he spoke, Livy closed her eyes to hear his words. "Not a monster. He didn't start out to be a monster.

"In the beginning, he was like a little kid, excited to travel to the Core. Friendships developed. Especially between him and Ian, Lander's grandfather. If we suspected anything was amiss, we would never have come to the Surface with him."

Castor huffed out his nose again, then continued; his voice still soft. Facing the window again, as if he couldn't get enough of the sky beyond.

"Aurelius became obsessed with our longevity and our Stone Sovereigns' abilities. He pressed us to allow his staff to take blood, conduct tests. He said it was for our protection, to keep us safe from Surface illnesses. But after the test results were came in, everything changed." Castor shook his head and turned to face Livy.

"But that's the past. We need to focus on today. Right now, your emotions are all over the place. Like you said, you're angry and confused. But you won't stay confused. You'll find some solid ground once the truth is exposed.

"What happened between your father and us happened a long time ago. Maybe your father regretted what he did. Perhaps that's why he does so much for others now."

"But if he was responsible for the deaths of your people, giving money to charities can't change that."

Castor nodded. "That's true. But nothing can change the fact that he's your father."

Livy smiled through unshed tears, struggling to balance her belief in her father with what she was learning. "Thanks. You know Daddy would have a fit if he knew I was talking to you ... I mean if what you're saying is true. And ... you talk of forgiveness. He doesn't. He thinks humans should be responsible for themselves and it's up to those of us who have much to share with those who don't. But there's no God we answer to, there was no real life Noah, just future generations of humans."

"He's not the first person I've met who felt like that. Back before we Core Dwellers took shelter from the flood in the tunnels, Noah promised his God was getting ready to send judgement. Well, we all know how that turned out. What do you think?"

Livy chewed the side of her lower lip. "I know Parrish believes. And he's got me thinking. But to be honest, I have more questions than answers at this point. I don't think I'm ready to talk about it. It's hard enough thinking all I know about my father might just be a lie, without trashing his beliefs at the same time."

Castor shook his head. "I'd never advocate trashing anyone's beliefs, however I do enjoy the challenge of discussing the basis for those beliefs. But we weren't talking about your father; we were talking about you."

"I think that's a discussion you're going to have to save for another time," Parrish said, walking up to stand behind his father. "We're approaching the airport and we'll be landing soon."

CHAPTER 30

The brothers, Livy, Becky, and Michael gathered in the small lounge. Becky dropped her bag next to Michael's wondering where Parrish and Parker's parents had gone. Her curiosity about Lander had jumped levels when she heard Castor and Desma couldn't travel to Zephryn in case Livy's father recognized them. And ... if that happened, they'd all be in big trouble. The mystery surrounding Lander, this curious Elm family, and their history with Aurelius Hunt deepened. Becky chewed her lower lip as she considered the implications.

And then there was Livy. Becky still wasn't certain whose side she would be on if her father was behind Lander's kidnapping.

Becky flicked her gaze to where Livy stood conversing in soft tones with Parrish. *Yep. That's a hard one to read. She really likes Parrish ... but can he count on her to side with him against her father if things go south?*

Livy walked a short distance away to call and arrange for a ride on her father's yacht but returned several minutes later, a scowl setting a line between her brows. "Again, just like with the jet; we missed the yacht. It's docked at the island and won't be available until tomorrow." She stamped a foot and released a hiss of breath.

"Anyway, I've arranged passage on the next ferry. We need to be on the dock in twenty minutes. And … the good news is… my father's limo driver will be waiting at the docks to take us up to the mansion."

"Then we'd better get going." Parrish ran a hand down Livy's arm. "It'll be alright. We can take the ferry. I mean it's not like we need a private yacht."

Livy groaned and shook her head. "You don't understand. The ferry … well … the next ferry is going to be transporting several middle school groups to the island to visit the wildlife park. We're going to be stuck for nearly forty-five minutes with more than one hundred middle schoolers."

Becky snorted a laugh. "You mean you're not afraid to face your father—the mighty Aurelius Hunt—and yet you are uncomfortable riding a ferry with a bunch of kids?"

"That's not it. The kids … they know me. All three groups are from local schools today. I've been doing this school tour thing since I was a kid myself." She met Parrish's gaze with a small smile. "Just be ready. We're going to be the center of attention. And if these kids learn we're … you know … a couple, they are going to deluge you with questions."

She glanced at Becky, Michael, and Parker. "Just don't say I didn't warn you."

Desma and Castor walked over. "We're all set," Castor said. "We rented a car and we'll be staying at the Grande View Hotel. It's not far." He met each person's eyes before nodding. "Okay. Remember, you are not alone. Desma and I are close if you need us. You all have our cell numbers?"

Becky rolled her eyes. *Castor and Desma are worse than my parents. I guess with good reason. Sheesh! Lander … what have you gotten me into?*

Livy looked down to her phone. "The shuttle to the docks will be leaving in about five minutes. We'd better go."

Desma hugged Parker and Parrish. "Stay safe." Desma wiped her eyes. "Just ... just ... don't take any chances. And remember to call me or your dad if you need *anything*. And remember, don't trust Aurelius. He lies." Her eyes flicked to Livy and she shrugged. "He does."

Castor gave each son a man hug, then took Desma's arm and led her to the outer doors that faced the main highway.

"Okay, friends of Livy now bound for Zephryn Island, our ride is waiting out the back door." Livy waved her arm in the air like a tour guide as she marched in the opposite direction Castor and Desma had headed.

The clouds from earlier had dissipated, leaving a clear blue sky with plenty of sunshine to reflect off the turquoise water like diamonds scattered at random as Livy, Parrish, Parker, Becky, and Michael boarded the sleek ferry for Zephryn Island.

Sea gulls circled and dipped, their raucous calls almost drowned out by the rowdy noise of middle school youth as they boarded the ferry behind the companions and scattered around the lower deck seeking seats. Several sprinted toward the stairs to the upper level only to be herded back by a young teacher. "No. Not up there," she called. "Everyone needs to sit together on the lower deck. Robby, that includes you."

Livy, with a scarf covering most of her face and a floppy hat shading the rest, pushed Parrish toward the stairs once the youngsters slunk past them toward the rest of the school children. "Quick, while they're distracted. We'll get to the upper level and have a quiet ride."

Ten minutes later, Becky stood at the aft railing between Parker and Michael, watching the pier shrink as the ferry sped toward Zephryn Island. The faint odor of saltwater drifted up from below. A stiffening breeze grabbed Livy's hat and pulled it from her head, pink ribbons flapping. Parrish reached for the thing, but it escaped his grasp. Michael caught it and with an exaggerated bow presented it to Livy.

"Thank you, Michael." Livy dropped into an old-fashioned curtsey.

Becky smiled, but just on the surface. It wasn't until they left the airport behind that she grasped just how dangerous this trip could become. She had read many articles about Aurelius Hunt, had even studied him in an economics class at the local university for AP credits. His R&D compound was noted to be a fortress rivaling any secure government facility and only employees and a select few were granted access.

If Lander is there, we don't stand a chance. I wonder ... her gaze shifted to Livy again ... *has she ever been there? Does her position as Hunt's daughter grant her access to his professional domain?*

Becky pursed her lips and wrinkled her nose. It was going to be an interesting next few days. Very interesting.

Livy's father's limo was waiting in the reserved zone outside the double doors of the small ferry terminal at the Zephryn Island docks.

The chauffeur bowed. "Good morning, Miss Olivia. It's nice to see you. We were surprised when we got your call. Your father didn't say anything about you coming. We thought you were at school."

Livy gave the man a bright smile and a quick hug. Roger had worked for her father since she was a little girl and she was fond of him, his wife, and their two little boys. "Good morning Roger. It's good to see you as well. How are Nora and the boys?"

"Thank you for asking, Miss. They're all doing fine." He stood in a rigid pose and watched her with a closed expression. Waiting.

"I know. You're right. Father doesn't know I'm here. It's sort of a surprise." Livy waved her hands with enthusiasm, emphasizing her words.

Roger's stern expression melted into a smile. "And I suppose calling to have the limo pick you up here rather than a golf cart is a surprise as well?"

"Well ... you see ... I brought several friends with me. And I promised them we would do things right and in style while we're on Daddy's island. We're only staying for a few days, and I was certain daddy wouldn't mind." She smiled sweetly.

Roger helped Parker and Parrish load their luggage into the white stretch limo Town Car while Livy, Becky, and Michael took seats inside. Once the bags were secured, Parker and Parrish joined the others.

As soon as they were moving, Livy pressed a button raising the sound-proof glass partition. "Roger can't hear us now so now's a good time to talk.

"It will take about twenty minutes to get to the main house from here. When I called Ms. Beckman, my dad's administrative assistant, and requested the limo, I arranged for everyone to stay at the mansion. Parker and Parrish, you'll share a suite. Michael, you'll have your own room. Becky, you'll also have your own room. I hope that's okay with everyone."

"How far is the mansion from your father's R&D complex?" Becky asked.

Livy drew in a sharp breath. "You know about that?"

"I've done my homework. I know that in addition to Aurelius Hunt Industries' corporate offices on the south east end of the island, there is a secure R&D complex where few are permitted access. Can you get us in there?"

Livy's gaze dropped to study the hands clasped in her lap. "I've never been allowed in there." Her eyes squeezed shut for a moment before she opened them and fixed Becky with a determined look. "But there's a first time for everything, right?"

An awkward silence fell over the occupants of the limo, the only sound, the mild hum of the engine. Livy stared out the window and Becky wondered yet again if Livy was going to cave before they had a chance to try and find Lander.

The beauty of the island tugged at Becky's heart. The intense, almost surreal colors reminded her of Maui. They drove past the Welcome Center where wide swaths of flowers stood out against the various greens of grass, shrubs, and palm trees. The building reminded Becky of a southern mansion, only on a grander scale.

Another ten minutes brought them to a gate with a guard shack. A man wearing black cargo pants, a charcoal gray button-down shirt, and a charcoal gray ball cap with an island logo and the letters AHI on the front opened the gate and waved them through. Michael elbowed Becky. She shifted to face her friend and questioned him with her eyes. He frowned and pointed at the guard as they started forward. Becky couldn't miss the significance, the man not only had a firearm holster on his belt, he carried a rifle.

"That's quite some security at the gate." Becky left the statement hang in the air.

Livy turned from the window and met her gaze. "Yes. My father has been the target of various jealous competitors since I was a child. He's always taken a firm stand on security."

"Where's the R&D complex in relation to where we are now?" Michael asked.

Parker responded by pointing ahead and to the left. "It's behind the mansion."

Livy's eyes went wide. "You remember that?"

"I don't," Parrish said giving his brother a side-ways look.

"I was older when we lived there." Parker's gaze roamed

to the right. "And up ahead, past the mansion, is the sand beach." A shiver ran through Parker. "Sorry. Not the best of memories."

They left the bright sunshine behind as Roger slowed the vehicle to take a sharp curve through an area of thicker vegetation. Coming out the other side, Becky blinked at the light that seemed to reflect off everything as they approached a smaller version of the Welcome Center.

Roger maneuvered the long vehicle past expansive flower beds in rainbow colors and up to the front of the mansion. The moment the car doors opened, hot, humid air, the sweet fragrance of frangipanis, and a symphony of bird song filled the back of the limousine. Livy pushed the control and the privacy panel slid back into place.

Livy and Parrish climbed out on one side while Becky, Michael, and Parker exited on the other side of the Town Car. Roger carried Livy's and Becky's luggage up the three steps to the veranda which ran the length of the house, while Parker, Parrish, and Michael brought their own.

As Roger placed the bags on the porch, a tall, thin man dressed in black slacks and a gray polo shirt opened the heavy wooden door and stepped out. The same logo as on the guard's hat decorated his breast pocket.

"Miss Livy. It is a pleasure to see you again." The man bowed, exposing a spot on the top of his head where his blonde hair was thinning. He stood, silent for a moment, his eyes focused on his feet. He looked up with a wavering smile. "I am sorry Miss Livy; I owe you an apology. Though you hoped to keep your arrival a secret, I unfortunately let it slip. Mr. Hunt is delighted. He asked me to welcome you and your friends. Please come in out of this heat. Roger and Kirk can get the bags and take them up to your rooms. Your father is waiting in the conservatory."

CHAPTER 31

As Livy, Parrish, Parker, Becky, and Michael strolled into the conservatory, Aurelius Hunt turned his attention from the large, multipaned windows overlooking the park-like landscape and the bluest of water beyond. A welcoming smile lit his face. He set the drink he held in his left hand on a round, glass table with spindly legs, and walked over to greet them.

"Livy! I was surprised when I heard you were home. This is an unexpected pleasure. Didn't you return to school?" Aurelius hugged his daughter, then wrapping his fingers around her upper arms, set her back from himself and looked her in the eye. "I thought you were past that reckless phase and had settled down with the goal of graduating with honors. Now, here you are, home ... and ..." His gaze roamed over the group. "And with four other young adults." The charismatic smile reappeared. "Obviously skipping classes as well."

Razor-sharp, blue eyes met Becky's and she began to understand the comments she had read about the man's ability to read minds. His penetrating gaze pierced her as if he could see into her mind and read her thoughts. He was not what she expected. Casually dressed in white chinos and a navy-blue polo shirt, Aurelius Hunt's appearance may have been that of a slightly built, well-mannered, older gentleman, but his mind was sharp and his eyes seemed to catch everything. Becky shivered despite the warm, heavy air.

"Why don't you introduce your friends, Livy?"

While Aurelius Hunt's attention followed Livy's introductions, Becky took a moment to appreciate the beauty of the conservatory. Victorian in style, three walls, including the half dome at the far end of the room were composed of leaded glass panes set into an ornate, green framework. A vast dome of the same glass and green style rose a good thirty feet above their heads.

Livy moved to Becky's side. "And this is Becky … ah, Rebecca Sheridan. Becky, this is my father, Aurelius Hunt."

A flush of adrenaline fluttered through Becky and she plastered a stiff smile on her face. "Oh … of course. Um … it's a pleasure to meet you Mr. Hunt."

"The pleasure is all mine, I assure you. I'm always delighted when Livy brings friends home. It's been so long since she has done so, we must celebrate your arrival." He turned his head, his gaze, once again, landing on everyone. He held up a finger to indicate he needed a moment, then checked his watch.

"My, my, my. Just look at the time. It's nearly 11:00. Well, no bother. By the time we get there, it will be perfect timing for lunch."

Livy's eyebrows shot up and she glanced at Parrish before turning and facing her father. "Dad? Where is *there*?"

He clapped his hands together and chuckled. "That, my dear, is a surprise. Come along, everyone. As soon as I learned you were here, I set in motion plans for an exciting afternoon for you all and we must get started." He chuckled again, almost like a little kid with a new toy.

No. Certainly not what I expected.

Aurelius's hand-stitched leather loafers tapped across the green and cream-colored marble tiles as he led everyone from the room.

Becky gave Michael a sideways glance as they followed Livy's father down the hall back to the vast, three-story foyer where they had entered a short while ago. Michael grinned, shrugged, and mouthed, *an adverture, right?*

The man set a rapid pace. Rather than heading to the limousine as Becky expected, they marched down a small brick path through a grove of trees. Bird song saturated the warm, sun-filled air like a symphony. Leaving the copse of trees behind, golden sunbeams revealed swaths of flowers in vibrant hues of red, orange, yellow, and cream set in rainbow patterns in expansive beds. Becky slowed to take in the splendor surrounding her.

"Becks, come on." Michael's hissed message pulled Becky from the diversion and she jogged to catch up to the others as they approached a private dock, hidden from the public areas by a rocky breakwater.

The path followed the curve of an incline then led to a printed concrete pad and a wooden dock. Waves lapped with a sloshing sound against the side of the sleekest and largest yacht Becky had ever seen. Sunlight glinted off the polished white of its sides.

"Beautiful, isn't she? A Heesen." Aurelius waved at the white yacht, the pride in his voice unmistakable. "Netherlands, you know. Wonderful yachts. At slightly over 163 feet, and a max speed of 23 knots, the *Mist of the Depths* will have us to our destination in no time."

A young man dressed in gray chino shorts and a silver polo approached with a wide smile. "Welcome home, Miss Livy."

He took Livy's hand and guided her up the steps to the yacht, Parker and Parrish followed.

Becky hesitated, uncertain if she should follow or wait for the man to come for her. She pursed her lips. *Yeah right. Like I can't climb some steps without help. No way.* Hearing Michael's chuckle behind her, she turned and punched his arm.

"Hey, Becks. What was that for?"

She smirked and proceeded up the steps. "Just on general principles."

"You're going to pay for that, Becks. When you least expect it."

"Sure. That's what you always say Michael. That's what you always say."

Once everyone was on the main deck, Aurelius waved toward the lower deck. "Bedrooms are down there. You'll find bathing suits, cover-ups, towels ... well whatever you need, including sunscreen. Once you're ready, come up to the sundeck. I'll wait for you there. It's too beautiful a day to not take advantage of the weather."

Becky's eyebrows shot up as the man winked. *Did he really just do that?*

"We'll enjoy the sundeck for as long as we can. At least until the afternoon storms roll through. Most of my guests prefer to be up there when the weather's nice. There's a fully stocked bar and a whirlpool."

Becky, Livy, Parrish, Parker, and Michael descended to the lower level. Livy whispered for the others to follow her into the largest bedroom.

"What is going on, Livy?" Parrish asked, anger sparking in his eyes. "Is this some kind of a game to your father?"

Livy stepped back, bumping into the king-size bed. "No." Livy shook her head. "My father isn't like that."

Parrish pressed forward. "Isn't he? Livy ... do you even know him?"

"Stop. Sssss!" Becky stepped between the two, held out her arms and made puppet hands, slapping her fingers to her thumbs signaling 'shut your mouth' at Livy and Parrish. She scowled at each in turn. "We need to play this out however Livy's father conducts it. It's the only hope we have of finding the truth. At least he's playing nice … hasn't thrown us off his island." She focused on Livy. "Do you think he knows why we're here?"

Livy pulled her lower lip between her teeth and shook her head, her eyes narrowed. "No. I don't think so. I mean, how could he?"

"And is he normally this … um … *exuberant* with your friends?"

"No. I don't know. I haven't brought any friends to the island since I was in middle school … and it was different then."

Livy plopped down on the bed, her hands running in a nervous pattern over the pale-yellow coverlet. "He gets like this sometimes. When he's excited about a breakthrough. Ever since I was a child, I always knew when work was going well. He'd be so …" She glanced up at Becky. "*Exuberant.*" Her eyes went wide. "Oh no. Could it mean …"

Parker hissed an oath. "Of course. It means he kidnapped Lander and he's thrilled to finally have the only remaining Stone Sovereign on the Surface under his control."

Parrish punched the dark wood door of a floor to ceiling closet. "We have to confront him. Now."

"No," Becky said. "I want to save Lander as much as you do. Maybe even more. But we can't let Mr. Hunt guess what we're up to or he *will* toss us off his island and then we'll have no way of finding Lander. We need to make nice, keep him happy, and move when the time is right."

"Becky's right," Michael added. "She usually is." Michael's bulk overshadowed Parker and Parrish as he stepped in from the doorway where he had been standing.

Becky still couldn't believe he had come with her. They'd

been friends since middle school and his support now warmed her.

Parker ground the heels of his palms into his eye sockets and he huffed out a breath. "You are right. Becky's right." He met everyone's eyes. "We'll do what Becky says."

Parrish reached out and took Livy's hands, pulling her to her feet. "I'm sorry Livy. Really. I was out of line." She stepped close to him and he wrapped his arms around her. "Are you okay with this? If not, say something now. Whatever we do has to be okay with you."

She sniffed and nodded. "I'm okay. I need to know the truth … even if it hurts." She tilted her head back and gazed up at Parrish. "But promise me this, if we don't find Lander here, you will keep what my father did in the past … in the past."

Parrish nodded. "Yeah. It's better for us that way too."

A half hour later, dressed in swimsuits and holding drinks, they listened as Aurelius Hunt entertained them with stories of African safaris, boat races, and building a world class network of businesses.

They dropped anchor in a secluded cove on the west side of the island where Chef Rosario served Roast Chicken with Fennel Panzanella and Apple Pecan Arugula salad followed by fresh fruit for lunch.

Becky nearly choked on a piece of apple when Hunt announced he was dropping Livy and her at an exclusive day spa in Coral City called The Hours for an afternoon of pampering. She tried to protest, but Hunt would not back down. "It's been years since my daughter has brought friends home. I'll not be denied the privilege of pampering you all. And … while you ladies are being pampered, the young men and I will do some deep-sea fishing."

"That's great, Dad." Livy turned to Becky and rolled her eyes.

"Wow! Mr. Hunt," Becky said. "That's great. Can I get braids?"

He smiled like a kindly grandfather. "Of course, my dear. Whatever you want."

The next couple days turned into a whirl of activity as Aurelius Hunt led the companions through a nonstop series of activities: A tour of the animal preserve, a gourmet dinner on the mainland, skeet shooting from the upper deck of *Mist of the Depths*, until Livy finally confronted her father.

After he handed his rifle to a crewman, she placed her hand on his arm. "Dad, we need to talk. You know I love you, right? And I do appreciate all you planned. It's been fantastic having this time with you."

Livy's hand fisted on her father's arm and tears glinted on her lashes in the bright sunlight. A spear of alarm shot through Becky as a first distant rumble of thunder sounded. *Oh no! She's going to tell him. He's been so sweet she's breaking.*

Livy cleared her throat and continued. "But ... but ... you see." She licked her lips as her eyes flitted to where Parrish sat. "We ... we sort of wanted some time to ourselves ... doing nothing. This afternoon I think we'll just head out to the sand beach and hang out.

"Oh, and don't worry about supper. We can take care of ourselves. Okay?"

Relief flooded through Becky. She rolled her shoulders, releasing some of the tension that had built across her back in the last thirty seconds.

Aurelius Hunt folded his hands before his face as if beginning a prayer. He closed his eyes, breathed out a sharp breath of air through his nose, and nodded. He rested his chin on the tips of his fingers and nodded again.

"You're absolutely right, Livy. You came here to have some down time with your friends, and I've taken over. I guess it's just my nature to take control and drive things. I'll leave you kids to it. Besides, I have a most important project I've let slide for the last few days."

He shook hands with Parrish, Parker, and Michael, then planted a kiss on Becky's cheek before wrapping his arms around Livy in a gentle hug. "I love you, Livy. Have fun with your friends. But please, can we get together again before you leave? Perhaps another meal?"

Thunder rumbled yet again as Livy nodded.

CHAPTER 32

Exhaustion and hunger plagued Lander, holding him in a semi-conscious state after he woke. He gazed unseeing at the already familiar white surroundings. Uncaring. He blinked then closed his eyes. Lethargy turned his world into a gray nothingness where even the act of lifting his arm from the floor where he lay seemed to require too much energy. How much time had passed since Talen returned him to his room held no meaning for Lander. He had slept then woken several times.

Groaning, he forced up into a sitting position and crossed his legs. "Hey! Anybody there." Though the words came out in a dry whisper, the sound of his own voice grounded him.

Come on, Lander, focus.

Lander's eyes widened. "Pop-pop?"

You're better than this, son. Remember what you were taught.

Lander groaned again and scrubbed his face with his hands. "What you taught me? Oh, Pop-pop, it's more like what you didn't teach me. Why didn't you tell me? Prepare me for… this …? For how my parents died?" He scrubbed his hands over his face again.

"Stupid, stop talking to yourself or they'll think you've really lost it. Get a grip, Lander. Stop." A hysterical chuckle burst from him. "Yeah, like anyone would care."

He pressed upright. The will to survive pushing him.

Come on, Lander. Focus. Move. If you don't move, you've already lost.

The voice, though unknown, was as familiar to him as the beat of his own heart. "Mom?"

Look by the door.

Uncertain what was happening, Lander shifted his gaze to the door and pulled in a sharp breath. A silver thermos sat on the floor next to the thin, dark line that marked the edge of the doorway.

He approached it with slow, hesitant steps. Thirst battled his instincts to treat this like a trick, but when he dropped to his knees, opened the thermos, and sniffed, the lack of odor and the sloshing of the liquid triggered his need. He raised the stainless-steel rim to his lips and gulped more than he should have.

Cool wetness coated his tongue then dribbled down his parched throat. He groaned. He wanted to wait a bit before drinking more in case the water had been drugged, but his need for water overrode his concern and drove him to tip the thermos and drink deeply.

A heavy rumble of thunder shook the building dragging him back to reality and Lander pulled the thermos from his lips. *Slow. You'll get sick if you drink too much too fast. If it's drugged … well at least I'm not dying of thirst.*

The fog in his brain cleared some and he wondered if he had imagined Pop-pop's and his mother's voices. *Probably. Dehydration can do that.*

He scanned the room yet again as he ran his tongue over his teeth. "Okay. Pop-pop Ian trained me to be strong." He climbed to his feet and jogged around the small square as another growl of thunder shook the building.

Though he struggled against his anger at Pop-pop, the realization hit him; Pop-pop had pushed him so hard ever since he was young for a reason. To make him tough. And he needed to be strong now. If he wasn't, he would collapse under the weight of who and what he was. The thought pulled him to a staggering stop.

"Okay, voice in my head. I get it now. Though I may not win this war, I'm not going to give up without a fight."

He ran around the outer perimeter of his room, sprinted across, flicked fire and created fireballs, turned invisible. But the thing he worked on most was fortifying his shield.

Time passed. Storms came and went. He slept. When he awoke, the thermos again sat by the door, filled with fresh water. A paper plate with a sandwich on it sat next to the water. The scent of peanut butter filled the air. Lander inhaled the PB and J and drank half the water before resuming training.

He flicked fire and built it into intense balls of smoldering flames before allowing them to dissipate only to repeat the exercise again and again. Taking time and analyzing what he was doing, he built shields, then constructed second and third layers within the bubble-like barriers surrounding him. He achieved three layers with consistent success, but when he tried for a fourth layer, the whole shield crumbled.

With an intensity born of need, he pushed past his limit during each training session. Gasping and pulling in large gulps of air he collapsed to the floor. Letting go of his focus, he slowed his breathing and drifted into a dreamless slumber of exhaustion.

Each time he awoke, he ate the sandwiches and drank the water that appeared as if by magic while he slept. And he continued practicing. He worked his gifts while extending the time he held his shield in place. Though he had no accurate way to measure the time, he counted in his head.

When he achieved his goal of holding the shield in place while creating fire balls for a count of 100, a sense of accomplishment brought a grim smile to his face. He could do this. He would do this. *It gets easier with practice, like my focus is a muscle. The more I use it, the stronger it gets. What else can I do?*

Anger at his grandfather's lack of training leached through him. Not as strong as before he began to understand, but still strong enough to clench his fists and grind his teeth. And he wondered again about the voices he heard. *Well … I guess I'm not going crazy since I haven't heard them in a while. How long? Yeah … a while … how long is a while?*

"Hey, Pop-pop … are you there? Any chance you can tell me more about what I can do? Like … is there more than fire, shield, and invisibility." He paused, looked up at the ceiling as the tell-tale rumbles of another storm growled in the distance. "I'm not complaining … I mean they are really cool. But … is there something more?"

The next time he woke, food and fresh water sat at the door as had become the routine. He shook his head as he chewed the last bite of sandwich. *It's weird that I never wake when they take the thermos.* His chewing slowed. Like a bolt of lightning from the frequent storms that rattled the building, a thought speared him. *They drug me while I'm sleeping … so I sleep deeper … longer. They can do whatever they want. Of course. Why didn't I realize this sooner? I really am stupid.*

He chugged down a mouthful of water, capped the thermos and tossed it into the padded door. *Idiot … stupid … argh …* He pounded the heels of his hands into the sides of his head. Anger swirled, notched up to fury … at Talen, at the vampiric doctor and icy nurse when they drew his blood. At Hunt. But mostly at himself for being so stupid. He created pictures in his mind: The doctor laughing like Dracula while a hunched back nurse jabbed needles into his arm and throat.

He pushed up the long sleeves of the loose-fitting shirt and studied the veins of his inner arms. An oath Pop-pop would have washed his mouth out with soap for using, exploded into the silence around him. His arms looked like the arms of the junkie he had seen in a film about addiction in Health class.

Thunder rolled back and forth like it was bouncing off mountains around him. He screamed. Jumping to his feet he punched the padded wall. Hot anger coursed through him and he screamed again.

He turned in a circle and shouted as the deep-toned voice of a rolling thunder trembled the air around him. "I'm not going down without a fight," he yelled into the padding of the ceiling.

He coughed and almost choked on his own saliva when a husky voice answered from the doorway. "I hope not. That would be way too easy ... and not very satisfying."

Lander's eyes zeroed in on the deep brown of Talen's eyes. A look of supreme superiority stretched a smile across the man's tan face, exposing white teeth.

"Time for a workout, freak." Talen tossed the handheld device that activated Lander's anklet in the air and caught it. "Want this, don't you? No one's watching now ... why don't you try and take it ... see if you can. I promise I won't activate it. Come on freak. Just you and me. Here ... now, Mr. *Last of the oh so special Stone Sovereigns.* Let's see what you've got.

"Your mom was fierce; you know that? She burned my uncle ... alive. I listened to him scream in agony. Oh, yea. She was a murderer. And I took great pleasure in putting her down."

Reason fled and Lander sprang across the room at Talen. The man laughed and laid Lander flat on his back with a quick punch to his stomach followed by an upper cut to his chin.

Pain shot through Lander's gut and jaw but it wasn't as bad as he expected. *Stupid. Stupid. Just what he wanted.* He turned to his side and spit out a glob of blood.

Talen shook his head and laughed. "Oh, freak. You're a funny one. You're gonna have to do better than that if you want to beat me. This time I cut you some slack. I won't be so gentle next time." The man released another deep laugh. "Well, fun's over for now. Mr. Hunt is waiting."

Lander pushed up from the floor and grimaced. Talen waved him out the door then followed him down the hallway toward the room Lander had visited twice before. Anger still churned his stomach. This man had killed his mother. He even laughed about it. One way or another Lander was going to end him. *Just need to be smart about it. Pop-pop made me strong … and smart. I can do this.*

Lander clenched his jaw, cringed at the pain, then settled into it. It was just pain; he could handle pain. He was done crying and wimping out; it was time to get serious. Today he would make it past the locked door and get outside. Once outside, no one could catch him. This was what he had been trained to do. Whatever it took. He closed his eyes, quieted his rampaging thoughts and listened. Remembering his grandfather's lessons he focused. Pulled up an enveloping shield and doubled it. No one was going to tase him today.

This time, the click of a door sliding open sounded loud in his ears. Primed, Lander shifted to face the sound and opened his eyes. A new opponent stood before the door that sealed behind him.

"Good evening, Mr. Devlin." Hunt's voice blared through the speakers and Lander suppressed the urge to cringe. "I must apologize for making you wait so long before visiting again." He chuckled. "My daughter and a few of her friends arrived for a visit the day before yesterday ... just after our little meeting and your ... unseemly escape attempt.

"Their arrival was such a wonderful surprise. She's away at school most of the time these days, so I couldn't resist the chance to spoil her a bit. Despite what you might think, I'm not a bad man. I love my daughter ... and it's been a long time since she brought friends home for me to meet." He chuckled. "And, if I am correct—and I'm rarely wrong—one of the young men is her *special someone*. Ah yes ... time will tell.

"The day they arrived I couldn't resist taking them out on *Mist*. Yesterday we toured the island, enjoyed a picnic lunch, visited the animal preserve, etc. I treated them to several surprises. And today, after a super morning, my daughter blew me off. It seems they wanted some time to themselves. Something about doing nothing ... or sitting on the beach ... whatever." A deep sigh hissed through the speaker. "I needed to get caught up with work matters anyway. Well, as they say, better late than never. On to the business at hand.

"Are you ready to continue our experiment, Mr. Devlin?"

"I thought we would try something different tonight. As you might have noticed, Mr. Jackson isn't carrying a Taser. He is a martial arts expert. Consider his hands and feet his weapons of choice. I'm curious to see if that *shield* you have constructed will be able to stop him. Let's find out, shall we?"

No! Let's not. Lander steeled his nerves for what he needed to do, then turned both hands palms up. Before Jackson took two steps toward him, Lander flicked fire and created two fireballs. Without waiting to see what the martial arts expert might do, he threw the fire, one ball at the man's head and the other at his legs. He could block one but not both.

Again, Lander formed flaming balls. He twisted and

flung both at the exposed cameras. Movement. Jackson. Lander jumped back, avoiding a flying kick aimed at his head. His shield bent, but held strong as the man compensated, twisted, and landed back on his feet, one pant leg smoking.

Again, Lander reinforced his shield. He pulled his hands back into his body, then pushed outward, directing the shield at the man with force, just as he had done to break the door open the other day. The shield crashed into Jackson, he landed hard, his neck at an awkward angle. He lay still.

Heat rose in Lander, he fought against the anger seething within him, seeking release in violence.

Lander.

He shook his head. *I'm hearing things. This isn't real.*

Lander. You have to stop. Breathe. Just breathe. I'm here. I'm going to help you. Relax and let your instincts do what Ian trained you to do.

The heat leveled off and Lander blinked away warm, wet tears. "Mom? Is that you?"

Listen and do what I say. We don't have much time.

CHAPTER 33

Wisps of smoke and the acrid odor of smoldering plastic permeated the air. Lander coughed then covered his mouth with a hand. His gaze skittered around the room before falling to the still figure lying on the floor.

"Is he ... is he ... dead?"

Lander. Focus. Get ready. Lander ... Now!

I know. I know.

The latch clicked and the door began to slide. Talen glared as his arm slipped through the widening gap. He pointed the device that activated Lander's anklet. Without thinking, Lander flung a layer of protection around his ankle as he surged forward and grabbed Talen's arm, wrenching the black box from his grasp, yanking the man off his feet, into the room. Lander backed away from Talen, dropped the device, and formed two fireballs.

The fury in Talen's eyes promised retaliation, but Lander couldn't stop. Bile rose in Lander as he released the first ball onto the black box at his feet and pitched the second at Talen's chest. The man screamed. Lander formed a third ball as he leaped over the writhing Talen who batted with both hands at the smoldering embers on his chest. Stumbling out the door, Lander came face to face with a group of six armed guards.

A thought, an instinct—Lander wasn't certain which—but he accepted it. An instant later, he merged the remaining fireball with his shield. He gazed out at the men surrounding him through a billowing sheet that glowed with blue flames. Bullets hit the barrier and dropped onto the floor in puddles of liquid metal.

He didn't know how much longer he could hold the shield in place without his Stones of Power; already, the adrenaline-induced energy he had tapped into was fading.

He sucked in a breath, then exploded the shield. The force of the blast flung the security guards into walls and down the hallway. Trembling, Lander focused again and disappeared. He stepped over an unconscious man lying in his path and started to retrace his steps from the other day.

No. Not that way. I'll get trapped again. He backtracked and, seeing a dark hallway to his left, darted that way. He slowed. It looked as if he now ran toward a dead end, but seconds later, he realized what he had mistaken for a wall was a metal door.

Shouts erupted behind him.

Please, please, let it be open. He hit the panic bar and the door swung open with a hiss, triggering a high-pitched alarm. Lander lost his grip on invisibility. His body trembled as the last of the adrenaline washed from his system. Eyes blinking, he studied his surroundings. *Need to hide. Need to hide.*

He stood in a shadow-drenched alley between two white cinderblock buildings, the pavement still warm beneath his bare feet. Above him, a full, round moon looked close enough to touch. Scarves of thin clouds raced past the silver orb. To his left, large moths battered against bright, yellow lights illuminating an empty parking lot. To his right, the alley ran up to a security gate. Beyond the gate a brick walkway, lighted by old-fashioned streetlamps and edged with flowering bushes and trees, led to another building. He started to sprint toward the walkway but stumbled to a stop. *Reality check! No running for the time being.* He groaned, then limped forward at a slow hobble.

The voice returned. **You need to get to the mansion ... Aurelius Hunt's study. It's not far now. Beyond the fence; up the brick path.**

Ignoring the instruction, Lander limped to the gate. *How am I going to get past that? If I try, the anklet will trigger. I'll fall unconscious and Talen'll just scoop me up like yesterday's roadkill.*

He wanted to drop to his knees and give up, but a small electrical box alongside the gate caught his attention. *Worth a try.*

Breathing hard, he stood for a moment and gulped in draughts of warm, moist air. He needed to catch his breath and slow his heart rate. He fought the urge to cover his ears as the blaring alarm continued to assault his ear drums, and summoned deep reserves to focus. Lifting his hands, he sparked fire then sent shafts of energy into the box. Ten seconds later, the box exploded.

Running out of time, and uncertain if he had taken out the whole fence or just the gate, he pulled up a weak shield and touched the fence. When nothing happened, he pushed the gate. The thing swung open with a smooth movement and he stepped through, hoping the Wasp wouldn't trigger and send him to la-la land.

He let the shield drop and started down the brick path, his eyes on the hunt for a spot to hide and recuperate some of his energy so he could focus again. He turned to his left and, leaving the level walkway, began to climb an incline covered in bushes. As he slipped between the shrubs, the heavy, sweet fragrance of tropical flowers permeated the air.

They'll know ... they'll smell. He stopped. A slight breeze shifted the branches of trees farther up the hill, wafting the flowery scent away from the alley. *Okay ... maybe not. Remember what Pop-pop taught you. Okay helpful breeze keep blowing.* The breeze stiffened and Lander allowed a weary half smile to emerge. *Thank you.*

You're going the wrong way. You need to get to the mansion.

"Yeah. Yeah. I hear you." He pulled in and released another breath. "For now, I need a place to hide ... until I can focus and go invisible again."

A door slammed. Raised voices cut through the sound of the alarm and the underlying drone of insects.

Lander dropped into a crouch. Twisting onto hands and knees, he crawled uphill through the thick bushes, praying the darkness and wind would cover his movements. The voices grew louder, and he dropped to his stomach. He tried to focus but was too weak to do more than flicker.

The voices receded. Those chasing him must have seen the broken gate and continued down the walkway. He rose back into a crouch, then pressed up to a hunched-over run. He needed to put distance between himself and his pursuers before they returned to scour the hillside.

The moon had dropped to a lower position in the sky by the time Lander pushed upright ... and realized his mistake. Standing on the top of the rise, the silver light behind, he stood out like an easy target. He shifted into a crouch, turning. The sound of a rifle shot echoed off the surrounding mountains.

Lander's thoughts slowed. *What was I ... something bit ... stung ...?* He reached to his neck where a feathered barb had punctured the skin. His legs turned to rubber and he fell to his knees, then tumbled head over heels down the side of the hill. Bushes and trees zipped past him as he rolled and toppled like a limp, rag doll. He thumped into a rock and his world went dark.

Lander. Lander! Wake up! Lander!

Confused thoughts collided with each other. Lander struggled against the fog in his mind. *Pop-pop must have ... made me ... spend the night? Outside? Where?*

Lander!

The voice triggered a stomach-churning mix of pain and panic. Lander turned and swallowed back the scream that sought release. His right side burned as if he had fallen onto one of his fireballs and when he tried to pull in a deep breath the agony intensified.

Memories shifted and reality flooded back. He blinked, disoriented by bright sunlight filtering through tree branches high overhead. *It ... wasn't ... it... night?*

Lander.

"No." He blinked and shaded his eyes with a hand. "You're nothing but a product of my imagination. Stop talking to me. You con- con- fuse me."

Lander, please listen. You have to heal and get to the mansion. Do you understand?

"No. I don't understand. I don't understand any of this. I just want it to go back to before ... before Pop-pop ... No. This can't be real."

Lander. Stop. Don't go down that road ... it will not help. Ian taught you how to heal, right?

Lander sniffed and wiped his nose with the muddy sleeve of his shirt. He nodded. "Are you my mom?"

Because I love you Lander, I have been sent. But you must be strong now. Focus and heal. You must flush the drug they shot into you from your system then focus on your ribs. When you crashed into the rock, you either broke or bruised ribs. I can't do it. You must.

Lander wanted to curl in on himself and cry. But the voice—whether she was his mother, or an illusion created by his overstressed brain—was right. He focused.

His system had already flushed most of the drug out of his body, so he shifted his focus to his ribs. Using gentle fingers, Lander probed the spot. The external examination confirmed his internal awareness. The ribs were bruised but not broken. Warmth flooded the area as he directed impulses of healing to the blood and tissue surrounding the bones.

Nearly twenty minutes passed before Lander climbed to his feet. A slight soreness persisted, but he could move with ease. Exhaustion rode him in a way he had never experienced before. But he was free—at least for the moment. And he had the voice to lead him.

Pulling in and releasing several deep breaths, Lander scanned the area where he had landed. Green surrounded him in shades he'd never seen before, from light lemony green to deep blue green. He picked his way down the remainder of the hill. Flowers bloomed in abundant colors, their fragrance permeating the air with an almost overwhelming sweetness.

Follow the curve of the hill. It will take you to water ... and food.

Pushing his way through the undergrowth beneath a clump of the tall, local trees, Lander looked up and pulled in a sharp breath at the beauty before him. A small waterfall split into two streams and splashed down a series of rocks into a small pool. Moss covered rocks sat around the edge. The heat that had drawn out beads of sweat on his upper lip faded in the cool shade of the tiny recess.

He moved forward taking care to place his feet where he would leave no tracks. Once he reached the rocks, he jumped onto the first then hopped from one to the next until he reached the pool's edge where he squatted, scanned his surroundings, and cupped water to his mouth. Though not as cool as he expected, the water was clear and tasteless. *Perfect.*

He drank without reserve. The soft splatter of the falling water soothed his frayed nerves and he looked for a suitable place to rest. His eyes snagged on red berries and he wondered if they were safe to eat.

"Hey ... M – M - *Mom?* Are you still here?"

He thought he heard a smile in her voice. ***For a little longer. I can help you ... but then I must leave.***

"Um ... do you know? Are these berries edible?"

Yes ... and tasty.

Using a large leaf, Lander collected a pile of berries then scooted into a shady hollow formed by an outcropping of rocks overlooking the pool. Sitting cross-legged, he inhaled most of the berries, leaving the rest for later.

"Can we talk now?" He shifted around until he settled with his back against the cool rock that formed the back wall of the tiny cavity.

Yes.

Lander closed his eyes. He had so many questions. *What do I ask first?*

"That guy ... um ... the one I hit. Is he ... is he dead?"

What's done is done.

Lander processed the response. Guilt at the thought he had become what Talen accused him of being—a killer—churned like soured milk in his stomach. He prayed he hadn't killed the man and swallowed down the shame, storing it away.

"You never gave me a straight answer; are you my mom?"

I was.

"Soooo ... if you're *dead* how can you be here talking to me now?"

I was sent. You are destined. You must return to the Core and save our people. This is why I was sent.

Lander pondered her words. The whole idea that he was *destined* seemed too impossible to believe. "What do you mean *destined?*"

That I cannot say. You will understand when the time comes.

He scratched the side of his face. *Yeah, right. Like that's not evading the question.*

"If you can't tell me that, can you tell me why it's so important I go to the mansion?"

Aurelius Hunt took your Stones of Power ... Jerod's— your father's—stones. You must get them back. They will be in his office in the mansion ... along with those he took from me. You must recover both sets before you attempt to descend to the Core.

"I had my dad's—Jerod's. And ... Hunt has yours. Did Pop-pop Ian have stones too?"

Jerod and Ian shared the Devlin family stones. When we escaped, Jerod returned his to his father. Didn't Ian tell you this?

"I didn't even know these ... *Power* ... stones existed until after he died."

The buzzing of insects, the splashing of water, and the soughing of wind through leaves filled the air as Lander pondered his mother's words.

You are so strong, but your power will never manifest fully unless you control the Stones of Power from both family lines. That is why you must find my stones as well as yours. Do you understand?

"I ... think ... so. It's just too much to take in right now. But ... I think I understand.

"Are you ... are you an angel?"

Of course not. Humans don't become angels when they die. That's just nonsense.

The voice went silent for a few minutes. ***My son, I have delivered the message I was sent to deliver. I must leave you now. Remember, I love you. So does your dad. Be safe; be strong. When you get to the Core, seek out the truth. There are those who will try to deceive you. Trust Noah's God.***

CHAPTER 34

As the sun sank beyond the peaks of the high mountains behind Lander, bathing the hollow in deep shadows, he succumbed to his exhaustion and climbed back into the tiny stone alcove above the pool. Sitting cross-legged once again and facing east, he considered his mother's words. Since Pop-pop's death, his life here on the Surface had been dumped into the toilet ... *and flushed.* Now, he was trapped on Hunt's island, hunted. He had to do something; he needed to strike back and the idea of slipping into Hunt's own home and taking back what belonged to him appealed to Lander. *But leave the Surface for the Core?*

Becky's face rose up in his mind, the way she smiled at him at the aquarium ... her banter when he had spent so long in the gem exhibit at the museum. Though they hadn't known each other long, the thought of possibly never seeing her again sent a pang through his heart.

When you get to the Core, seek out the truth. There are those who will try to deceive you. Trust Noah's God.

He shivered as the words sent uneasy tendrils of premonition through him. Birds rustled in branches high above, their sharp calls lacing the air. Small animals skittered through the underbrush to drink at the pool. Leaves rattled as the wind picked up. Lightning flashed in the distance, revealing the underbellies of churning clouds.

Still Lander sat, wrapped in his thoughts. ***You are so strong, but your power will never manifest fully unless you control both your father's and my Stones of Power. That is why you must find the stones.*** Paralyzed by his fears and doubts he struggled against a growing sense of destiny.

Lightning streaks pierced the sky and thunder rattled the ground as it echoed through the mountains. Lander shook himself out of his daze and watched as sheets of rain blocked out everything beyond the opening of his rock shelter. An unexpected sense of purpose had sprouted in him while the storm approached. He had made his decision. Once the storm passed, he would work his way around the lower foothills and head back to Aurelius Hunt Industries. Back to the mansion that sat at the end of the brick pathway.

Lander squatted behind a group of bushes on the manicured lawn of a gentle incline overlooking what had to be the mansion. As the final ragged edges of broken clouds flitted past the moon, silvery light illuminated the house. It reminded Lander of pictures from his history text of southern antebellum mansions.

Floodlights bathed the mansion and the perfectly designed landscape surrounding it. Lights that weren't on the night before. *Must be for my benefit.*

The front of the house overlooked a vast lawn that led to

a sandy beach where waves now sparked with silver high-lights.

Practicing the patience Pop-pop Ian had drilled into him, Lander watched without moving, silent and invisible, as several people entered and left by one of the side doors. When Talen walked out, limping slightly, self-loathing at the injury he had caused mingled with a sense of accomplishment at escaping the man.

Fifteen minutes later, the mansion seemed quiet. No one else had come or gone. Lander pushed upright, stretched, crouched, and sprinted toward the building. Once he reached the outer edges of the lighted area, he slipped behind the massive trunk of a live oak. Though he was focused and invisible, he didn't want to take the chance his shadow might be noticed.

Everything seemed quiet, the fierce wind from earlier had settled into a refreshing, light breeze, helping to mask his movements. He slipped around the bole of the tree, scanned again, then sprinted to the side of the mansion where the brick walkway he had been on the other night curved up to a porch. He took the two steps in one leap, crossed the porch with silent tread, then pressed his back against the wall. While pulling in several breaths and releasing them slowly through his nose, he shook out his hands and rolled his shoulders, then flattened into the clapboard siding again.

Voices came and went. When the light coming through the window in the door went out and the absence of voices lasted several minutes, he slid to the door, turned, and peeked in through the curtained window. Black granite counters topped ornate, pale yellow cabinets and reflected a low light set over a double sink. Lander wrinkled his nose and shook his head at the enormous kitchen.

He moved away from the door and plopped down in a shadow darkened corner where the railings of the porch met the wall. When the dark of night began to show the lighter gray of approaching sunrise and everyone in the house was asleep, he would sneak in. No sense pushing his luck now. He closed his eyes and settled in to wait.

Lander blinked. Time to move. A faint brightening of the sky out over the ocean hinted at the coming sunrise. He pushed up onto his feet then stretched, working out the kinks that had formed as he sat unmoving for the last few hours.

As he hoped, the door to the kitchen was unlocked and opened without a sound. He slipped inside, pulling it shut with a slight click behind him.

His stomach rumbled and he opened cabinets until he found a huge refrigerator, its doors disguised to look like built in cabinets. Pulling out a bin, he found a stash of apples. Grabbing one, he bit into it, holding it with his teeth as he rummaged again. He pulled the cover off a glass container and found a pile of sliced roast beef. He scooped out a handful, set the apple on a counter and pulled apart the meat, eating it two slices at a time in the light of the refrigerator. With a sigh of relief at the full feeling in his belly, he finished the last bite of apple and tossed its core into the trash receptacle located in a pullout next to the sink. Resealing the glass container that held the meat, he replaced it on the shelf and closed the door, plunging the room back into deep shadows. Now to find Hunt's study.

Without wasting energy to become invisible in the quiet darkness, Lander crept across the kitchen, past a pantry and through a large dining room with a table that must have been able to seat thirty people. The door from the dining room lead to a long hall. As he stole up the passage, a slight brightening in a grand open foyer to his left hinted that time was short.

The fragrances of fresh growth, budding plants, and fertilizer drifted to Lander. His nose itched and he rubbed it with the back of his hand. After a quick glance down the hall-way, Lander opened doors to his left and right, checking out the rooms he passed. Nothing that looked like a study. He turned the handle on the last door to his left before the passage widened at the entryway to a large, glass conserva-tory. *Locked. This must be it.*

He pulled in a breath and lifted a quick prayer. He focused as if to spark fire, but kept the intent sharp and tiny, then lifted the pointer finger of his right hand to connect with the lock on the door. A second later, the door swung open. Releasing his breath, he scanned the dark passage behind him before slipping into the room. He tried to pull the door shut, but the latching mechanism had been ruined by his break in.

Lander's eyes shifted around the shadow-drenched room. He flicked a small flame on his palm. The space was larger than he expected, with dark wood shelves and oriental rugs in muted tones. He took two steps forward. One of the rugs, plush against his bare feet, prompted him to curl his toes into the soft pile.

A burgundy leather couch and two matching wing-back chairs, along with several small, round tables constructed of the same dark-hued wood as the shelves, sat in front of a massive fireplace to his left. A bank of windows before him overlooked the veranda, lawn, and the ocean beyond. Pearlescent gray of the coming dawn brightened the sky over the water. To his right stood a large desk; beyond it, an alcove with two smaller leather chairs was set into a wall of shelves.

His movements quick and smooth, he shifted behind the desk and releasing the flame on his palm, pulled open draw-ers. Though he had expected them to be locked, each opened without a sound. *Nothing … Nothing …*

He shuffled papers, eventually just throwing them on the floor as his heart rate climbed and his muscles clenched. *Where are they?* He huffed out a breath, his eyes shifting to the windows. In the next few minutes, the first rays would paint the horizon. He ran trembling fingers through his hair.

Stumbling, he ran from table to table, throwing open drawers. Still nothing. Looking up, the alcove caught his attention. *If I were a super rich, evil, multi-billionaire, where would I hide evidence of ... whatever ... argh.*

He stopped, squeezed his eyes shut and clenched his fists. *Think! Think! Where ...*

He opened his eyes, before him sat the alcove. A quick intake of breath followed on the heels of an idea. *If I were ... I would ... I'll bet he has a secret panel.*

Skirting around the desk, Lander plowed into the alcove. He shifted both chairs and the round table between them, practically tossing them into the main room, then began knocking on the wood paneling. Not five minutes later, his efforts were rewarded when his hand landed on a wooden inset that shifted under slight pressure. A section of bookshelves in the study swung open with a soft grating sound. Jumping over a tossed lamp, Lander peered into the hidden room. Within sat a small desk and chair set as well as a burgundy leather chair next to a tiny round table.

With another glance at the brightening day beyond the windows, Lander scurried to the hidden desk. This one was locked. He focused, then shot an intense bolt of fire into the keyhole. The front of the drawer blew off. Taking care to not burn himself, he reached in and grabbed the ragged sides of the drawer. As he pulled it open, relief flooded through him. Sitting apart on a green felt liner were his stones, next to them sat two more. His mother's.

With trembling fingers, he picked up all four Stones of Power, cupping his two in his right hand and the others on the palm of his left. As the familiar bluish-green glow grew in his stones, his mother's stones began to glow with a red cast. He drew in a breath as a surge of power shot through first his hands, up his arms, then through his entire body. He wanted to shout, the sensation surged with such strength, but he clamped down the urge and turned to the bank of windows.

It didn't take more than a minute to ascertain they were thick and solid with no opening mechanism. And using his power to break through them would draw attention.

I'll have to go back the way I came.

He stood at the door with the shattered latch, listening. Two voices drifted up the hall. If Lander wasn't mistaken, they came from farther away ... *maybe the foyer* ... and sounded familiar. One stood out as *very* familiar. *Becky? No. Why would she be here? And ... Michael?* The voices got closer. There was no mistake.

Lander slipped out the door into the hall and whispered, "Becky?"

CHAPTER 35

L ander? Oh my ... Lander!" Becky rushed down the hall and slammed into Lander, nearly knocking him over as he flung out his arms and clutched the Stones of Power in his hands. "It is you. Oh ... oh! Lander! I was so worried!"

She wrapped her arms around him, her face pressed into his chest, tears wetting the fabric of his shirt. The fragrance of coconuts that was so much a part of Becky permeated the air and Lander breathed it in as memories of their times together blossomed in his mind. She sobbed.

Taking care, he wrapped his arms around her, his fisted hands on her warm back pulling her to him. He rested his chin on the top of her head and wondered how she could be here ... on Aurelius Hunt's private island. *Not possible. How?*

"Well, bro, I bet you can't even imagine how worried Becky's been seeing how she's just ignoring you now. I mean it was so rude to just up and disappear with those bozos the other day. Nearly broke her heart." Michael walked up then glanced back over his shoulder. "But as lovely as this romantic reunion is, I don't think this is the best time or place for it."

Becky pulled away, running the back of her hand across her wet cheeks. She looked up into Lander's eyes and hers went wide. "Your hair! What happened to your hair?"

Lander shrugged. 'It's not that bad, is it?"

The smile that lit her face sent his heart racing even faster than it had been.

A second later, her lips flattened and her eyes sparked. "If I get my hands on those goons who took you …" She tilted her head and her expression softened as she cupped his cheek with the palm of her hand and gazed at his face. "I don't know how we found you or what you're doing here, but Michael's right. We have to get you out of here. Now."

The sound of clapping echoed up the hallway. "Well done. You've found our missing *patient*. I don't know who you are or how you got in here," Talen growled, "but no one's going anywhere.

"You two trespassers need to step away from that *boy*. He's quite ill and in quarantine. Not supposed to come in contact with others."

Lander slipped Becky his mother's stones. She lifted her eyes to his, questions there. He pursed his lips and gave her a look he hoped she understood, then pushed her from him. Shifting his stance, he balanced a Stone of Power on each palm and met Talen's stare.

Talen chuckled and raised the second control box for Lander's anklet. "Who do you think will be quicker, freak." He lifted his thumb to a position over the second button, the one that would render Lander unconscious.

"Even if you could get off a fireball or two, imagine the danger you would put these *friends* in by doing so. Why don't you behave? Drop what you have in your hands and come with me before someone gets hurt."

Talen signaled to the two men behind him. With practiced moves, they trained Glock pistols on Becky and Michael.

"Mr. Talen, what is going on here?" Livy's voice sounded loud and shrill as she strode up the hallway, her chin raised and her eyes cold. She pushed past the three men to stand next to Becky. Parker and Parrish trailed Livy up the hall, stopped behind the guards their faces creased as if they had eaten something foul.

"Miss Hunt? What ..." Talen's voice lost some of its edge as Livy glared at him, her brows drawn down and her mouth a stern line. "I'm sorry you had to witness this confrontation. Please, don't bother yourself with it. I've got this under control. Just caught some trespassers. They will be turned over to the Coral City police and prosecuted." He paused and glanced at Lander, Becky, and Michael before turning back to Livy. "Your father would be upset if he learned I allowed you to involve yourself in security matters."

"These *trespassers* are my *friends* and are here at my invitation. How dare you point guns at them. My father is well aware of their presence here and has been entertaining them these last few days. Rest assured, Mr. Talen, he will hear about this ... this *abuse* of power."

Livy turned from Talen to face Lander. She winked then moved in close and mouthed, *use me as a hostage*. She wiggled her eyebrows.

Lander's eyes went wide. He swallowed hard but nodded. Livy returned the slight nod. Quick as a thought, Lander dumped the stone in his left hand into his right hand, grabbed Livy's left arm and pulled her to him, spinning her around so her back was to his chest.

Talen was already moving, his hand flexed, thumb plunging.

"No!" Lander pressed his stones to Livy's neck. "Unless you want to see your boss' daughter turned to ash, drop that thing."

All movement stopped. Lander focused on Talen, but he

could feel the hurt and disappointment flowing from Becky and Michael. It didn't matter. Livy's strategy was his only chance. Becky and the others would need to trust him.

"Lander?" Becky's voice drew his eyes to her. What he saw confirmed it. Becky shook her head. "What are you doing?"

Behind the guards, Parrish had pulled his cell from his shorts pocket and was whispering to someone. He caught Lander's gaze and relief flooded through Lander. Parrish understood. He knew what Livy was doing. In time Becky would understand too.

Lander's gaze returned to meet Talen's. "Well … are you going to do what I say, or is she going to suffer?"

Talen released an oath and dropped the control device to the floor.

Lander struggled against light-headedness. He thought he would pass out as he tried to pull air into lungs that refused to cooperate. His hands trembling, he held Livy in front of him like a shield, and moved forward a step, Livy moving with him. "Now, Talen, you're going to take us to the mine entrance." Relief surged when his voice remained strong and didn't crack.

Talen snarled, exposing even, white teeth. He motioned to the man on his right. "Get Mr. Hunt. Inform him of the situation. Tell him I'm cooperating … for the moment. Be certain he understands the gravity of the problem."

The man pushed past Parker and Parrish then sprinted down the hall. A few seconds later, the large double doors in the front foyer slammed shut.

Lander continued to press forward one step at a time while Talen backed up keeping the distance between them from growing. Michael and Becky slipped past Talen and the other guard to join Parker and Parrish. When they reached the grand foyer, Livy whispered to Lander, "Go out through the foyer. The limo's there."

Talen's nostrils flared. "Are you helping this … *boy*, Miss Livy?"

Lander felt Livy stiffen at the question. "What? How could you even think that?"

"What did you whisper to him?"

"Nothing! I told him he'd better let me go before my father gets here. What else would I say?"

They continued moving down the hall. When they reached the entryway, light poured in through the leaded panes of glass in the doorway, casting colored rainbows from the crystal chandelier in random patterns on the wall.

Lander paused, surveying the area.

"Now what?" Talen sneered. "You lost or something?"

Lander motioned with his chin. "Out the door. Now. Everyone."

They crossed the broad veranda and descended the two steps to the brick walkway that led to a circle of concrete that served as a small parking area.

A shaft of sunlight cast a silver beam across gray-blue waves rolling in soft mounds toward the shore, already threading heat through the air. A slight morning breeze ruffled Lander's shirt, bringing with it the tang of salt. After moving forward a few feet, everyone came to a stop. Before them, as if awaiting their approach, sat a shiny, white, stretch limousine.

Stifling another tremor that threatened his grasp on his stones, Lander lifted a quick prayer. *Hey ... God ... it's me, Lander. I know I haven't prayed much; not like Pop-pop Ian. But if you could please help me get through the next hour or two without getting caught or hurting anybody ... help me get to the Core. It's where I'm supposed to go, right? I would truly appreciate that. Oh ... and thanks for sending my mom.*

"Keep moving," Lander said in a voice he hoped sounded confident. "To that ... car ... limo ... whatever. The white thing." *Great ... nothing like sounding as if I know what I'm doing.*

They approached the limousine, Talen tracking close to Lander's side. A grin of superiority lighting his face. "Now what, freak?"

Mustering a mask of self-assurance, Lander said, "We're going. You're staying here." He turned his head and lifted his chin at Michael. "Can you drive this thing?"

"As long as the key is inside."

"Check it."

Michael hopped into the driver's seat then sent a smile and nod in Lander's direction.

"You have no idea what you're doing," Talen growled. "Give up before someone gets hurt. Do these *friends* of yours know you're a murderer? Have you told them that?"

Lander swallowed back the bile working up his throat, his eyes going wide. "No! I didn't … didn't … it was an accident. I just wanted to get away. I didn't mean to …"

"Sure. Sure." Talen played with the device in his hand, tossing it up and catching it.

"Stop!" Lander's shout sounded shrill in his ears.

Talen chuckled. "Aww. Are you afraid I might do something like … this?" His thumb shifted over the control.

"I said stop." He shoved his stones into the side of Livy's neck.

"Ouch!"

"Sorry," he whispered.

Talen raised his hands in submission. "Okay, kid. I'll behave."

Lander inclined his head in Parker's direction. "Find something to tie these guys up."

Parker and Parrish scanned the area. Parrish took off toward the dock. A minute later, he ran back, a coil of rope in his hands. Less than a minute later, Talen and the other guard were on their stomachs, hands tied behind their backs, the ropes run between their wrists and their ankles.

Parrish chuckled. "They looked like baby calves trussed up at a rodeo."

Lander smiled at the picture and released Livy. "Okay, that's good enough. Everybody in."

He shifted his focus to the vehicle. Parker slipped into the seat next to Michael who had started the engine. Parrish moved in to sit on the long couch. Becky held the back door open and waved him inside. "Get in."

Lander glanced back at the trussed-up men for one last look. Talen twisted his head to the side, wiggled on the ground, and smiled at him, this time with a feral hint of coming retribution. A chill raced up Lander's spine. He shivered, then turned and shoved Livy into the open door. He dove in behind her. "Go. Go. Go."

Michael already had the gas pedal pushed to the floor before the door even closed. It swung wide as Becky stretched out to grab the handle. She grunted and, as the long vehicle fishtailed, used the force of the movement and her weight to yank the heavy door shut. With a shout of triumph, Michael sped down the drive.

Parrish helped Livy slip out from under Lander then pulled her in for a tight hug. "You were awesome. I never would have expected this side of you."

A tiny smile turned up the sides of Livy's lips and she leaned into Parrish for a kiss.

"Hey," Michael said. "I know how much you two enjoy expressing your undying love, but I need directions. Livy?"

She pulled back from Parrish and focused out the windshield. "Up ahead …"

"Whoa!" Michael sputtered. "The gate. I forgot about the gate."

"As I was about to say, Michael. You need to slow down so we can make it past the guard at the gate. Lander? … Lander?"

After Livy moved to sit next to Parrish on the charcoal gray leather couch, Becky had slipped to the floor, turned Lander over, and cradled his head on her lap.

"He's out cold." Becky's eyes darted to Livy's. "That Talen guy must have triggered the device."

Becky ran her fingers down the side of Lander's bruised face, his long lashes dark on cheeks that were too pale. Her heart ached at what he must have suffered. "What did they do to you?" she whispered.

Barefooted and wearing nothing more than a light cotton shirt and loose pants, he looked frail and young, his arms black and blue as if he was a drug addict.

Michael's voice broke through Becky's thoughts. "Hey, Livy … that gate you mentioned … well, it's coming up. What do you want me to do?"

CHAPTER 36

Michael, slow down." Parker took command in a voice that brooked no questions. "We need to get Lander and Becky up on seats and strapped in." Parker stood on unsteady legs and slipped between the front bucket seats into the back of the limo. "Slower, Michael. Stop if you have to, but don't let the guards see us."

Mottled sunlight streaked through the windows like a strobe that slowed, then stilled.

"Okay, Parker. We're stopped. But the guys from the mansion can't be far behind us." Tension bled through Michael's words, sharpening them.

Parker glanced at his brother then flicked his attention to Lander. "Parrish."

"Okay, Becky. You did great. But now I need you to get up and strapped in. Parrish and I'll get Lander."

Parker and Parrish pulled Lander upright, set him on the couch, and belted him into the seat next to Becky's. She raised grateful eyes to Parker and mouthed, *thank you.* Lander's head lolled to the side and she slipped beneath it, allowing it to rest on her shoulder.

Parker nodded. "You good, Becky?"

She allowed a tight smile to surface. "I'm good. Thanks."

"Parrish." Parker returned his focus to his brother who was settling in next to Livy, clicking the end of the belt into the catch. "Mom and Dad have hired a helicopter pilot who's willing to land on the island. They didn't even question me when I told them Lander was heading for the Core, like they already knew. They're going to meet us at the mine entrance."

Parrish nodded. "Dad probably did his thing with his stone. Makes sense. I just hope we can make this happen without anyone getting hurt."

"Me too, Brother. Me too."

Parker returned to his seat and buckled in as well. "Everyone ready?"

"All ready back here." Parrish wrapped an arm around Livy's shoulders.

"Okay, Michael. This is it. Drive through. Don't stop. This vehicle can take it. It's built like a tank. So, unless they stand in the road and refuse to get out of the way, keep going. But don't run anyone down."

Becky caught movement on the road behind them. "They're here! Michael! Move!"

Michael stomped on the gas and the Town Car barreled forward. Seconds later they sped down a straight portion of the drive toward the guard shack and gate.

"Hold on!" Michael screamed, his voice pitched higher at the end, like a young girl's, as 'on' turned into a full-fledged screech.

Becky, with the instincts of a mother, flung her right arm across Lander's chest.

The guards standing on both sides of the lowered gate looked as if they wouldn't back down, until their eyes went wide, and they dove into the shrubbery. The limo sailed through the wooden bar like a knife through butter.

"At the *T,* turn right, then turn right again at the next turn off," Livy called out in a breathless voice. "You're not going to like this, but we'll need to break through another gate to get to the mine."

"No problemo," Michael glanced back, a wild smile on his face. "I don't remember the last time I did something so invigorating. Terrifying ... but invigorating."

Becky released a pent-up breath and chuckled. "Michael. I've said it before, but I'll say it again. You are insane!"

Michael laughed a wicked villain laugh.

Parker released his seat belt and wove his way into the back again. He stopped in front of Becky. "I don't know if I can help Lander, but I have an idea. Do you mind if I try?"

Swallowing back her concern she nodded. "What do you have in mind?"

"Just a trigger to try and wake him up."

Becky undid her belt, shifted her shoulder out from under Lander's head, and slid down the couch, leaving the seat next to Lander open for Parker. He slipped into position.

"What are you going to try?" Parrish asked, leaning in toward his brother.

"I'm not sure, but I think maybe a pulse. Like when I draw a gem from a stone. At least I thought I'd try that."

Parrish nodded. "Sounds like a good idea. Need me to do anything?"

"Nah, I've got this." He sat for a moment, holding his hands palms up as if trying to decide where to place them. "Becky. Michael. I know you guys do the church thing. How about asking the big man upstairs for some help?"

"Especially since that Talen guy and his goons, even if they stopped at the gate, must be closing in on us now." Michael said. "Livy, is this the place where I go right again?"

"Yes. If you go straight, you'll end up at the AHI Animal Preserve … see there. The big sign?"

"Got it," Michael said.

"Praying." Becky allowed a hint of anxiety to leach into her voice and she closed her eyes. Though she had only known Lander for a short time, their connection already ran deeper than any she had before, except for hers and Michael's. But his was more like a brother's. What she felt for Lander wasn't what a sister felt. And now, the thought of losing him tore at her insides. *Blessed Lord, God of all creation. You hold us in the palm of your hand. Please guide Parker, give him wisdom. Help us to get to the mine safely. And please let Lander wake up. We're running out of time and if he doesn't wake up soon we're gonna be in a whole mess of trouble.*

Becky opened her eyes and nodded. Releasing a puff of air through pursed lips, Parker leaned in and set his hands to either side of Lander's head. His eyes lost focus and a second later Lander blinked.

Becky hadn't realized she was holding her breath until she pulled in a gasp. "Lander? Are you … alright?" *Stupid question! Of course he's not alright.*

He squeezed his eyes shut then opened them again, his focus on Becky. "I think so. What happened?"

"That Talen guy must have had another device. Somehow, even tied up, he triggered it, though I don't know how. You dove into the limo behind Livy and collapsed. Parker did something and you woke up."

"Hey! Guys! We're coming up on the other gate. Looks like they got the word we were coming. There's a group of guards. They're lined up across the road … and … it looks like they've got guns."

Livy chewed her lip, her hair bouncing as she shook her head. "No. The guards don't keep firearms on the island. They must be tranq guns. They use them to tranquilize animals … in the preserve … like when they need medical attention."

"No tranquilizer dart is going to penetrate the bullet proof glass on this stretch," Parker said. "Just keep going, Michael."

As they approached the line of men, they slowed to a crawl. A large guard with a handlebar mustache who stood in the middle of the road, stepped out in front of the others and motioned for them to stop.

"Keep going," Parker said again. "As long as we don't stop, we'll get past them. They'll have to move. If we stop, we've lost."

"He's right," Lander said as he leaned forward to scan out the windshield.

Livy jumped up. "We'll never break through the barrier at this speed." She juggled past the others to the front seat where Parker had been sitting. "There's got to be a way to make them move off the pavement."

"Becky?" Lander said.

She met his gray eyes and shuddered at the determination in them.

"I need my stones."

She choked in a breath, uncertain, then it hit her. The stones he had given to her back at the mansion. She undid her seatbelt, rose up, and fished the two stones from the back pocket of her shorts. Meeting his eyes, she handed them to him.

Pushing up onto his feet, Lander pocketed his mother's stones and scooped up his two as he wobbled down the aisle between the couch and the bar. "Let me out."

"No!" Becky grabbed at his hand. "We came to rescue you. If you go out there, they'll … No!"

A semi-sad smile drew his lips up at the corners as Lander nodded, sending Becky's heart racing even more than it had been. *He's smiling? Smiling! For me!* She blinked back tears that crawled out despite her efforts.

"It's okay, Becky. Don't worry. I don't plan to get caught."

Lander clutched the stones in one hand and stumbled across to the back door. "Okay, Michael. Stop. This won't take long."

"If you say so."

Lander opened the door. It swung wide as the vehicle came to a stop. He jumped out and jogged a few steps on the warm concrete to keep from face planting. Palming a stone in each hand, he turned to face the men blocking the road as a faint rumble of thunder growled in the distance.

The trademark blue-green light sprouted in the stones, infusing the air around them, setting Lander's hands to glowing. The guards, almost as one, shifted to train their sights on Lander. Too late. He focused, lifted his arms out to his sides, and pulled up a shield. Strength flowed through him from the stones, enhancing his ability. Potency leached from him into the impossibly strong barrier. What he had been able to accomplish without the stones paled in comparison to what now shimmered before him.

Lander walked forward, pushing the indistinct blue-green wall before him. Tranqulizer darts dropped, clattering on the concrete. He passed the front of the limo, pulled in a breath, and flung his hands forward, willing his shield into the men who still fired their guns, unaware of their danger.

The wall rushed ahead. Like a storm surge, it swelled, hitting the men and tossing them onto their backs like so much driftwood, rifles flying beyond.

Gritting his teeth and struggling to not think about whether the bodies he moved were alive or not, Lander slipped his stones into his pockets on top of his mother's and began to pull the men in front of the limo off to the side of the road. Michael climbed out to help, but Lander waved him back. "I've got this. You just get ready to move." The thought that his friends would discover Talen had told the truth—that he was a murderer—set his stomach to twisting. He swallowed the bile that rose up his throat at what he had done ... what he was doing.

Please, Lord, let them be unconscious, not dead. Please not dead.

In the distance, several vehicles chewed up the road, racing toward Lander and his friends. Lander climbed into the Town Car and shouted to Michael. "Go."

CHAPTER 37

The limo's tires squealed on the concrete, it began to fishtail, then lurched forward like a battering ram aimed at the gate. Though this one was an upgrade from the ornamental gate securing the mansion, the Town Car made quick work of it. Sparks flew and metal screeched as the gate and part of the fence dragged along to either side of the car's front bumpers. Then the car bounced like a child on a trampoline, sending shock waves through the interior as they rode over the remains of the gate. Michael gave it more gas and they picked up speed again.

Five minutes later, they took a sharp turn to their left and passed the turnoff for the white, cinderblock building where Lander had been held captive. A small, nondescript sign read, AHI R&D, No Admittance without authorization. The parking lot Lander had seen the night he escaped sat to the left of the building and two other buildings peeked out from behind it.

Lander glanced back over his shoulder wondering if he could see the mansion from here, but the thick foliage blocked the view past the building.

They took another sharp turn, this time to the right, then they were climbing up into the mountains covering the northwest corner of Zephryn Island. The air turned thick and dark and condensation formed on the windshield as several rumbles of thunder echoed off the surrounding mountains.

"Wow!" Livy whispered. "This is beautiful. I can't believe I've never been up here before."

"That's because your father never wanted you to know the truth of what he found in these mountains." Parrish brushed a lock of hair behind Livy's left ear. "But now it's time to learn the truth."

"Time to learn the truth, right?" Becky said. "Lander. Are you up to telling us what happened to you?"

The last thing Lander wanted to do was relive the last several days; the experience was bad enough the first time around. But he nodded. His friends had come to his rescue and he owed them that much. And though it would be painful for Livy to hear, Lander trusted that her willingness to help him meant she was also willing to learn the truth about what her father was doing in his R&D complex.

He started his story with the kidnapping and waking up on the metal table. When he talked about the first testing, Becky leaned into him and gave him a hug. "Why? Why would Mr. Hunt act like that?"

Lander shifted his gaze to Livy and saw the same question in her eyes. *How could her father treat anyone that way?* He saw the pain behind the question. "Because in his mind I'm not human."

Lander sighed, remembering the doctor's excitement after studying his bloodwork. "My DNA is … different. He and those working with him feel justified in their actions. Whatever he does to me," his eyes shifted to Parker then Parrish, "or Parker or Parrish or any Core Dweller is justified because he is doing it for the good of mankind … humans."

Livy buried her face in her palms and Parrish massaged her back.

"He told me once that he's not a bad man; he's a good man who loves his daughter. From his perspective, using Core Dwellers for research that could improve the lives of countless humans is heroic."

"No its not!" Livy raised her head, her eyes sparking with anger. "He thinks he's justifying his actions, that he's some kind of hero; but to be honest, it's more about how much money he can make with his research. It always has been. I accepted that about him a long time ago. I was proud of him for his human-itarian efforts ... even welcoming school groups to tour the animal preserve ... but that was only a public image. Something to polish and show off." She raised haunted eyes to meet Land-er's. "I see that now ... I guess deep down I've always known that."

Tears dribbled down Livy's cheeks and she turned into Parrish's shoulder with a sob.

Lander wanted to console Livy, tell her that her father wasn't a monster in sheeps' clothing. But he couldn't. The pain of what Hunt did to him was too fresh, too raw. And it wasn't just the physical abuse. Hunt and Talon had called him a freak, not human. Lander swallowed the bile that threatened to choke him.

They crested the pass between two mountains as the clouds started to break apart, the bulk of the storm rumbling toward the southwest. The road dropped along a gentle grade down into a high valley.

"Will you look at that." Michael's voice was filled with wonder.

The sun rode along the bottom edge of the shredding clouds, its rays visible and vivid like the fingers of God as they skimmed across a manicured setting that reminded Lander of pictures in a book about English manors he had borrowed from the library once. Everything was vibrant hues of green, from lemony yellow green to deep blue green that was almost black.

Castor's words played in his mind. *Aurelius led us through a narrow crevice and out into an impossibly vast brightness. When we saw the sun for the first time, we thought it would blind us, the light was so intense. We had only ever experienced the muted light of the Core. It was all so green ... so overwhelming ... and beautiful.*

This was what his parents had seen when they first came to the surface. This valley.

Lightning flashed a final jagged fork down into the mountain facing them, drawing Lander's attention to the mouth of a large, dark tunnel. It gaped at them like the maw of some mythical monster. The mine.

Lander shivered. Fear jittered up his spine. *What am I doing here? Why didn't I leave the island when I had the chance? Because my mom told me I had to go to the Core? My mom? I don't even know if that voice was anything more than my own imagination. The Core? Who am I kidding?*

Becky must have sensed his growing agitation. She reached to grab his hand, cradling it in both of hers. "Are you okay?"

Lander shook his head. "No. I don't know." He sucked in a loud breath. "What if I'm wrong? What if I shouldn't have dragged you here? What if you get hurt ... or one of the others gets hurt?"

Becky gave him a sidelong glance. "What if ... what if ... what if? Stop that. *What ifs* are nothing more than a guilt trip built on doubts. Lander, everybody has doubts. You can't let your doubts be the thing that drives your actions. You believe in God, right?"

"Sure ... I think so. Well, not like Pop-pop Ian did." Lander shifted his gaze from Becky to the scenery sliding by as they descended into the valley.

"That's pretty weak, Lander." He couldn't miss the frustration in Becky's voice.

Trust Noah's God. *But could he trust? Trust enough to travel to the Core.* In that moment of decision, the longing to visit the world of his parents flooded through Lander with an irresistible force. He wanted to be the special person Pop-pop always said he was.

"You're right Becky. My trust is weak … but it's still alive. I want to see the Core. I want to trust Noah's God … the God of Pop-pop's Bible. And there's no ifs before those."

Warmth bled through him at Becky's broad smile. "So, Core-boy, what do we do next?"

Michael's laughter from the front seat filled the limo. "*Core-boy*! I like that."

"*Core-boy?*" Parker grimaced. "You ever call me that *Tattoo-boy* and I'll show you what we Corish are really capable of."

"Enough," Livy shouted. "We're almost to the mine entrance. How are we planning to get past the guards?"

"News flash," Michael said. "I don't see any guards. Do you think they're hiding? Waiting to spring some kind of trap?"

"Once we broke through the second gate, they had to figure we were heading here and not trying to get off the island." Parker squinted his eyes and scratched his chin. "This doesn't make any sense."

"You guys have done enough." Lander leaned forward, his elbows on his knees. "You've gotten me to the valley. Just drop me off, turn around, and get out of here. I can sneak into the mine on my own. Remember, I can turn invisible. It'll be easier this way. I appreciate all you've done, but I'm better on my own from this point forward."

Michael pulled to the side of the road.

"Come back to Camden with us." Becky's voice broke on the last word. "We'll hide you there. You can take time to think through what you want to do. Why rush into going down to the Core. You don't even know anybody there." She paused, chewed her lower lip, then said, "Stay. Stay with me." Her wide, deep brown eyes pleaded with Lander.

He closed his eyes and shook his head. His heart broke at the thought of leaving Becky. He pushed up onto his feet and climbed out of the Town Car. Becky stepped out after him and grabbed him around the waist from behind. Her warm body pressed into Lander's back and he groaned. *God? Why can't I stay with Becky? I'm not even a true Core Dweller. I was born and raised on the surface.*

Lander turned, wrapped his arms around Becky, and rested his chin on the top of her head like he had done back at the mansion. Every part of him longed to stay with her like this, breathing the soft fragrance of coconuts. But he couldn't; and he wouldn't lead her on with false hope.

While Lander and Becky stood hugging, everyone else had filed out of the limo and stood in a half circle around them. Lander cleared his throat. "There's something you need to know." He let go of Becky with one hand and tilted her chin up with his fingers so he could look into her eyes. "It's the reason I have to go to the Core. Even though I don't want to. If I could, I'd stay here, here with you." He scanned the faces around him. "With all of you. But I can't."

His gaze searched the crystal-clear azure sky. The storm clouds were nothing more than a hazy darkness on the horizon. The position of the sun revealed the time he had to explain things was evaporating.

He pulled in a deep breath, let it out with a huff and started. "When things were bad and I was losing hope, my … my mother's voice. Well, a voice that said it was my mother spoke to me. She told me I had a destiny and … that destiny was in the Core. Something is happening there and I … have to … help the people there."

"Whoa, dude! That's heavy," Michael said as he kicked at the stones beneath his feet.

"And you believe this was real?" Doubt flattened Parker's lips and Lander knew he wouldn't understand.

"Yes. She told me things ... helped me." He lowered his gaze to Becky again. "She told me to trust Noah's God, Becky. I don't think I can say no."

Lander watched the transformation in Becky play out on her features. They softened. She nodded. "I understand." The sorrow returned. "But ... do you think you'll come back to the Surface after ... after you do what you need to do?"

"Come back to you? If I am at all able, I promise I will come back to you, Becky."

A bittersweet smile flitted across her face. "I believe you will keep that promise."

The thumping of a helicopter echoed across the valley. "That's either Mom and Dad or Livy's father and his guards. We need to cut this short now." Parker turned back to the limo and reaching in, grabbed a brown paper bag. Facing Lander, he said, "You look like crap, but this should help. I hope the shoes fit. Becky said they're the size shoes you bought in Camden before."

Lander stepped away from Becky and peeked in the bag. Inside were a black hoodie, a black logo tee from the band Red, a pair of jeans, underclothes, and leather shoes. He lifted his eyes to Parker. "Thanks."

Parker gave him an awkward man-hug, then slipped into the limo.

Livy approached Lander, her eyes pools of guilt. "I'm so sorry for ... for."

"It's okay. You didn't know. You have nothing to feel guilty for."

Parrish stepped up next to Livy and wrapped an arm around her shoulders. "I keep telling her that." He hesitated for a moment, then reached out and took Lander's hand. "Take care of yourself. Our parents will probably head right to the mine. Keep an eye out for them and … keep them safe. Okay?"

Lander nodded. Livy stood on tiptoes and planted a kiss on his cheek. "Remember what you said to Becky. You have to come back to her. You promised." She spun around and vanished inside the Town Car. Parrish gave Lander a quick nod then climbed in behind her.

Michael pulled Lander into a bear hug and thumped his back. "What Livy said, right? And when you do come back, we're going for matching tattoos. Got it?"

Not trusting his voice, Lander nodded.

As Michael returned to the front seat, Lander turned to Becky and wrapped his arms around her again. She tilted her head and he lowered his lips to hers. Electricity jolted through him as her soft lips met his. He wished the moment could go on forever as the kiss deepened. After a minute, she pushed back, her hands shifting to hold his biceps.

"You're an idiot Lander Devlin. But I love you. Please be safe." She searched his eyes one last time, then turned and ran to the limo, joining the others inside.

The engine hummed and Michael turned the vehicle around. Lander watched as it vanished over the rise. He jogged to a clump of trees with flowering bushes beneath and changed into the new clothing, stuffed what he'd been wearing into the bag, and shoved it under a bush.

Stepping out from the midst of the undergrowth, he fingered the stones in the pockets of his jeans, taking comfort in their accessibility, and turned his face toward the mouth of the mine. "Well, God. I hope you're backing me up here. Because I have no idea what I'm doing."

CHAPTER 38

Residual humidity from the storm's passing combined with the sun's warmth to draw beads of moisture out on Lander's temples and upper lip. The tee-shirt clung to his upper torso and sticky sweat accumulated where he had wrapped the hoodie around his waist. Lander's breaths came sharp and heavy as he worked his way across the valley floor, skirting the thick undergrowth at the edge of the groomed landscape.

Birds chattered and sang, and, in the distance, a lion roared in the animal preserve. The sound drew gooseflesh out on the back of Lander's neck and arms despite the moisture laden heat of the day.

A half-hour later, Lander crouched behind a large shrub covered by a twining vine. He breathed in the heady, sweet fragrance of the vine's unique yellow-green flowers. He took a few moments to enjoy the beautiful scent while he slowed his heart rate and breathing and watched the mine entrance for any activity.

After several minutes, he pulled in a final deep breath,

focused and turned invisible, then sprinted for the darkness within the semi-circular entryway. The sun's warmth vanished once Lander moved into the dark shadows of the huge entryway. Twenty feet in, he pulled up next to a heavy chain link fence and gate, similar to the one they had broken through earlier.

He scanned the area. *No one?* Shrugging, he released his invisibility. *Maybe that's normal.* As his eyes adjusted to the shadowy half-light, Lander bent and examined the lock. *Nothing special.* Beyond the gate, a tunnel, tall and wide enough for large construction vehicles to navigate, ran forward in a straight line. Bare incandescent light bulbs hanging from the ceiling, cast faint light until they faded in the distance.

Lander turned his attention back to the lock. He thought it would be a quick and easy break in, but the heavy metal of the lock proved resistant to his spark of fire.

"Perhaps I can help with that."

Lander's heart thumped and his breath caught in his throat as he swung around, clutching one of his stones and going invisible.

A deep chuckle drifted to him and Lander squinted into the brightness at the tunnel's mouth. "Castor?"

"We thought you might need a little help." Castor's burly form appeared as a silhouette emerging from the sunlight. To his right, another figure approached, smaller. "We didn't think you would choose to come here though. Assumed you would want to escape the island. When Parker called us to fill us in, I thought he was joking at first."

The other figure's head turned, scanning the tunnel entrance. "I never thought I'd see this place again. Well, maybe not *exactly* this place … it's changed since we were here last."

"Desma?" Lander's mouth dropped open. He couldn't wrap his mind around Castor and Desma's appearance here on Aurelius Hunt's island. The one place in the world he would least expect to see them despite what Parker had said. "What are you two doing here?"

"Like I said, we came to help. But I have to ask, why are you here instead of on a boat putting as much distance between you and Hunt as possible?"

Castor moved past Lander and bent to examine the lock. "You can answer that after we get past this gate. There are about a half dozen vehicles headed this way. They were stopped by Hunt's white limo when the chopper flew over the road leading to the mine.

"Let me see if I can melt this."

Lander opened his mouth, questions vying with each other to be asked, but nothing came out.

Castor pulled a stone from a pocket of the light windbreaker he wore. His eyes lost focus and his stone glowed a soft golden color. A few seconds later, the lock began to ooze, like melted chocolate. Castor grunted, then knocked it off the gate with his elbow.

"The limo? You saw the white limo?" Lander sputtered as his brain kicked back into gear. "It was stopped? Did you see anyone?"

"No. Why?" Hesitation and suspicion laced Desma's voice.

"Because my friends were in the limo. Parker and Parrish were with them."

"What?" Desma's eyes narrowed as she glared at Lander. "You should be with them. You're the Stone Sovereign. Their protection was on you." She began spouting off in Corish.

"Desma." Castor raised his hands in a placating gesture. "Don't blame the boy. The best thing we can do now is get him to the Vortex. Come on."

As Castor pushed the heavy gate open enough for them to slip through, the sound of engines echoed in the sunlit entrance. "Hurry."

Desma wormed through the opening with Castor at her heels. "Come on, Lander."

Lander glided past the melted lock, took a few steps, then turned to face the gate.

"What are you doing?" Castor yelled.

"Don't stop. I'll catch up. I'm going to slow them down a bit." Lander pushed the gate closed and examined the lock. He didn't know if the idea churning within his mind would work but he had to try. Castor had told him once that as a Stone Sovereign he could do whatever Castor did. Lander focused and directed the energy he used to spark fire into the lock. Rivulets of sweat tracked down the sides of his face, but within seconds, the lock had fused.

"Yes!" He fist-pumped the air once and as shadows began to gather, blocking the sunlight in the entryway, he pivoted and sprinted after Castor and Desma.

It didn't take him more than a minute to catch up. The two had reached the end of the tunnel where it opened into an immense cavern. They stood with mouths gaping. The ceiling, lost in deep shadows above, had to be at least one-hundred feet high. A dozen construction vehicles sat in a row to Lander's left. About thirty feet in front of Lander, a body of water reflected the dim lights. In the distance, he could make out the form of a bridge across the water.

Desma pulled in a noisy breath. "This wasn't here sixteen years ago."

"Which way do we go?" Lander asked as his stomach dropped like a lead balloon. If things had changed so much, could Castor and Desma get him to this *Vortex* before Hunt and his people caught them. As if to reinforce his fears, loud voices came from the tunnel.

"This way." Castor sprinted toward the water. He skirted around the right edge, heading for the bridge.

Lights came on overhead as they ran across the bridge.

Lander put on more speed and cast a shield around Castor, Desma, and himself, remembering the sting of the Wasp. He wished he had taken the time to remove the anklet, but it would have to wait now.

"Lander?" Hunt's voice drifted over the water. "It's time to stop running."

Castor motioned Lander to keep running. Beyond the bridge, they approached another tunnel. "This way." Castor waved into the tunnel.

Desma ran in a few feet then stopped. "Lander, flick fire. We need light in here."

"This is it." Castor bent over, breathing hard, his hands on his knees. "There's an elevator here now, but this is the tunnel we came in through when we first came to the Surface." He pulled in a couple deep breaths and nodded. "Aurelius probably installed the elevator to slice time off the trip to the Vortex."

"He always planned to go back, didn't he?" Desma huffed. "That's what you and Ian knew. He left some men behind so he could go back." Her eyes went wide. "He never expected to lose Ian ... and Cyanne and Jerod. He thought he'd manipulate them and be able to travel back and forth at will."

"That's what Ian and I figured," Castor said. "And that's why it was so important that he not find Ian and Lander. Now, the safest thing to do is get Lander to the Core where Aurelius can't reach him. Come on. Let's see where this elevator takes us."

The hollow sounds of feet running over the bridge echoed through the tunnel, a close reminder that they were running out of time, as Castor hit the button. A breath of relief whooshed out between Lander's lips as the heavy metal doors creaked open and lights went on inside the largest elevator he had ever seen. Though the massive vehicles they had passed in the cavern wouldn't fit in, most of the others could.

Lander bounced on his heels and jogged into the elevator,

Desma and Castor behind him. As the doors began to close, Talen skidded to a stop in front of closing doors and, reaching in, forced them back open.

Palming his stones, Lander focused. He sparked fire, then stopped, letting the charge die. Castor and Desma stood between him and Talen. He refocused and set a shield of protection between the couple and Talen instead.

Hostility radiated off Talen, sending a tremor through Lander. Worse yet, Aurelius Hunt, his hand grasping Livy's elbow, moved into a position behind his head of security dragging his daughter with him. More than a dozen guards filed in on Hunt's heels, herding Becky, Michael, Parker, and Parrish before them.

A satisfied smile washed across Hunt's face. "Ah, Mr. Devlin. I see I have your attention. Very good. Now, if you will please back up, I believe we can all fit on the elevator. It's time we talked about what you will do for me."

CHAPTER 39

Lander's breathing grew labored as the very air seemed to leach from within the elevator at Hunt's words. Castor bristled, anger seeping from him as his eyes locked on Hunt. "Aurelius, it's been a long time. Not long enough."

Hunt's eyes widened. "Castor? Is that you? And ... do I see the lovely Desma there in the shadows behind you? This is an unexpected pleasure." His gaze flicked behind him and when he faced front again, he shook his head, his smile broader than before. "And, of course, the two young gentlemen with gray eyes must be Parker and Parrish. My how they've grown! You have done well avoiding my searchers these sixteen years. And yet, here you are. Once again on my island ... here of your own choosing, attempting to save your young Stone Sovereign. Such loyalty is ... touching.

"But since Mr. Devlin has elected to return to the Core rather than escape my island, I have decided to allow him to discover his roots. It is past time I checked on the investment I planted there when we left; and, for the first time in many years, I have a Core Dweller capable of transporting me back to the Core. It is, in its own way, more exciting than any testing I could have performed in my lab. A real test of his talents."

He stepped back and to the side, pulling Livy with him. "Everyone, please join Mr. Devlin in the elevator.

Hunt waved his men forward. Once they filed past, he propelled Livy before him and entered as well. "Mr. Talen?"

Talen shifted past Castor and pressed a button on the control panel. The elevator shuddered, then began to move. A few minutes later, Talen wormed his way back to stand next to Lander. Lander stiffened as the man wrapped long, strong fingers around his wrist.

Talen glanced at him sideways through slitted lids. "I'll take those stones now. All four." Though spoken softly so only Lander could hear, the tone of Talen's voice promised violence if his words weren't obeyed.

Lander clenched his jaw. *If he thinks I'm just going to hand my family's stones over without a fight, he's badly mistaken.*

Talen's grip intensified on Lander's wrist, as if the man was trying to break bones. Lander struggled to yank his hand back and attempted to step away. Talen's hold was unbreakable. Anger churning like a fire in his blood, Lander looked to the man's hand then lifted hate-filled eyes to Talen's smirking face, wanting nothing more than to wipe the insufferable grin off Talen's face. Lander's stomach knotted as Talen pulled a Wasp controller from a large pocket on the left leg of his cargo pants.

Lander looked down to the Wasp still fastened on his leg but when he lifted his gaze Talen shook his head. He flicked his eyes to Becky then back to Lander and nodded.

The knot in Lander's stomach tightened. An anklet was strapped to Becky. She must have sensed his attention because at that moment she turned her head, her eyes wide and sad. *I'm so sorry*, she mouthed.

Lander closed his eyes, struggling to cap a bubbling fury that rose like the lava of an erupting volcano within him. He wished he had never met Becky. If not for him she would be safe in Camden, not here in this elevator heading toward who knows what, with a Wasp fastened to her ankle. Hunt's voice broke through his roiling emotions.

"Ah ... here we are. Castor. Desma. I think you will be pleased to see the improvements I've made to expedite access to the Vortex. What took three days before, can now be done in a matter of minutes."

The elevator doors slid open and Aurelius Hunt led the group out into another immense cavern. How far they were below the surface now, Lander could only wonder as Talen propelled him to a place next to Hunt.

"He refused to give me the stones, Mr. Hunt." Talen's focus remained fixated on Lander. "Should I demonstrate the effectiveness of the new Wasp?"

"No!" Lander's and Hunt's voices blended together in protest.

"Leave her alone." Michael elbowed the guard on his right and moved to stand in front of Becky. "What do you people want anyway? This is crazy!"

Michael dropped into a fighting stance, his lips drawn back exposing clenched teeth. The tension in the air sizzled as fifteen guns trained on him.

"Michael, no. Stop." Becky grabbed Michael's arm, turning him to face her. "Please. Just cooperate. They promised no one would get hurt if we don't fight them."

A grimace contorted Michael's face and he lifted his gaze to Lander's. Lander had no doubt, Michael didn't believe that promise. Not one bit. But the muscular youth threw his hands in the air. "Okay, Becks. If that's what you want. But if they hurt you ... I can't promise anything."

"Good. I'm glad that's behind us." Hunt scanned the

group, his eyes settling on Lander. "Now, Mr. Devlin to avoid any further disturbances, I suggest you hand the stones in your possession to Mr. Talen. I will hold onto them for now. As you will need them to transport us to the Core, they will be returned to you at the proper time."

Swallowing a bitter brew of fear, anger, and frustration, Lander handed his stones to Talen, then fished his mother's from his pocket and handed them over as well.

"Well done," Hunt said as Talen gave all four stones to him. "Now, let us continue. It is a bit of a walk to the next elevator."

A half-hour and two elevator rides later, they stood in a much smaller cavern. The air here felt dense and heavy, old, even though ventilation holes could be seen at regular intervals on the ceiling, looking like nothing more than far away stars shining on a cloudless night. The thought of the unconceivable weight pressing down from above sent a chill through Lander. But what drew his attention were the flickers of pulsing light arising from a hole in the floor across the room from the elevator.

Despite Talen's forbidding look, Lander wrapped an arm around Becky's waist and guided her forward toward the flashes. They approached the edge and Lander felt Becky stiffen. His own muscles drew tight at the sight. Within the hole a maelstrom swirled. Around a black center whirled pink, blue, and green lights, shifting and flowing in and out and around like the winds of a tornado.

Vertigo flushed through Lander. It was like trying to maintain his balance while looking down into a funnel cloud from above. The hairs on his neck stood on end at the power emanating from the hole.

Desma's whisper reached him over the hissing noise of the whirlwind of lights before him. "The Vortex."

This is the Vortex. This is what I'm supposed to travel through? …

While protecting everyone else with a shield? No. I can't do this! Impossible. I don't know what I'm doing. Oh, Lord, creator of the universe. You created this too. You know I can't do this. Help me.

Hunt clapped his hands, a look of delight brightening his face as it glistened first blue then pink in the flares. Lander couldn't be certain, but he thought he saw the man's skin melt away, leaving nothing but a skull highlighted by the flickers.

Castor had moved to Lander's left, setting a large, warm hand on his shoulder. "You are a Stone Sovereign, Lander. You were made for this. The Vortex may look daunting, but you are strong. Do not fear."

Unable to trust his voice, Lander sucked in a gulp of air and nodded as he pulled Becky closer to his side. She wrapped an arm around his back and squeezed. "Castor's right, Lander. You are strong. I trust you." A half-grin surfaced. "But you know me. I trust God even more. Just like Pastor Stevens taught us. He is with us even now."

A warm peace flooded Lander at Becky's words and he nodded. "Yeah! Just like Pastor Stevens would say if he was here."

Hunt released Livy and she hurried into Parrish's embrace. They wrapped arms around each other. Desma approached the two with hesitant steps. She hugged Parrish, and, after studying Livy for a moment, she hugged her too. Then Parrish, Livy, Parker, Desma, and Michael walked to the edge of the Vortex alongside Lander and Becky, where they too gazed at the swirling lights.

Talen shouted orders and the guards moved to various cabinets against the wall to the right of the elevator and began to collect more weapons and equipment in preparation for descending to the Core.

Hunt, still smiling, moved to stand between Lander and Castor. "Well, Mr. Devlin. Are you ready? My men and I will be set to go in just a few more minutes."

Castor turned to face the man, his eyes wide. "Your men? How many are you planning to take?"

"Those who are here with us."

The words drew the other's attention; soon all eyes were on Castor and Hunt.

"Lander's never done this before and you expect him to transport so many safely?" Castor growled his protest.

"Of course. I have no doubt he can transport not only my men and me, but you and Desma as well. That's why you're here isn't it? You want to return?"

Lander fought the bile that rose up his throat, swallowing it back. He glanced over his shoulder at the black hole that seemed to have no bottom. *What am I supposed to do? Just jump in? While keeping everyone shielded?* Nausea swirled through him again; even Castor thought he couldn't get everyone through safely.

Releasing Becky, he turned to Castor. "I don't know how to do this. Please, tell me what to do."

Castor reached past Hunt and grabbed Lander's arm. "You've set shields. Form a big one around those you are transporting, then fix your focus on keeping it solid, thick. You are strong … stronger than your parents or Ian … and you have four Stones of Power. Trust God and trust your instincts. I don't think Aurelius is going to give you any choice in the matter. So be strong and do what only you can do."

Hunt stepped away from the edge. Talen and the other guards gathered around him, each guard armed and carrying a large pack on his back.

Talen walked up to Becky and grabbed her arm, pulling her away from Lander. "You're coming too, girlie." He met Lander's angry eyes. "I'm going to take care of your lady friend, freak. Do what Mr. Hunt tells you and she won't get hurt."

Lander wanted to pull Becky back, into his arms where he could keep her safe from Talen, but if he tried anything, Talen wouldn't hesitate to use his Wasp. The thought of Becky experiencing the sting like he had, set Lander back a step, right to the edge of the swirling lights. He glowered, but said nothing.

Hunt raised his hands as if he was about to give a benediction. "Right! I believe we are ready to begin this momentous adventure.

"Castor. Desma. If you are joining us, come stand with my men."

Castor looked to Desma. "Are we going?"

"I want to. But I thought you wanted to stay on the Surface."

"Oh, please." Hunt said, impatience lacing his voice. He lowered his hands, setting them on his hips. "Make you choice without delay. I will wait no longer."

"Castor?" Desma's gaze flicked to Parker and Parrish. "I need to go. Maybe I'll be able to return later, but for now, I need to do this."

"And so do I." Castor said. "If I deserted Lander now, I could never forgive myself." A crooked smile graced his lips. "And Ian would probably haunt me. We go together."

The two walked over, hand in hand, and joined the group set to go to the Core.

Hunt's gaze swept over Livy, Parrish, Parker, and Michael, who gathered together farther from the Vortex. "Once we are gone, you may leave Zephryn Island. That includes you Olivia. Your actions the last few days have proven you are no daughter of mine. While I am gone, you will continue to enjoy my support, but when I return be prepared. You will be cut off without a cent from me."

He turned and walked up to Lander, pulling the Stones of Power from his pants pockets, his eyes set in lines of suspicion. "I am certain you know how to use these. And since your girlfriend will be joining us, I suspect you will not try anything that would threaten her safety. But, just in case ..." He waved a hand toward one of the guards.

In one smooth movement, the man shouldered a rifle. A

sound like rocks shattering echoed around the cavern. Michael's eyes turned into saucers and his mouth hung open as blood began to seep down his right leg.

"No!" Lander's shout mingled with the fading echoes. He started toward his friend, intent on healing the wound. A scream of pain from Becky pulled him up sharp. Talen stood over her, the Wasp controller in his hand. Then four guards moved into position blocking Michael from Lander's sight.

Lander fell to his knees. His head throbbed and his heart shattered. "Please. Don't do this. I'll do whatever you want. Just let me heal Michael. Please! And don't hurt Becky. Please don't hurt Becky!"

"Good. We have an understanding, Mr. Devlin." Aurelius Hunt strode forward to stand in front of Lander. "This is the way it's going to work. We will bring your injured friend with us. *If* you cooperate ... and ... *if* he survives the trip, I will allow you to heal him once we reach the Core. Do we have an agreement?"

Lander nodded, his focus split between Michael's bleeding leg and Becky. He wanted to kill Talen as the image of Becky crouched, tears in her eyes, her hand on the anklet, rooted in his mind.

"Do. We. Have. An. Agreement?"

"Yes. Yes," Lander gritted out between clenched teeth.

Hunt waved and the four men blocking Lander walked to Michael, picked him up, and jogged back to stand with the others.

"Now, Mr. Devlin. My destiny calls."

Lander pushed to his feet. Ignoring the promise of violence in Talen's eyes, he helped Becky to stand. His arm around her, he staggered to the edge of the hole.

Hunt handed him the Stones of Power. Lander focused. Within seconds all four stones glowed, two blue-green and two red as blood. The power of the stones flooded through him, sparking his nerves and setting his blood on fire. He set the shield, felt it circle around the group standing behind him. Without looking back, he closed his eyes, pulled Becky in closer, and leaped feet first into the black hole at the center of the Vortex.

cswachter.com
facebook page: C. S. Wachter
For more information
and updates on what's coming next.

Review?

Reviews help others make informed decisions about
the books they choose to read.

If you enjoyed *Lander's Legacy* please consider leaving
a review on Amazon, Goodreads, and/or any site of
your choosing.

Thank you!

Other books by C. S. Wachter

THE SEVEN WORDS

The Sorcerer's Bane
The Light Arises
The Deceit of Darkness
The Light Unbound

Demon's Legacy: A Worlds of Ochen Short Story

A Weight of Reckoning – Sequel to The Seven Words

www.ingramcontent.com/pod-product-compliance
Lightning Source LLC
Chambersburg PA
CBHW020407260626
47156CB00007B/2270